BALEFIRE

Other B&W titles by Nigel Tranter

›BALEFIRE›

NIGEL TRANTER

B&W PUBLISHING

British Library Cataloguing in Publication Data:
A catalogue record for this book is available from
the British Library

Cover illustration: Detail from
Robert the Bruce and De Bohun
by Eric Harald MacBeth Robertson
Photograph by kind permission
of The Flemings Collection.

Printed by WS Bookwell Ltd

I

SIMON ARMSTRONG raised himself a little higher on his elbow, and groaned. Groaned with both physical and spiritual hurt. His right leg was not only horribly gashed, but the thigh-bone was broken. An English halberd had done that. He was bruised all over, his entire body a throbbing ache. Moreover, the glancing blow which had knocked off his morion had grazed temple, cheek-bone and jaw. That was what had laid him unconscious. And now, conscious again, he groaned.

How long he had lain there on that reeking hillside he did not know. The battle had joined about four of the afternoon. It might be six now, or even later. And none of his companions would tell him. Around him, one even on him, they lay, in infinite variety of posture, in their scores, their hundreds, Scots and English, alike only in the strange unanimity of death. Limbs sprawled and bent and projected, heads lolled, gauntleted fingers pointed mockingly, and, most curiously, innumerable bare feet, mud encrusted, appealed grotesquely to the driving rain-clouds that represented heaven—for the Scots had largely discarded their footgear in order to purchase a better grip as they came slithering and sliding down the slippery slope of that ill-omened Branxton Hill. And the litter of their pikes, the damned, disastrous, encumbering, eighteen-foot French pikes that had been their ruin and betrayal, lay like a forest struck by a tornado, sheared, broken and splintered, in every direction, transfixing the men who had borne them more than any of the enemy. Here and there, admittedly, a figure stirred a little, as Sim Armstrong was stirring, and groaned too—but pitifully few they were. Surrey, relaying King Harry's savage instructions, had ordered no quarter and no prisoners.

But it was not his personal state, nor yet the shambles that lay around him, that was responsible for the young Borderer's

1

groan. His glance, misted red as it was, and unsteady, was turned downhill and to the right to where, some two or three hundred yards away, the main battle still raged. If battle it could be called now. A grievous change had come over the scene since last he had had opportunity to glance that way. The clash of sword against hacking, shearing halberd still resounded above the shouts and the screams and the slogans and the challenges—but how shockingly decimated were the ranks around the King. Or not around, but behind the King—for still their foolish, headstrong, gallant, lovable James Stewart fought like his own Rampant Lion in the very forefront of the battle, as he had been fighting for hours, heavy armour and wounds notwithstanding. From his vantage-point on the hill, Simon could see, over the heads of the great press of the English that now surrounded the Scots centre, how James, his broken lance long discarded, still hewed and slashed and thrust, where the press would let him. But manifestly that royal arm was flagging, its blows wilder and ever less telling. As were those of all at his back. For what were even five-foot swords against long axe-headed eight-foot halberds to tightly hemmed-in men? Especially conventional cutting swords, round-pointed; short pointed jabbing swords might have saved them, as they had saved the Spaniards at Ravenna in like case—but not these knightly blades. Most of the Scots around their king were immobilised indeed until it was their turn to die, packed too close to fight.

How were the mighty fallen—how few the proud standards that still fluttered in the wind and rain above the shrinking hard-pressed band. The Royal Standard, red lion on gold, still flew, reeling and drunken, blood-stained and tattered—from his coat-armour it seemed to be in the hands of young Keith now, the son of the Marischal. How many hands had held up that banner that grim afternoon, before having it snatched anew from suddenly drooping nerveless fingers? Even as Armstrong gazed, the young Lord Keith sank down under a hail of halberd strokes, and the toppling flag was seized by another, a huge man dressed in the tartans of a Highlander—

Hector Maclean of Duart, wielding a great claymore like a windmill. But the chief's presence there brought only another lump into the Borderer's dry throat. The fact that Maclean was fighting now at the King's side could mean only that his own Highland brigade, the right wing of the Scots army, under Argyll and Lennox, had been shattered and broken also.

Simon raised his throbbing, burning eyes to peer still farther rightwards, eastwards, where these rolling green Flodden hills sank and dwindled towards the rushing Till in its steep valley. But he could make out little, through the driving rain and the reek of the battle, for the September night was prematurely falling. It would be dark in less than an hour, and already the slopes near the Till were blotted out, as were the foothills of great Cheviot to his left. But at least he could see that no gallant Highland array now graced those shadowy eastern braes— only confused and struggling small groups and parties scattered amongst a desolation as terrible as that which surrounded himself.

A great triumphant shout from hundreds of throats brought Simon's gaze back to the central stage. The King was down— disappeared at last under the smiting, hacking throng. Maclean and the Standard still remained, high on the ever-growing mound of the Scots dead. But the King . . .

But, no—there was the slender valiant figure, so slight beside the huge Highlander, raised up again by urgent hands. But James was sore stricken, obviously, reeling, his helm gone, right shoulder sagging, right arm useless. Yet he had his dripping sword in his left hand, and was striking out again, however clumsily. Something like a cheer was conceived in Simon Armstrong's throat—but was born from his lips as a choking sob.

The folly of it, the man despaired between clenched teeth— the utter, insensate, hopeless, magnificent folly of it! There was no breaking away, no yielding, no retiral or retreat. Nor had there been, from the first. Men, the flower of Scotland, stood until they fell. And then were stood astride, or upon, in their turn, till others fell over them. The King's array was surrounded, yes. But it had not budged an inch since first it had been halted by the blast of the English cannon, the sky-darkening hail of arrows, and the worse than uselessness of the vaunted pike phalanx formation on broken ground. It had only shrunk, and gone on shrinking. Fifteen thousand men had formed this great central division, the noblest and the best of the land. All remained—but a bare thousand stood upright. It was King James's own command, when he ordered the descent from Flodden Hill. There would be no surrender, no retreat, no re-forming to fight another day. All would be put to the test; all would stand or fall by the result. To that end all were dismounted, that none might be tempted to flee. Forty-five thousand horses and more waited riderless up above there, on the hilltops. Few indeed would ever carry a Scottish master again. None of them would carry Scotland's chivalry off fatal Flodden Field.

A mere half-dozen ragged banners streamed now, supporting the Lion Rampant, where before there had been a hundred. Simon could still make out the boar's heads of Huntly, the gold escallops of Montrose, the crescents of Seton, the buckles of Rothes, and the red shields of Hay. But where were the emblems of Douglas and Cassillis, of Crawford and Herries, of Caithness and Sempill, of Atholl and Glencairn, and scores upon scores of others? Where was the young Archbishop of St. Andrews, James's own natural son? And the Bishops of the Isles and Caithness? Where was the Chancellor, the Constable, the Lyon, the Standard-bearer, the Treasurer? All cut down, trampled and gone. Where, aye where, were the forty fine French captains, sent by Louis to instruct the Scots in the new art of warfare with pikes three times the length of a man? Gone, too. Would they had gone, and their accursed pikes with them, those French instructors on whom James Stewart had placed more reliance than on his God, before ever the battle was joined!

Simon, lying there on the blood-soaked hillside, saw his king go down the second time. And as he fell under the halberd's stroke, an upthrust sword plunged in deep beneath his steel

4

gorget, and there remained. No man might live so stricken, paladin as he might be.

The wolfish savage shout rose again, and maintained, and there was a mighty surge forward of the English van. Maclean went down—even though the Standard was saved again. And over and upon the King's body Surrey's knights rushed, their steel avid for the royal blood. Up and down, up and down, their swords smote and lunged and beat, madly, as though they would never stop. Unsuccessful at blinking away the hot tears that flooded his eyes, Simon Armstrong buried face on arm, and so lay.

When next he raised heavy head it was no longer to concentrate on that devoted company still in the grievous drawn-out process of dying with their dead monarch. The Lion of Scotland still flew, and no man was deserting it. Nor could any now, indeed, hemmed in completely as they were. But Simon Armstrong was not of that fated array. He had been in Douglas of Drumlanrig's company—Douglas the Bold, who now lay only a few yards away, glazed eyes staring unblinking up into the driving rain—in the Lord Home's Border array, the left wing of the Scots army. It was not incumbent upon *him* to die beside the Royal Standard. His wing had not been defeated. Home, Warden of the Marches and Chamberlain of Scotland, far from failing, had chased the Cheshire men opposing him right off the field—even if thereby he had broken up his own phalanx. But who ever heard of Borderers fighting on foot, in ranks of pikes, like German mercenaries? Drumlanrig's men had been left by Home to face Lord Dacre, and right well they had acquitted themselves. But the collapse of the array on their right had thrown upon their depleted ranks the full weight of the English second line under Surrey's son, the Lord Admiral. The Scots reserve should have come to their aid, but they chose rather to go to the help of their king instead—and who would blame them? Drumlanrig's Borderers, of Hawick and Teviotdale and Ettrick, standing fast, had gone down under the avalanche, selling their lives dearly. Here was no failure . . .

5

And Simon Armstrong of Stirkshaws was young, a mere twenty-five, and life was too precious just to throw away, now that the die was cast, the King was dead. His own death would serve nothing. So his urgent gaze surveyed the rest of the desperate scene—or at least such of it as the swiftly advancing dusk permitted. To his left, amongst the shadowy whin-dotted foothills of Cheviot, innumerable small affrays engaged, Borderers against Borderers—Scotts and Elliots and Turnbulls against Northumbrian Herons and Fenwicks and Blacketts. Yes, and Scottish Liddesdale Armstrongs against English Tynedale Armstrongs. But everywhere the Scots had the worst of it, because they were unhorsed, at the royal command, and no such edict crippled the English mosstroopers. Indeed, this lack of horseflesh nagged now at Sim Armstrong's bemused brain, as it had nagged at his fellows' throughout the battle, undermining their morale—for the Borderer and his mount were one. It turned Simon's eyes now uphill, back to that ridge two or three hundred feet above, where his black mare awaited him in company with all those thousands of other horses. In the mist and the mirk he thought that he could just make out mounted men up there now. Perhaps Home's people had returned from chasing the Cheshire men, and having remounted, would yet come thundering down upon the English in the valley . . . ?

If he could somehow get up there . . . dragging this accursed leg behind him? Get to his horse. Even if he had to go all the way on hands and knees . . .

Gritting his teeth, Simon heaved himself up into a sitting position. A heavy man lay across his good left leg—Wattie's Dod, one of his own herds. Ill tidings he would have to bear to Jean, Dod's wife—or widow, rather—if ever he won back to Stirkshaws. Dod had been on his feet and smiting when he himself went down. Perhaps he had died seeking to save him, his laird? Others of his name and race lay thick around. They could have been doing the same. All were dead. Dispatched after they had fallen, no doubt, by a ruthless enemy. More wives to acquaint with their widowhood. Was he lucky to have

6

escaped thus far, then? Or would he have been better dead with the rest? It was the dead's day, this ninth day of September, fifteen hundred and thirteen. Why should he, Sim Armstrong, be odd-man-out?

Nevertheless, shaking a dizzy head, the young man sought to shift Dod's body from his leg. But he seemed to be as limp as a kitten. Dod was a big man. Heave and tug as he would, he could not move the dead-weight. Tears of weakness, helplessness and a sudden rage started to his eyes.

Better dead or no, in a few moments Simon was turning over on his stomach, and, teeth bared, grinning at the hurt of it. Once over, and rested awhile, he dug in his elbows, leaning over another body as fulcrum, and sought to draw and wriggle his leg loose.

It was an agonising business, and time and again he had to desist lest he swoon right away. But at length he worked himself free, and lay panting.

When he raised his head again, it was with face set firmly to that hill. The forlorn struggle around the Standard still raged below him, but he did not glance that way again. A man may drain the dregs of emotion quite dry.

Painfully, arduously, inch by inch, Simon started to drag himself upwards, perspiration starting from his brow and mingling with the blood that trickled down from his temple. His right leg was as though on fire. Every nerve and muscle of his body protested. The slope was not actually steep, but it was horribly slippery, with blood as well as with the mud and rainwater. But the slope itself was not the worst of it. The surmounting and negotiating of the ranks and piles and mounds of the slain was the sterner ordeal—that, and the picking of a way through the tangle of pikeshafts that thrust in every direction like *chevaux-de-frise*. A hale man would have found it no light task. Weakened by loss of blood, and with a broken leg to draw behind him, only a fierce and elemental urge for life itself kept Simon going. He did not need to be told that to rest, to relax, just to lie where he was, would in all probability number him amongst the dead in very truth before that night

7

was out. This was not his first taste of battle and its aftermath.

How far the man managed to hoist himself up that hill of carnage he was never in a position to know. He seemed to be at it for an eternity, and the Inferno itself, he knew, could offer him no worse. Distance and time was not to be measured in inches and minutes, but only in agony and sweat and blind determination. He envied those dead with everything that was physical and corporeal in him—but the inner essential flickering flame that was Simon Armstrong himself would have no truck with them, even as he crawled on over them, using them. He knew no pity now, no sorrow, no regret—only the need to live. And he hated those dead because they *were* so dead, and would keep him from living if they could.

It was a dead man who defeated him, in the end, nevertheless. Somewhere, the purgatory of his progress brought him to a burn, a small stream that flowed, not chuckling but thick and angry and red-stained, down and across his path. Its channel was narrow, and only two or three feet in depth. But for Simon Armstrong it might have been Tweed itself. At its crumbling rim he wept in vexation and bitterness, for nowise could he drag himself down into it, across and up the little bank beyond. Other men had tried, and failed—that he could see. And then, a little way up, he perceived something else—a corpse that lay right across the stream, like a bridge, supported there partly by the pike that transfixed him and partly by another body in the burn itself. Biting his lip, thither Simon crawled.

The projecting pike was a nuisance. Nevertheless the young man had got most of himself across when his dead ally suddenly betrayed him. The body rolled over and collapsed. Scrabbling desperately with hands and knee to save himself, Simon crashed down on the grassy bank, and slid partly into the water. And pain came roaring at him like a leaping ravening lion, beat him down and overwhelmed him in a red torture, before merciful oblivion swallowed him up.

Consciousness is a relative thing. There are shades and levels and degrees of it, not all of them welcome or honest or kindly. Sim Armstrong experienced most of them throughout the dark watches of that foul night—and the imprint of them was etched upon his mind for eternity.

He knew no order or sequence in his consciousness, no coherence or consistency. Only pain and fear and horror and a great and compelling awareness of evil. Nor was all that evil, that ill, within himself, he knew, great as was his trouble. The evil was all about him—and not just in the cloying silence and corruption of death. Silence, stillness, would have been good, welcome. But all through that dire night some part of the man's mind listened and heeded, listened to the groaning, the cries for mercy, the thin beseeching and desperate pleading—and the suddenly stilled shrieks. Aye, and to the hoarse laughter and cruel mockery, the quarrelling and snarling over spoil, the fierce dragging and kicking and savaging, the drunken roystering and triumph. He was aware of lights that flitted and hovered, fires that blazed, and even the stench of burning flesh. Humanity could reach its lowest at night on a lost and won battlefield. Flodden Field, thanks to Bluff King Hal's guiding hand, potent even from faraway France, was notable in this respect as in others.

How far spent was the night before Simon regained sufficient consciousness to drag himself clear of the water is not to be known. Possibly it was fairly early on—for the effort and torment of so doing sent him swooning off again, and even after the next bout of awareness there still seemed to be an eternity of the baleful darkness. And though he managed to hoist and haul himself out of the stream itself on to a little ledge of grass, he could by no means pull himself up out of the little cleft which the burn had dug for itself. Perhaps he had cause to be thankful for that, for he was thereby tucked away and hidden in deepest shadow. Many spoilers and strippers of the fallen came close, horribly close—but none came actually looking into the burn-channel. They had no need to, indeed, with more accessible slain lying there in their thousands.

The rain had stopped, and at long last the stars paled with the dawn. Simon was wholly conscious now—and none the happier for being so. That he had survived the night there and then seemed scant cause for thankfulness. Nor did the new day bring its accustomed hope. He had no wide vista in his trench but, as the light increased, that segment of the field that he could see below him offered no reassurance, no gleam of comfort to the wounded man. Indeed, the scene looked infinitely more grim, more terrible, than before the darkness had fallen. For then, at least, the serried ranks of the fallen had looked like soldiers, warriors; now they only looked like corpses—for great numbers had been stripped naked, and lay violated, white, obscene-seeming, amongst the curling mist-wraiths of morning. Nor was the spoiling process yet completed. Everywhere armed men moved and quartered and searched, singly and in groups and bands, stooping, tugging. With most of Scotland's nobility and gentry lying there, the harvest was rich. Rich enough indeed for bloody fighting to be occurring widespread amongst the scavengers themselves. Swords and daggers were in every hand—to hack off stiff and difficult limbs and members, to quieten any vanquished who were not yet suitably dead and tractable, and to defend against or challenge rival spoilers.

Simon Armstrong lay waiting. It was only a question of time, obviously, till someone stumbled upon him—and then it all would be over. He could not move now, save back into the water. Drown himself? Better even a scavenging foeman's steel than that. A small dirk still was sheathed at his belt. He drew it, and hid it beneath his pain-racked body. At least he could die like an Armstrong, striking one last blow as he went . . .

He did not have long to wait to put his resolution to the test. For some little time he had been aware of voices, somewhere behind and above him, drawing ever nearer, with the chink of harness and mail and the clop-clop of horses' hooves. They were working down his burn, for sure. They would come upon him any moment. It so happened that the few men amongst whom he now lay were all ordinary fighting-men, tartan-clad

Gordon gillies of Huntly's indeed, from Aberdeenshire, unprotected by any armour and so killed mainly in the first telling flight of English arrows. Amongst them, he, clad in even the modest finery of a Border laird, must stand out at once for plunder.

A sudden hoarse shout from right above him tensed all Simon's muscles. He gripped the haft of his dirk fiercely. Now! He must not bungle this last, this so final effort. He must turn just at the right moment, when they were stooping low over him, but before they had realised that he was not dead, before the inevitable sword slashed down upon him. He must not let his cramped and stiff right arm fail him, nor be hindered by the wretched weakness of his body . . .

"Abel—see here!" a broad Northumbrian voice cried. "One they have missed, b'God! And no bare-shanked Highlander, this one."

"Ha! You're right, lad. A gentleman of coat-armour!" That was an older voice. "Aye—and by Saint Wilfred, an Armstrong at that! See you the Bent Arm of Armstrong."

That was the badge and blazon of Simon's house, the sword arm of Siward the Strong, painted on his cuirass.

"Armstrong or other—here is better pickings than from half-naked savages!"

"Aye. But have a care, lad. He might be of our own side. Of the North, and no Scot. Where is his helm?"

To Simon's missing morion had been attached the national colours of Scotland, so necessary for identifying friend from foe in hand-to-hand conflict.

"I don't see it . . ."

"Up here on the hill? Amongst these accursed Highlandmen?" another objected. "Would a good North-country Armstrong have fallen here?"

"Chasing fleeing Scots, he might . . ."

"A plague on't!" the first speaker cried. "What difference? He'll make as rich picking, English as Scots!"

"Surely. Why so particular . . . ?"

"Wait!" the older voice commanded. "Pickings, may be. But

think you not that some proud lady might not pay more for her lord's body brought home to her castle, than the mere pickings of his corpse? Let me see him."

Those words, less than noble in themselves, saved at least one life, perhaps two. For they awoke hope in Simon Armstrong's heart, hope of life, however slender. And since his desire for life was strong, behind all the suffering, and instinctively vehement, he acted upon it. Those words, whatever else they implied, indicated a prudent man, a man who used his head, not just a brutal blood-crazed oaf. To such, an appeal might be made—not to his mercy but to his wits, his prudent self-interest. In the moment that the speaker leaned down over him, Simon made his desperate throw for life. He turned over, face upwards—and left his dagger hidden beneath him.

"Sir," he gasped, "my ransom . . . will buy you . . . more than . . . a widow's thanks!" Simon took a shuddering breath as the other started back. "A thousand gold lions," he got out.

"Lord save us—he lives!" the other exclaimed. "Hold your hand, man." That last was cried to a younger man-at-arms whose sword had already jerked upwards.

Simon saw, though indistinctly, a big bearded man clad in morion and breastplate, and with it a blue livery on which was borne a plain gold cross saltirewise. With him were four younger men, similarly attired. Two had drawn swords in their hands; the other two led horses laden with booty.

"A thousand . . . gold lions," he reiterated, more weakly than he would have wished.

"Oho—so that is the way the cock crows!" the bearded man said. "You talk of ransom. You are of the enemy, then—the Scots?"

"Does it matter?" Simon asked thickly. "The gold . . . is the same."

"God's curse on him—he *is* a Scot!" the man with the readiest sword cried. "Kill him!"

"Aye—finish him off!"

"Wait!" the older man insisted again. "*I* give orders here, knaves! Of which Armstrongs are you, sirrah, that are so free

12

with your gold?"

"I am Simon Armstrong of Stirkshaws . . . in Upper Teviot-dale. Of the chiefly . . . house of Mangerton."

"Stirkshaws? I have heard that name. A rickle of stones and a doocot, in a Tividale bog?"

"A goodly heritage of . . . twenty ploughgates and a slated hall. Enough . . . to pay you your thousand gold pieces . . . and more." The last of that was little more than a whisper.

"M'mmm." The questioner stroked his beard. It was agonising for the fallen man to lie there helpless while life or death was decided for him. But what more could he do, or say—since he would not beg for mercy?

"A murrain on him, Abel—it is ordered that we take no prisoners!" one of the others contended. "If Earl Surrey were to hear o' this . . . !"

"Aye—and belike we'll never see a penny of the fellow's gold," a second complained. "Better the pickings that we're sure of. See that gold ring on his finger . . ."

"By Saint Wilfred—will you hold your prating tongues!" their leader exclaimed. "A man may not think for your gabble." His thought processes seemed to be reasonably unimpaired, nevertheless, for almost abstractedly, as with his mind on greater matters, the bearded man stooped down and tugged at the ring on Simon's finger.

The wounded man neither aided nor resisted him, fighting his own battle with pain and delirium, with pride and the urge to go on living. The signet-ring that had been his father's and his grandfather's before him, engraved with the arms of his line, slid without much difficulty into the other's hand, was considered casually, and passed on into a capacious pocket.

"You name Saint Wilfred . . . ?" Simon got out, striving to keep his voice steady, even if all else of him was reeling. "That could mean . . . that you are of Hexham? And by your cross and colours, you are churchmen. Five hundred lions, then . . . to Saint Wilfred's Priory of Hexham . . . above your own." That was the best that he could do. His head seemed to be opening and shutting like a bellows. His wits would barely

13

work for him, stark as was the need. Consciousness itself was slipping, slipping. He could not be sure even that he had indeed uttered those last words. If he tried very hard, might he be able to repeat them . . . ?

But it seemed that he must have enunciated them. For the big man was speaking again. "Aha—a godly Scot, and pious!" he cried. "Generous, too—a man after my own heart!" Was it only Simon's bemused imagination, or did the fellow sound almost jovial now? Imagination, undoubtedly, for the great bearded head was nodding ridiculously, and going on nodding, up and down, up and down, in a grotesque caricature of amiability. But of course his own head was nodding too, now, on his emblazoned breastplate, and he could no longer keep his leaden eyelids raised over his swimming eyes.

Desperately Simon fought to retain his failing senses. "We can do no other than accept this generous offertory," the other seemed to be declaring. "We may not rob Mother Church. God forbid! My Lord Prior will be much gratified. Much gratified . . . much gratified . . . much . . ."

With a supreme effort the wounded man sought to discipline and clear away the foolish words that were chasing themselves round and round his splitting head. He raised a vague and shaky hand. "My leg . . . is broke," he said. That was not indeed what he had intended to say—if said it he had, indeed. He was schooling unruly slack lips to form other words, any words, when rough hands seized his shoulders, to draw him up out of that stream-channel.

And the tide of that other stream that he had been bordering for so long immediately surged up tumultuously, jealously, to engulf him. Simon Armstrong sank away into blissful oblivion once more.

14

II

SIMON was aware of the sun shining pleasantly warm on his face long before he opened his eyes. Indeed, he became aware of other things too, before unwillingly he admitted to consciousness, even to himself—that the pain in his leg was not quite so fierce, that he no longer lay partly in cold water, that the horrible sounds of the stricken battlefield no longer assailed his ears. In fact, when he had prevailed upon himself reluctantly to listen, he had to acknowledge that the only sounds appeared to be homely and pleasant ones—a tuneful cheerful whistling against the rhythmic, comfortable and uncomplicated background of horses steadily cropping grass. That, and the trilling of larks. Attend as he would, he could make out no more ominous sound.

Cautiously, distrustfully, he opened his eyes, and after a few moments staring at an innocent blue sky flecked with fleecy clouds, allowed his glance to sink to survey the closer scene. He was lying in the mouth of a little wooded dene that opened off a green narrow valley under rolling hills, amongst ferns and thorn trees. In front of him a young man, in the blue livery with the gold cross, sat on the grass, arms and helmet laid aside, whittling at a stick with a dagger, and whistling. Around him miscellaneous booty and plunder was heaped—armour, weapons, clothing and ornaments. Four or five horses grazed near by. That seemed to be all.

Simon was content just to lie there, not questioning, hardly even wondering—though he noted that his leg was bound up now, with rough skill, two broken sections of pikestaff being used as splints to secure it in position. The pain therefrom was definitely less. He was desperately thirsty—but that could wait. For the rest, he was alive, no effort was being demanded of him, and the sun shone.

But presently the man in front of him, of about his own age, crop-headed and stocky, turned, and observing that his charge's eyes were open, spoke. "So you ha' decided to live a mite longer, eh?" he said.

Since that was almost an echo of the sentiments that had been forming themselves in his own mind, Simon nodded slightly. He did not venture into words.

"Aye. Well, I'll thank you to make up your mind, Master Armstrong," the other declared, and forcefully. "If you're for dying, die now before you are any more trouble to us, I say. It has been weary work enough getting you this far, God knows! We could ha' been better employed."

Wary-eyed, the Scot watched the man, but did not answer.

"Die now, and at the least we can turn to work o' more profit, see you." The whistler evidently deemed it necessary for the prisoner fully to understand the situation and the trouble to which he was putting his captors. "But die on us after we get you to Hexham, an' we lose all. No ransom, an' our labours wasted. A pox on it—I'd as well run you through now an' ha' done with it!"

Simon accepted that as a grumble rather than any immediate threat—though he recognised it as a line of thought that could endanger him. He turned his head away.

He could see a considerable distance up the valley, which pursued a fairly straight course for a mile or two before being interrupted by out-thrusting shoulders of great Cheviot itself. This must be the glen of the College Burn, then, somewhere above Hethpool—an area not unknown to Scots anxious to win discreetly back to their own territory after visiting the fat lowlands of Northumbria. In which case they were a few miles south by west of Flodden Hill—on their way, presumably, to Hexham amongst the Tynedale hills, from what this guard said.

The fellow seemed to feel the need to talk, however little co-operation he received from his charge. Perhaps that was a sign that he had been left on his own for some time. From the sun's position it would be past noon. Simon calculated that he must have been unconscious for five or six hours at least.

"How are we to know that your folk will pay for you, even if you live?" the Northumbrian went on, in gloomy rumination. "Or that they ha' the gold? I say it is a poor hazard, and chancy, to be taking all these risks for. Abel Ridley is a man hard and soft in the wrong places, say I!" He spat accurately at a questing bee, and his glance slid over the wounded man's person. "Hurting bad?" he wondered, in a different tone.

Simon half-shrugged, non-committally. "I am thirsty," he said thickly.

The other sheathed his dagger and got to his feet. He picked up his morion, carrying it in his hand and started down the little slope—obviously going to use his helmet to fetch water from the river. But, at the edge of the thorn trees, he stopped suddenly, drew back discreetly into cover, and so stood.

Soon Simon could see what had arrested him. A string of mounted men, leading horses laden with plunder, was passing up the valley. By the style of them they were evidently English Borderers making for home, well endowed. Yet his guard, as clearly, wanted no truck with them. Moreover, if his attitude was furtive, strangely so also was the air of the men riding past. They kept glancing behind them, and hurrying their beasts on, most patently anxious to be elsewhere, uninterfered with, just as soon as might be.

Simon recognised how it was, of course—he was Borderer enough for that. The Earl of Surrey would be claiming all booty as prize for King Henry—who was known to be a grasping man. He would by no means approve of all this individual enterprise. Moreover, undoubtedly he would be striving to hold together his army, possibly to follow up his victory by an invasion of Scotland, now lying wide open. This hiving off and departing of groups and bands, making for home, would suit him ill. For certain he would be seeking to stop it.

But it was the time-honoured Border custom, nevertheless. On both sides. The bold swift blow, the spoil, and then home— that was ever the marchmen's idea of warfare. Indeed, the Borderers were apt to be somewhat out of sympathy with kings and their large-scale battles anyway, preferring their own methods and loyalties, their own raids and feuds and codes of conduct. These Northumbrians were merely living up to their traditions. That weaker bands should avoid stronger, with hard-won gear to be got safely home, was understandable, and also in the tradition.

When the party was safely past, Simon's guard slipped down to the riverside, and returned with a helmetful of water. Gratefully the wounded man drank, raised up on his would-be slaughterer's arm.

"My thanks," he panted.

"Dry work, dying!" the other grinned. And returned to his whittling and his whistling.

Presently another and still larger band passed with a clatter of hooves and armour up the valley, also laden down with spoil. "A busy road, the College Water, this day," Simon commented grimly.

"Aye." That was short. "Would we were as nimble at taking it."

But the young man's patience was not tried for much longer. The sound of horsemen approaching from behind them turned his head round, as the big bearded man, who seemed to be named Abel Ridley, with seven or eight others, all in the livery of Hexham Priory, arrived back, not openly up the valley, but more discreetly over the rolling tree-dotted foothills from the north. Like the others, however, they also led a string of captured horses, some of them handsomely caparisoned beasts, well laden.

Now there was no delay. While the grazing animals were being hurriedly loaded up again, Simon was hoisted, with more care and gentleness than might have been looked for, up in front of Ridley's own saddle. The hurt of it all but over-whelmed him, nevertheless, and they were trotting on their way up the track by the riverside before he came sufficiently out of the consequent red mist of pain to be very well aware of what went on. In fact, the jolting of the horse's motion was so hard on his leg that throughout that nightmare ride the Scot's normal perceptions were considerably dulled. The

18

sequence of events and the country traversed remained always thereafter vague and uncertain in his mind.

Ridley, within whose strong leather-sheathed arms he rode, was talking to him, demanding something of him. ". . . you understand, man? You will say that? Declare that was what you told us, should we be challenged?"

"Eh . . . ? I . . . I have not heard you aright, I fear. What would you . . . ?"

"Tut, man. You are to say, if any of my Lord Dacre's men catch up with us, that you told us that you were of Tynedale. An Armstrong of our own English North. That we are but taking you home, wounded. Surrey, they say, has already hanged certain captains for taking prisoners, contrary to his commands—and hanged the prisoners too. Dacre would not do that, I think, respecting the Lord Prior as he does—but you he would slay, for certain. And all our labour wasted. So you will do this, see you?"

"Claim to be an English Armstrong—of Tynedale? Would I be believed . . . ?"

The other shrugged. "Perhaps not. But at the least you will absolve us from the charge of taking Scots prisoners."

Simon nodded, seeing no point in refusing. "Very well. I have far-out cousins in Tarsetdale, of the North Tyne. Say that . . . I am Armstrong of Gleedlee . . ." Even to enunciate that was an effort.

"Good," the other acknowledged, "Gleedlee, in Tarsetdale. I think that perhaps you are a man of sound sense, Master Armstrong!"

Thereafter, as they rode jingling up the peaceful valley of the College, between ever-rising hills, captor chatted to prisoner quite companionably—even though the latter was not in a state fully to take in all that he was told. It transpired that Abel Ridley was one of the stewards of the wealthy and powerful Hexham Priory, whose lands extended far and wide in the dales of Tyne and Rede and Coquet. With a party of ten men he had formed one of the Prior's contributions to the Border contingent of Lord Dacre, Warden of the English Marches, in

19

Surrey's army. He had lost two men in the battle—but he did not seem to be greatly concerned about them, for nobody had seen them fall, and it was quite possible that they might turn up once all the confusion was over. Indeed, though Simon may have been wrong, he rather gathered that the Hexham company, perhaps all Dacre's array, had not been in the thickest of the fighting at all, by good fortune or good judgment. Dacre himself, it appeared, was under a cloud with Surrey, for some reason. But it had been a glorious victory, for all that—even though Surrey had not been certain that he was in fact the victor till morning light had revealed only the massive host of the Scots dead left on the field. King James had been out-witted, outmanoeuvred and out-fought, he and his lords fighting like common men-at-arms and leaving generalship to fate.

Simon was neither in a condition nor a position strongly to counter this conclusion.

Despite his talking, the Hexham steward did not fail to keep a sharp watch around them as they rode. And clearly with good reason—if he was anxious to avoid questioning company or rival booty-seekers. For surely never had those empty Cheviot hills been so throng with folk. The entire English Border army seemed to be streaming away south and west, in twos and threes and dozens and fifties, each with their share of dead men's gear, carried on dead men's horses. The larger parties tended to hold to the valley floors and the best going, while the little groups kept safely up on high ground and rough hillside. Each tributary valley and gap on either side revealed more of the home-goers. Ridley kept at a discreet distance behind the fairly large band that was something like half a mile in front, and sought not to be overtaken by the lot behind.

Ridley's men were loud in their complaints that with all this traffic there would not be a bite of food to be picked up for miles—and their stomachs were direly empty. It seemed that Surrey had had no victuals for his army for three days. The land had been devastated by King James's host, which had been in possession for a week before the English forces came up. When the riders passed the lonely place of Southernknowe, at the junction of the Lambden Burn and the College, it was to find it a deserted and blackened ruin. The same applied a mile farther on, at Fleehope. At both, the Hexham men cursed the blackguard Scots, and glared at their prisoner menacingly.

But neither hunger nor vengeful bitterness were to be the worst of their troubles. Soon after Fleehope, the valley, circling the base of Cheviot, began to climb sharply. Soon the enclosing slopes had roughened and steepened until the horsemen were threading what was almost a rocky-sided gorge, through which the stream descended headlong in a series of waterfalls and spouting rapids. Ahead of them they could glimpse their route winding up and up till it passed below the mighty cauldron of Hen Hole itself, where the College Burn was born amongst gloomy precipices, whereafter they must take to the high open mosses and peat-hags of the watershed—actually crossing the Border for a little way into Scotland, where it thrust a brief salient eastwards towards the sea.

Simon knew the spot of old, and his heart was sore at the thought of it. To be on Scottish soil again, thus . . .

But his heart was to be sorer still in a few minutes—and not only his heart. When the larger party in front were directly under Hen Hole, and they themselves therefore something just under the half-mile from it, the great shadowy crater gouged out of the hilltop suddenly erupted horsemen, scores of horsemen, who spilled out and downhill into the gut of the valley in a yelling savage flood, lances levelled, pennons fluttering, swords drawn.

"Scots!" Ridley shouted, pulling his mount up on to its hind legs with a jerk that all but unseated his groaning passenger. "Scots! Back! Back, I say!"

But, swinging their horses round in the narrow space, the Hexham men discovered another troop of armed Scots streaming down behind them out of a hidden fold of the hill. Trapped, they stared this way and that. Not over-eager hands reached down for swords.

It was well for Ridley's people that there were groups of returning warriors both before and behind them on that climbing track—larger groups than their own, too. At the moment they were not the immediate target of the ambushers. They had time, precious moments, to consider their situation.

Abel Ridley, as Simon had judged back on the battlefield, was a prudent man who could use his head. He used it now, quelling curtly the babbled outcry of his men. Glancing forward and back, he perceived that the enemy at his rear were only half as far away as those in front. Also, that though they were fewer in number—at a rough computation, fifty against twice as many farther up—they had a much smaller band of English to tackle. There might be two dozen of his compatriots in the party behind, against three score ahead. Burdened as they were with booty and led horses, and caught in the restricted space of the valley floor, they would not stand a chance against the impetus of the downwards thundering Scots. The first charge would overwhelm them. Therefore, it behoved a prudent man to move while the moving was good.

Ridley dug in his spurs, pointing on up the valley, and plunged forward again.

But he did not lead along the track for more than a few score yards. At a point where the opposite valley side was less steep, thanks to the inflow of a tumbling burnlet, he turned his tall bay horse right-handed, splashed it across the main stream in a great splatter and spray, and set it directly at the hillside, rowelling its flanks cruelly with his spurs. Behind him his men followed unquestioning, urging their mounts at the daunting slope.

As befitted a man who used his head, Ridley was a realist. His eight men, dashing to the aid of the party ahead, could not materially have altered the situation, would not have won the day for his countrymen, situated as they were. Moreover, the patriotic battling and trumpet-blowing of yesterday were over and done with, the victory won—and it fell to sensible and responsible men to get home with their hard-won gains as best

22

they could. Here was no occasion for glorious and unprofitable dying in the face of superior numbers. Battling with broken remnants of the Scots army would avail nothing. And the welfare and enrichment of Holy Church being involved, left God-fearing men no choice anyway. Up with them, then, and out of this death-trap of a valley!

Scrabbling, slipping, scattering turfs and stones, launching glissades of rubble, the big doubly burdened bay forced its way upwards—while Simon Armstrong bit his lip till the blood flowed. Abel Ridley, amongst his other attributes, was a fine horseman most evidently, with a notable eye for terrain. Those at his heels, though their mounts were less heavily laden, were not all so expert—and of course they had the led horses to manage also. They followed as closely as they could in their leader's tracks, a sliding, stumbling, cursing crew—but the gaps between widened. There was a wild yell from behind, as one of the horses slithered on the treacherous slope, lost its balance, and went pitching over in a welter of lashing hooves, throwing its rider down before it and cannoning into the led beast behind. The man and both horses went rolling and bounding downwards, gear and booty scattering.

"Fool!" Ridley cried. "On! Let him be. Up with you!"

Zigzagging this way and that, the horses having actually to clamber to hoist themselves up, they clawed their way out of the trough of the valley. Another pack-animal lost its footing and went hurtling downhill—though the man leading it managed to loose it in time to avoid being dragged with it.

At length the worst was over, the actual gorge of the river was conquered and the upper hillsides slanted away westwards amidst tussocks and bracken at a lesser angle. Ridley drew up his trembling, steaming, sweating mount, to gaze downwards, panting. He had achieved what many would have deemed impossible—at the cost of one man, three horses and a quarter of their spoils. There was no sign of the casualty down there. Perhaps the stream, running in spate after a week of rain, had carried him away. One horse stood, drooping, saddlery awry, at the foot of the hill; one was trying to drag itself out of the water; the third lay kicking feebly in the shallows.

"A pity," the steward sighed—and transferred his glance elsewhere.

Downstream it was as he had anticipated. The party in the valley there had already been overridden, scattered and cut down by the Scots, who were now briskly at the heartsome gleaning of a rich harvest of plunder—though their leaders seemed to be urging them on upstream towards their colleagues engaged higher up. There, under Hen Hole, the struggle still raged, a seething turmoil of men and horses and clashing flailing steel, the clangour and shouting of it sounding clearly amongst the echoing hillsides. But it was apparent that the outnumbered English were dwindling fast, as men fell or broke away and sought to flee. That affair soon would be over, and it became wise men well to shake the dust of a thoroughly unhealthy neighbourhood from their feet.

Curiously enough, it was Simon Armstrong who perceived first the more immediate threat. Dazed as he was, only semi-conscious as he had been on occasion mounting that grim bluff, he was desperately trying to reassert the dominance of his mind over his bodily hurt, weakness and nausea, in the blessed moments of inactivity while Ridley waited for his followers, when his swimming eyes fixed upon more move-ment—not down in the valley, but nearer at hand, up here on the hillside. He peered—and bit off the exclamation that rose unbidden to his lips.

But his captor had felt his start and stirring within his arms, and turned his head quickly. A smaller party of Scots must have been ensconced on this western side of the valley, and high up—probably as a picquet to signal to their fellows hidden in Hen Hole when to emerge and spring the trap. These must have observed the Hexham group's bid for freedom, and now, to the number of about a dozen, were coming riding hot-foot towards them along the rim of the gorge.

Ridley, as before, wasted no time. Slewing his bay's head round, he kicked it into urgent motion, heading south by west, slantwise up the long face of Auchope Rig towards the low

24

ridge between that summit and Dod Hill. His people were not backward at his heels.

On this line they were riding at only right angles to their enemy's approach. But Abel Ridley was doing so designedly and out of no sort of bravado. By so doing he was following up a slight ridge, between which and the lip of the deeper valley was a wedge of more level ground, ever widening—and vivid with the emerald green of moss. If he could bog them down in there . . .

The Scots, however, were nothing loth to take to the soft ground, fanning out leftwards to intercept. They were slowed down, of course, inevitably, their horses plunging fetlock deep, black mud flying. But they came on, spread out now roughly in line abreast, yelling to the Northumbrians to stand and fight—as well they might.

Converging at an angle, rapidly the two lines of men drew closer. From his quick calculating glances, obviously Ridley was assessing closely his chances of winning clear in time—and drawing his mount's head ever a little more to the right in consequence. The margin was going to be narrow, either way—for him. Some of those behind him were going to have to fight, for sure.

Within the bearded man's embrace, Simon Armstrong was also doing some assessing—in so far as his bemused head would allow. Those were his countrymen, only a few yards off. If they had not already crossed the Scottish Border, they were very close to it. If he was to throw himself down from this horse now, somehow, the chances were that this Ridley and his men would have no opportunity to recapture him, to stop for him. Falling from a galloping horse, with a broken leg, would be a bad business. It might even be the death of him. But was his future so bright, as it was . . . ? And yet . . . ? It was not fear of hurt or death that restrained Simon Armstrong. It was something of the mind, not of the body. This man Ridley had, after a fashion, saved his life. He would have been dead *now*, but for him. The man had taken risks, gone against Surrey's orders, to save him—only so that he might win the greater

25

reward in ransom, admittedly. But still the fact remained. Did he not owe him something for his life? Could he deliberately seek to escape now, when he had offered ransom? Was there not a bargain struck, in some measure? If his freedom was restored purely by the actions of these fellow-Scots, well and good. If not . . .

All this darted and flickered through Simon's muddled mind in two or three seconds. And he sat still, within the other's arms.

The advancing men were near now, lances low, swords drawn, glinting in the sun. Near enough for the white lions on green, of Home, painted on their breastplates, to stand out. They were the Scottish Warden's own men of the Merse, then. "A Home! A Home!" they shouted.

Ridley was muttering into his beard. His tall raw-boned bay was going well, despite its double burden, its raking stride half as long again as those of the Scots' horses, on the softer ground. He was going to get past. There would be half a dozen yards between him and the leftmost of the interceptors.

Tense, rigid, Simon sat. He saw the contorted face of the nearest Merseman as he realised that his quarry was going to escape him. He heard him shout passionate demands to stop and fight. And then, as they thundered past, he glimpsed the other, reining his horse round so that it pawed the air with its forefeet, sods flying, in a fit of fury hurl his lance like a javelin across the yards between.

It was a near thing. The lance actually struck Ridley, but it was a glancing blow, its steel tip hitting the back of the Northumbrian's cuirass with a hollow clang, and sliding off and away—though the force of the buffet was sufficient to throw the steward forward in his saddle, crushing Simon against the horse's neck.

They plunged on. The shouting increased behind them, followed by the clash of blows. Some at least of the Hexham party had been intercepted. Abel Ridley glanced over his steel-clad shoulder. Then he reined up, and tugged his bay round.

Their followers had scattered, dispersed. Some had won

clear, uphill. Three were being actually engaged, others being chased. The led horses were an encumbrance. Two had already been turned adrift and were plunging off on their own. And after these, five of the Scots were galloping, in preference to those who had left them. As ever, the Borderers tended to see things from a practical standpoint—and plunder was ever of more use than dead men.

Abel Ridley, though prudent, was no coward. Escape, un-scathed, would have been the best and sensible course. But since that attempt had failed, he would fight if he must. The man who had hurled his lance at them had now turned his attention to one of the younger Hexham riders, engaging him with his sword, the Englishman fighting back. And even as they stared, a second Scot came boring down upon the pair.

Ridley spat out a single word, plucked his lance out of its socket, levelled it, and dug in his spurs.

They charged down upon the fighting couple. The Home had his back to them, thrusting and slashing furiously. The other oncoming Merseman undoubtedly noted their approach, and shouted a warning. But he was shouting, anyway, as were most other people, and the drumming of his horse's hooves probably drowned the noise of the steward's onset. Moreover, the two sworders were directly between him and Ridley's line of attack—and only seconds were involved.

Simon's obligation to Ridley was purely personal. No duty lay upon him to allow a fellow-countryman to be ridden down and slain, unwarned. Summoning every ounce of his scanty strength, he opened his mouth and yelled. What he yelled he did not know.

A cracked and broken shout it was, but sufficiently shrill to penetrate the clamour—and only just in time. Another moment or two and the lance would have transfixed its quarry. The man heard, glanced back—and jerked his mount violently around. Ridley plunged past, too late to alter course effectively, and the lance-point missed by inches. The young Northum-brian under attack, seizing his opportunity, changed a protec-tive parry into a blind backhanded swipe, which toppled his

27

disconcerted opponent right out of his saddle to the tussocky ground.

Ridley cursed, wrenched at his bay's head to pull it round—but was too late. The second Scot also strove desperately to change the direction of his charge, in this new situation, but likewise was not in time. They collided headlong amidst a splintering of lances, the clash of steel, and the lashing of hooves. The impact was prodigious—and complicated in its effect. For three other horses were involved, cumbering those few square feet of hillside—those of the attacked youth and his fallen assailant, and also his led horse. Three beasts went down in a chaos of flailing limbs, the big bay one of them.

And once again oblivion came to Simon Armstrong's rescue and enfolded at least his consciousness.

Why should the spirit of man fight for light and definition and awareness when dark and quiet and blessed nothingness are so much to be preferred on every count? Simon Armstrong knew, even when next he began tentatively to reach out feebly towards consciousness, that he was far better where he was, snug in the deep womb of insensibility, than in pain-racked perception. Yet he forced himself, time and again, against all inclination, to struggle back to the surface of sentience, back to sorrow.

It took a long time, too, and much casting and considering. They were riding again, that was clear, riding at a steady trot, not galloping, fleeing. He identified the bay horse still under him, too, and presently the man Ridley holding him as before, helmet gone now and bare head plastered with mud and blood. He was still a prisoner, then? His captors had escaped the Scots. But not all of them. Simon could see only four of the band remaining. And but two pack-horses. The rest were gone, then—left behind? Yet they had somehow held on to himself. Ridley must consider him valuable indeed.

They rode down a wide and fertile valley with cattle peacefully agraze on either hand. That would be either Coquetdale or North Tynedale, depending on how long he had been

28

unconscious. He hoped . . . yes, he hoped weakly, cravenly, that it was the Tyne—for then they would be the nearer to Hexham and to an end of this purgatory of riding, farther away from Scotland and home as it was.

The man's mind wandered, then, sickly to the thought of home, of his grey stone tower amongst the sheep-strewn hills where Borthwick joined Teviot, of his sister Ailie alone therein, whose heart would be wae for him. He sighed deeply for her— and perhaps for himself too. Poor Ailie, all her lee-lane. Poor Sim, too—poor Sim Armstrong . . .

Drops of water splattering up to his face brought him momentarily back to reality and the fact that they were splashing across a ford. He stirred—and Abel Ridley saw that his eyes were open.

"So you played me false, my master!" the big man said thickly, through swollen lips. "You'd ha' been the death o' me, eh? Crying out to your friends. I near ran you through for that, by Wilfred's blood!"

Simon knitted his brows. Also he shook his head urgently— but quickly desisted at the stunning pain of it. "No, no," he mumbled. "Not so." The unfairness of this, the injustice, was hard, hard, so that he bit his lip. "I . . . did not essay . . . escape," he claimed. "I bided . . . with you . . ."

The other snorted. "You had little choice!" he said.

They were riding through woodlands now, of oak and ash and hazel, already yellowing here and there to autumn. The tree-trunks were casting long shadows in a chequer-work of black and gold. That meant that it was late, wearing towards evening. The road had been as long as it seemed, then. Hexham would be thirty-five or forty miles from the College Water. Surely they must be near there now?

For some time Simon was aware of the ringing sound before he recognised it for what it was—he, whose head was ringing anyway. It was bells, distant, clangorous, insistent bells, pealing out wildly, tumultuously, across hill and dale and haugh and wood, coming to them above the tattoo of their horses' hooves, the clank of armour, and the creak of saddlery. Only a church, and a great church, could send forth that volume of triumphant clamour—the princely Priory of Hexham, proud mistress of the northern dales. This little party was not the first home with news of victory, then. The bells were beginning to peel all over Northumbria. By tomorrow all the English North would be clanging with the glad tidings of Flodden Field.

Soon thereafter, sooner than he could have hoped in view of the still distant sound of those bells, the clatter of hooves on cobble-stones and the echoes from surrounding courtyard walls announced journey's end to Simon Armstrong. He was aware of such things as fine stonework, glazed windows, fruit-trees and the cackle of geese; also of a deal of shouting and the chatter of voices. Then he was being lifted down from Ridley's saddle by rough hands—and straightway the hurt and agony of the process overcame all else, and he knew nothing more, certainly or coherently, until presently he realised that his state was wonderfully and blissfully improving. He was at rest, at last, and in a great bed, seemingly. Moreover, gentle ministering hands were now about him, not rough harsh ones, and soft voices sounded in his ears in place of gruff and ribald ones—though they came to him as through a veil, a throbbing clanging veil of sound, equally compounded of hammer-blows inside his head, and those damnable bells without. He wished, as he had never wished for anything before, that those bells would be still. The hammer-blows also, of course—but the bells were the worst, jangling, clamouring, beating out their endless rhythm of exultation. Other bells there would be ringing, too. Could he just catch a hint of them, coming echoing down the long Cheviot valleys out of the north—slow, sad, heavy bells, tolling out Scotland's sorrow and disaster . . . ? He strained, amidst all that chiming and clanging, to hear those other slow bells. But strive as he would, he could not hear them now. Not any more. Though, indeed, even the nearer urgent pealing was fading now, dying away. The hammer-blows too, slowly they sank and dwindled. Peace, blessed peace was smoothing his burning throbbing brows, smoothing, smoothing . . .

The man's unquiet spirit yielded, and slid away into dark tranquil depths.

III

SIMON ARMSTRONG was a captive now, indeed—and in a strange land, so much more strange and foreign than was merely Hexhamshire in Northumbria. It was an uncertain and chaotic world, but terribly real, compounded of black deeps and swirling red mists, of eddying fathomless tides and boundless empty arid plains and dead petrified forests, wherein was neither sense of time nor sequence nor any order or clarity—though certain impressions were vivid enough, recurring and terrifying. For aeons of time he wandered, lost and trapped in these grievous places, eternities dragging himself out of clutching dismal floods, plunging through endless miasmas, seeking escape from menacing and nameless threats. They were never far away, those dire and malevolent things, potent and persistent. In the main they were formless and monstrous dangers these, and none the less noxious for that; but sometimes they crystallised into flailing blood-stained halberds that pursued him of their own volition, enormous swords that thrust and smote, limbless men that trundled and rolled after him, and headless corpses who ringed him round and bore him down. None gave him rest nor relief in all those untold seasons of disquiet.

It was long, long before any glimmer of comfort or easement dawned in that murky limbo of night. But somehow, somewhere, something that was not inimical and evil and hurtful crept into the weary travail of Simon's captivity, something small and vague admittedly, but good, merciful. And persisted and established itself, away in some deep reach of the void in which he was imprisoned, small and remote but warm, like the memory of kindness. And there it glowed quietly, encouragingly, a tiny beacon of sanity and hope and friendliness, lit amongst the borderline hills of horror and hurt, a beacon that burned steadily, and grew in brightness as time, immeasurable time, rolled past and over him.

At what stage in his prolonged affliction the man began to give form and definition and character to this emanation of kindliness there was no knowing. But gradually, imperceptibly, the mild but steadfast influence to which he turned more and more, took shape in Simon's fevered and deranged perception, as feminine. Woman. Just woman, gentle, tender, constant, ministering.

And thereafter, somehow, the frightened, hunted, harried spirit of Simon Armstrong began to struggle, to fight back, not just to flee and cringe and hide from the dark things that haunted him. And always the woman was there, sustaining him, upholding him. It was not as a woman, a person, that he was aware of her, but rather as woman herself, essential and fundamental.

Then, one day, Simon, struggling with a vigour and urgency that he had never before achieved, fought to draw aside the cloying muffling curtains of that dolorous prison-land of his, seeking to follow her as she seemed to back away before him. And wondrously, gloriously, if only momentarily, he won out of the jealous enveloping folds, out into a place of light and air. His eyes open, he stared up at a woman indeed, who was bending over him.

Unblinking, he gazed, into deep brown eyes, warm and compassionate and calm, so blessedly calm for a man who lived with gibbering horror and fathomless evil. Drinking in the calm assurance of those eyes, Simon sighed with a great, an overpowering relief, and sank back into a darkness that no longer terrified.

After that, his awareness of the woman grew apace, and no longer just as a symbol, a presence. Though still entangled in the skirts of the dark, he was near to the surface now, escaped out of the blacker depths. Moreover, somehow the knowledge was born in him that one day he would win quite clear of it all. If he just waited quietly, harbouring his strength, one day the brown-eyed woman would hold out her hand, and he would reach out and take it, and she would draw him through

33

those grasping twining curtains, and he would be free. He bided his time, cunningly.

The day dawned, too—though it was not quite like that.

With the acceptance of utter exhaustion and prostration, Simon considered the dark-panelled low-ceiled chamber—or such of it as was straight in front of him, for by no means could he find strength to turn his head on the pillow. He lay on a great posted bed, with much white linen and warm coverings. A fire of logs flickered and hissed companionably on the hearth opposite. A brass vessel of autumn leaves and dog-hips stood on a table near by, along with a laving-bowl and cloth. For a time the man watched the play of firelight on the polished gleaming sides of these, with a sort of wondering satisfaction.

And then a worm of discontent began to twist and turn within him. Where was she? Had she left him alone—deserted him, now? He sought to turn his head, to look about him; desperately he strove—and could not do it. Tears of frustration and weakness rolled down his emaciated cheeks, so that all became dim and blurred. Even to blink his eyes clear required a major effort. But he could sniff . . .

Perhaps petulance was stronger in the man than will-power, at that moment, and achieved a fretful twitch of his head, however slight. And then she swam into his view. She was not gone. She was there, near him. In the room. Standing by a window. There was a man beside her—but Simon had no interest in the man. His eyes closed in satisfaction and relief. All was well.

But he opened them again very soon. She was still there, talking quietly with this fellow, this monkish man. And she was young and very comely, a tall lissome womanly figure, dark-haired, dark-eyed, generous-mouthed, dressed in a full-skirted gown of dark stuff, slashed at the front to show a brightly contrasting flowered petticoat, her waist encircled by a leather girdle from which hung a bunch of keys. Not that Simon Armstrong perceived all this there and then. But what he saw was enough.

34

Perhaps the quiet talkers heard his sniffs, for, turning, they saw that the invalid was watching them, and came over to his bed. The man was elderly, plump and genial-looking, dressed in the black robes of the Augustinian friars. The girl bent over the bed, smiling gently.

"So you have come back to us, at last," she said. Her voice was low-pitched, almost husky, unhurried. "I am glad. Very glad."

Simon took that in, and digested it. She was glad. But though he was glad too, he could not tell her so. He could not answer her, not by so much as a nod of the head. He was sorry about that, at the same time as he was glad.

She seemed to understand, however, for she touched his shoulder with the lightest of finger-tips, and told him not to worry, not to fret, not to do anything at all. Everything was well and as it should be. He would soon be himself again, strong. Meantime, he must lie still, and care for nothing.

While the friar nodded benign agreement, she leaned over and took the cloth from the laving-bowl and with it carefully, gently, bathed Simon's face below the bandaged brow.

To maintain any coherent perception of these new surroundings for longer than a few moments was more than could be asked of the sick man. He drifted away again. But perhaps his eyes were still open, nevertheless, for suddenly he knew a great distress. She was leaving him, going away. He would be alone again. Desperately he sought to stop her from going.

He must have achieved some sound at any rate, for, as she was passing through the open doorway behind the friar, she turned to look back at the man on the bed.

"It is all right. All right," she reassured him. "I am not going away, not leaving you. Never fear . . ."

But seeing the look of apprehension and alarm in his sunken eyes, she smiled again, threw a word or two after the departing priest, and came back to the bedside. She took the man's thin hand and spoke soothingly, almost crooning, as though to a child. What she said Simon knew not, nor cared. He was satisfied. She was going to stay with him. That was all that mattered. He could trust her. He could rest, now . . .

After that, things were better for Simon Armstrong. Fear and dread and doubt gradually died in him. He was still uncertain, unenlightened, about most things pertaining to his state, particularly of time, of the passage of hours and days—indeed, he was not interested in such matters. But he *was* aware that he was not alone any more. That he had a friend, and that she was there, near, when he needed her. He did not decide, in so many words, that he would restrain himself, would not call on her often, or unnecessarily. But the manhood in him was returning. Somewhere his male pride was beginning to stir again. To have an ally, now, was all his need. He would be a fighting-man again, one day—so long as he could be sure of an ally.

And then, as gradually, a new and niggling doubt was born and grew in the man's bemused mind. A treacherous, grievous, unworthy doubt that he could by no means banish. Could he be sure of the woman, after all? Was she to be trusted as an ally? Could he trust her any more than, say that fat friar, or those other men who sometimes came and stared down at him? At first he had been sure of her. But now he was less certain. For she changed, somehow, in her attitude towards him, one time from another, subtly. He could not tell how and in what fashion exactly it was that she changed—but he knew that she did. Gentle she was always in her ministrations, and attentive—but sometimes she looked at him differently from others, he sensed. Sometimes her tone of voice was changed. Not that words meant much to the man, yet—but the tone did. At times he knew her as purely patient, mild, kind; at others she seemed almost to be challenging him, to be urgent, demanding. Even in the way that she touched him, something deep within him, his stirring manhood perhaps, knew something of contrast, almost of conflict. And sensing this duality, this unreliability of mood and attitude, unease grew in the sick man.

Then, one day, he came to an understanding, solved the problem.

He had awakened out of a deep sleep, feeling infinitely

better, stronger, more alive, than he had done hitherto, and within moments was looking around for the woman. She was not there. Nobody was with him. Without realising it, he actually raised himself on an elbow on his pillow, the better to survey the room. Before, he would have felt querulous, neglected. But not this time. Now he considered his surroundings, for the first time with a seeing eye, noting the rain that was beating against the glazed window, the richness of the dark linenfold panelling on the walls, the white sheepskins on the floor that was neither rush-strewn nor sanded, but seemingly polished with wax. He was savouring these things, like the fine fire blazing between the winking brass firedogs on the hearth, when the door opened, and the woman came in.

"Aha, Master Armstrong," she cried. "Here is a happy sight! The sleeper awakes. Lazarus arises!" And she laughed musically.

Simon considered her also, intently. She was dressed differently, in gayer colours this time, in more eye-catching fashion altogether—for instance, the neck of her gown was certainly lower, above a high and tightly belted waist, and there was some sparkling ornament in her hair. None of which did any injustice to her dark loveliness. The man perceived that the young woman was more than just comely.

He sought to speak, and found words amazingly hard to come by. It seemed a long time since he had had cause to use them. "I . . . you . . . I thank you," he got out.

"Actually talking, too! This is indeed a day—the first words that we have heard out of you. I am privileged, sir!" And she sketched a curtsey as she came over to his bed. "Most men talk too much—even when they are fevered! But not Master Armstrong. I think that you must be a very deep one, sirrah!"

Simon did not belie the reputation she was giving him. He searched her face, her eyes, unspeaking. Her eyes—they were laughing, sparkling eyes, the eyes that he had remembered as calm, calm. And the brown of them was flecked with green, he saw now—he had not noticed that before. He sighed.

She chattered on as she straightened his bed linen, playfully

37

accusing him of dour Scots reticence, of deliberately keeping himself to himself, of preferring his own company. She had all but despaired of ever gaining not his life but his attention, she said.

Wary-eyed he observed her—and certainly her rounded womanliness was very much in evidence as she bent over him. But the man's regard tended to stray lower still, to her slender waist. At last he spoke. "Where are . . . your keys?" he asked, slowly, thickly.

Surprised, she paused. "Keys?" Her quick glance followed his slow one to her girdle, a handsome embroidered belt, silver-mounted. "Ah, I see. You think that I am your gaoler, Sir Prisoner? I' faith, no—I carry no keys. That is Esther. My sister. She is the housekeeper, the elder."

Her sister! Not this one at all? Could it be that? Two of them. Alike—but not alike. Sisters. And the other—the one that was different from this, had the keys. Perhaps it was all right, after all? Perhaps his friend, his ally, still was the same? Calm. Sure. A great surge of relief came over the man.

"Have no fear—I shall be a kind captor," the girl went on. "Can you not see that? Do I seem fearsome?" She eased him back on to his pillow. "But now, you must eat. We must bring food to make a proper man of you again. The breast of a fat capon? And mulled Bordeaux wine?"

Simon licked dry lips. "Your sister . . . ?"

"Fie, man—my sister will not hurt you. Her keys are not so potent . . ."

"No. She will not hurt you." The low-pitched, next to husky, voice spoke from the doorway. "Marcia speaks truth, sir."

He raised himself up again, unaware of the effort, under the other girl's restraining hand. The speaker came slowly over to him, smiling as slowly. And Simon smiled too, a near grimace though it was, twitching the hollow-cheeked bearded face.

"God be praised for this," she said gently.

Looking from one sister to the other, the man marvelled that two young women could be at once so similar and yet so strikingly dissimilar. Each had the same features, of high broad forehead, arching brows, fine eyes, straight rather short nose flaring to sensitive nostrils, and wide mouth above firm but delicately moulded chin. Each had lustrous dark hair drawn well back from the face, and a clear healthy pallor of complexion. Each was tall and well made, with long bones carried easily, gracefully. Of age, there could be only a year or two between them. Yet none but a deranged or barely conscious man would mistake one for the other. It was not physically that they differed notably, then, but in bearing and expression and manner. Probably it was in the eyes that the contrast was most marked; where Esther's, the elder, glowed deeply, calm, steady, her sister Marcia's flashed and sparkled brilliantly. Thus one girl's expression was tranquil, serene, while the other's was lively, vivacious. And while Esther's every movement was unhurried, her bearing restrained, her sister's was quite otherwise, implicit with a conscious femininity that held the eye. And both were of the sort to bewitch a man.

"He spoke to me, Esther—he truly spoke!" the girl Marcia cried. "Our captive has a tongue, after all. But I think that he fears you, and your keys!" And she laughed.

"Hush, magpie . . ." her sister was chiding, when Simon actually interrupted, hoarsely but urgently. "No," he said.

"No? I am glad of that," gravely Esther assured him. "But are you better? You are not in pain? Your leg? Your poor head . . . ?"

He shook his poor head. "My name . . . is Simon," he said.

"Simon! Simon Armstrong," Marcia took him up, repeating the words as though savouring them on her tongue. "A fair enough name . . . for a scoundrelly Scot!"

"Pay no heed to her, Master Armstrong," her sister advised. "Her tongue is the worst of her. Lie back, now. You must not tax yourself. You have been very ill, for many weeks. You must rest, and care for nothing—save to eat and grow strong again. You have swallowed no solid meats. That we shall remedy, forthwith. Come, Marcia—we shall see what the kitchen can produce."

"Our Simon needs company, needs inspiriting, as much as he needs victuals, perhaps?" the other girl suggested. "I shall provide the one while you go find the other . . ."

"No, you shall not, chatterer," Esther declared, mildly but firmly. "Father Crispin, you will recollect, said that he must suffer no excitement, no tiring. And you, Sister, would tire an archangel. Come."

Reluctantly Marcia shrugged shapely shoulders. "Well—one thing I insist upon, ere I go. That he tells us, this Simon, more than his own name. The name of his wife, say, back in Tividale . . . if he has one?"

"Shame on you, Marcia! Here is no question to . . ."

Simon shook his head, on his pillow. "I have no wife," he said. "Only a sister."

"So!" Laughing again, Marcia tossed her head. "You hear that, my dear? What did I tell you!" And with a lift of expressive eyebrows, she flashed dancing eyes on the invalid, before turning to follow her sister from the chamber.

The man reached up thin trembling fingers to stroke his chin, found it grossly bearded, and frowned.

IV

"SO you have not managed to cheat us, after all, young man!" Abel Ridley cried, towering hugely above the bed. "You ha' deigned to collect your wits, and come back to us, heh? And not before time, by Saint Wilfred! I swear you had me afeared that you were to be naught but a loss to us!"

"Hush, Father . . ."

"Hush-tush yourself, girl! I'll speak my mind. I've waited long enough, 'fore God!" the big man cried strongly—but his eyes twinkled. Looking up, Simon perceived that those eyes were grey, not brown like those of his daughters. "These wenches, Sir Scot, ha' kept me out of here all this time—lest I upset you, forsooth! Now, I'll ha' my say."

Simon thought this statement less than the truth—for had he not been dimly aware of the big steward's presence sometimes in those vague unquiet days that were past, leaning over him—just as that friar and others had done, likewise. But perhaps the man was referring only to these last two days? For it was the evening following the day when first he had really come to himself, had spoken to the young women, and partaken of solid food. Now, notably strengthened by the last, at least, he sat up amongst his pillows, the shadow of himself again.

"I have been of much trouble to you, Master Ridley," Simon acknowledged, speaking slowly, but clearly enough. "And to your daughters." He turned his eyes on the girl, who stood at the other side of the bed. Only the one sister was present, just then, the elder, Esther—and, better as he was, her nearness was still as a tower of strength to the man. "I am sorry. And grateful. Better, perhaps, had you left me on the field at Flodden Hill . . ."

"I feared the same myself, some time back . . ." Ridley was

agreeing, nodding, when his daughter broke in.

"No! Never! Father—you shame us!" she declared, less calm than was her wont. "Your baiting and teasing is untimely. Do not heed him, Simon—Master Armstrong. He but cozens you—cozens us both. He esteems it wit."

"Ha, lass—harp you on that string?" Her father looked at her sidelong, and tugged his beard. "So ho! Hear how she miscalls her sire—and calls you Simon, sirrah! But do not be misled—if I know woman, her concern is less in your welfare than in assuring her share in the fine thousand golden lions that your life will fetch us! Or was it fifteen hundred?"

"May you be forgiven that!" Esther said, flushing a little, but her voice even again. "To talk of money, now . . . !"

"I talk of it, woman—but you spend it!" Ridley chuckled. "Ever it was so. Beshrew me—would you have us to gain no profit soever of our venture against King Hal's enemies? An expensive sortie it was, too. Four good lads lost, your father with a broken head—and only two packs of poor Scots gear and this young man to show for it! We must make the most of him, I say!"

"My promise holds, sir," Simon declared. "A thousand golden lions, I said—and five hundred more for your Priory of Hexham."

"Aye, aye, lad—your memory is not affected, I see! But this was a long time back—weeks agone. Methinks there falls to be made some oncharge. Getting you here cost us dear. And ha' we not guested and nursed you all this time . . . ?"

"Stop!" the girl exclaimed, her brown eyes nearer blazing than glowing. "Cozening or none, I will not hear another word of this! Father—in sweet mercy's name . . . !"

"Dear God—do I offend again . . . ?"

"Sir—I accept your oncharge. 'Tis fair enough." That was Simon, intervening. "My life was the stake—a few pieces the more cannot repay my debt. In especial to your daughter . . ."

"No! No!"

"Yes. I would be happier, for my honour, that this should be. My estate, at a pinch, might raise another five hundred, I think."

"Spoken like an Armstrong!" Ridley acknowledged, handsomely. "Quiet, girl. My grandam was an Armstrong. Of the better sort, see you—from Morpeth. She was a notable woman. Maybe you have her, also, to thank for your life. When I saw your blazon . . ." He shrugged, and left the rest unsaid.

"Yes. My thanks. But . . . have you yet sent word to Stirkshaws? To my sister? For the gold?"

"Not so. What would you? We are honest folk, here in Northumberland. Would you ha' had us take the money and then trade them only a corpse, maybe? There was no profit in sending a message until it was clear that you would live. Moreover, belike your people would not believe and accept such message, without it bore your own handwriting and superscription? Might they not esteem it a cheat?"

"So Ailie . . . my sister, does not know? She will think me dead! Like all the others."

"I *said* that we should send word, at the least," Esther put in.

"Sending such word into Scotland is no light task, let me remind you, Daughter. The man who carries it takes his life in his hands. One such employ is enough."

"But you *will* send, forthwith?" Simon urged. "I will write the letter, ordering the gold, if you will give me quill and paper. There is no need to delay further . . ."

"Heed you his haste, lass?" Ridley exclaimed. "Our Scot has had enough of us. And of your nursing, girl."

"It will be weeks, months, before he can journey back to Scotland," Esther said quietly. "A broken leg does not mend so fast. Father Crispin says that he will not be out of this bed itself for many a day. He will have to be patient."

"Ummmm," said Abel Ridley. "We shall see. We need not be *too* tardy . . ."

"You could send the message, at least," Simon pressed. "So that my sister should know—know that I still live. And gather the ransom money. She will have to sell much cattle and sheep to gain it. I will write the letter . . ."

"The letter is the least of it. Finding the man to carry the letter into Scotland, to Tividale, will be less simple. A pedlar perhaps, or an Egyptian, might serve best. Or better still, a wandering friar. Someone who may move around across the Border, without suspicion. Yes, a begging friar would be best. Many such pass here, through Hexham, on their way from Durham to Jedworth and Dryburgh. Such should go safe, even from Home's raiders."

"Raiders . . . ?" Simon looked up. "Home? Does my Lord Home, then, still live? And lead his Mersemen?"

"Marry, does he not—the foul fiend flay him! He has led or set on, a score of forays into our peaceful Northumbria during this last moon, burning and harrying . . ."

"Forays? Then . . . then Scotland is not laid low? Crushed? Overrun?" The sick man's weak voice trembled.

"Alas, no," the steward admitted ruefully. "The pity of it— my Lord Surrey turned back from Flodden. He did not go on to conquer Scotland. He did not even move to capture Berwick. Some say that he had had his bellyful; some that he had an understanding with Albany, your king's cousin, who would now be regent for young James Fifth; others, that he fell out with his own commanders—and certes, I know that he had words with my Lord Dacre, our Warden. Who can tell? But the old carle turned round, and went back to London." Ridley did not mention that one of Surrey's greatest difficulties had been the melting away of his North Country levie, after the battle, laden with spoil, leaving him with but half an army.

"Perhaps we hit him harder than it seemed," Simon suggested. "We may have done better than we knew . . ." A faint flush had crept into the gaunt face, and the sunken eyes glittered. "Perhaps it was not such a terrible defeat . . . ?"

"Tush, man—you know not what you say! It was a defeat the like of which has never been known. On the field fell your king, the archbishop, two bishops, ten mitred abbots, a dozen earls, a score of lords, knights by the hundred, the provosts of half the towns of the land, and the heads of near to every noble and gentle family in your country. On our side, few of the

44

quality were so much as wounded."

"It may be that they left the fighting to the baser sort, then? For we died dear."

The older man shrugged, avoiding his daughter's eye—for had he not made that very same remark himself, one time? "As to that, I have not heard that it is the place of generals and commanders to ply pikes in the forefront of the battle, like common men-at-arms. As did your James and his barons. Here was folly, by all the saints!"

"Aye. Folly. But noble folly!" Simon sighed. "James Stewart lived a hundred years too late, I fear. Yet . . . yet your Surrey did not follow up his victory. And he is a sage and crafty warrior. Surely he was more shrewdly hit than you admit . . . ?"

"Not so," the steward contended strongly. "Statecraft, it may ha' been. Or divided counsels, belike. Not your Scots prowess of arms."

"But . . ."

"Peace! A truce—both of you!" the young woman intervened. "'Tis said that the Earl of Surrey himself knew not who was victor till the morrow of the battle, when daylight showed him in possession of the field. And such was his delight then, that, though he had berated his leaders the night before for poor fighting, he dubbed forty of them knights in the morning! So my Lord Dacre told the Lord Prior. So it may be that Simon is not so far amiss." Then she shook her dark head. "But here is folly likewise, to be sure! Fighting foolish battles the second time! Father—I will not have Simon excited and fretting, thus. It is the thing that must not be, Father Crispin said. It will use up his strength, bring on his fever anew. I will not allow it. You must go, now. You are no comfort to a sick man. You will go this instant!"

The big man grinned, and drooped an eyelid at the invalid.

It was Simon who protested. "No," he cried. "Do not go. There is so much yet that I must know, must hear. Who rules in Scotland? What of the Borders? Buccleuch—is he dead? And Ferniehirst? And Cavers, the Sheriff . . . ?"

"Hush, hush. All that you will learn in good time . . ."

"No. Tell me now. I have been too long ignorant. There is so much to learn. I do not even know where I am, save that it is near to Hexham in Tynedale!"

"You are in the Grange of Anick—my house," Ridley informed him. "I am steward, for the Lord Prior of Hexham, of the manors and demesnes of Anick, Acomb, Hallington, Fallowfield and Bingfield—no mean charge. And, marry—by the same token, I must go attend the affairs thereof, Master Armstrong, for a parcel of our beeves go to market tomorrow, and it will be dark within the hour. Another time I will enlighten you on the sorry state of your Scotland!"

"You will not forget the paper and quill—for my letter? Tomorrow . . . ?"

"Tomorrow I shall be at the market, and throng with affairs. But the next day, belike. The morrow's morn . . ."

"There is no hurry, in the world," his daughter asserted. "Now, lie back and rest—for you look liker a wraith than a man, I vow. If this is to be my father's effect on you, I will keep him away for much longer than the morrow's morn."

"No. I shall look for you then, sir," Simon insisted, as the other moved away, with a nod. But he sank back on his pillows, nevertheless, under the young woman's gentle pressure, and closed his eyes. He was tired, tired . . .

But it was not Esther Ridley who prevented her sire from coming to help compose that ransom letter two days following. In the interim, Thomas, Lord Dacre, Warden of the English Marches, on King Henry's orders, called on all lords of manors in his area, the Prior of Hexham amongst them, to provide levies for a great punitive raid over the Border. The Scots must be taught another lesson and have it brought home to them that Henry was not so preoccupied with his French wars that he had forgotten the old enemy. So Abel Ridley assembled a score or so of men from his bailiwick and went to join the Hexham contingent under the Prior's chief steward, Jem Harndean. Lord Dacre was ordering his force in two thrusts— one, under his own command, of perhaps a thousand men,

46

including the Hexham levies, to move across the Border by the time-honoured route from Redesdale, over the Carter Bar; the other, of three times that number, under his brother Sir Philip, to strike from far to the west, at Kershopebridge near Liddesdale, both to meet near Jedburgh, laying waste the land between.

Nothing loth, Abel Ridley rode off northwards in the grey November weather, on what promised to be a gainful and edifying expedition. His daughters declared that he was always readier for such a ploy than for the less militant aspects of Holy Church's business.

So Simon Armstrong had to possess his soul in such patience as was in him—and he had never been a notably patient man—and to steel his mind to futile and painful imaginings as to what was happening to his countrymen only thirty or forty miles away in the Scots Border valleys. In this he was aided by his nurses, who, in their different ways, were determined apparently that he should not fret nor pine. With their help, and that of Father Crispin, the Priory's apothecary, if with only moderate co-operation on his own part, he commenced his long slow climb out of the depths of weakness and debility to convalescence and recovery and the faraway heights of wholeness and the pride of manhood.

He recognised that many might have envied him his pilgrimage, and was not entirely ungrateful.

V

THE days passed, and lengthened into weeks. Abel Ridley came home again—a deal sooner than was expected, and but ill rewarded in gear and beasts for all his labours, to his own and his Lord Prior's disgust. The great raid into Scotland had been less than a success. Numerous farm-towns and little communities in Upper Liddesdale and the valleys of Rule, Jed and Kale had been sacked and burned, sundry peel-towers had been smoked out and thrown down, and harvested crops destroyed. But the booty had been paltry indeed from these small upland glens, especially for division amongst Dacre's four thousand, and the pickings of the richer, wider, more worthwhile dales of Teviot and Tweed and Ettrick and Yarrow had been denied them. Not only that, but even much of their gain from the lesser places had had to be discarded on the homeward march. The Lord Home and his bloodthirsty mosstroopers from the Eastern Marches, together with Douglas of Cavers, Sheriff of Teviotdale, and Kerr of Ferniehirst—who both seemed to have survived Flodden—summoned by the balefires on a score of hilltops, had turned up in such unexpected strength that Dacre had been forced to temper enthusiasm for his king's command with wholesome discretion. Not to put too fine a point on it, the English forces had had to retire hurriedly southwards from the Jedburgh area, and back over Carter and the Redeswire, harried by the Scots, being obliged to abandon much that would have delayed them in goods and cattle and even women, fruit of much zeal in King Henry's cause. This undoubtedly was what came of not having completed the work at Flodden Field. Whilst the Middle Marches, Teviotdale, Tweeddale and so on were admittedly practically devoid of able-bodied men as a result of the Flodden slaughter, Home's own Berwickshire contingent had got away almost scot-free, had been able to rally many broken men, and now

48

constituted a serious menace, denying the victors their legitimate rewards.

It all made gloomy telling—save to Simon Armstrong.

Lord Dacre had to ply a dexterous pen thereafter adequately to deal with the situation—for King Hal was not a man who appreciated doleful tidings and admissions of failure. Consequently he had rather to highlight the earlier stages of the raid in his dispatch, dealing with the destruction done on the Liddel, the Rule, the Jed and the Kale, and to draw something of a veil over the subsequent happenings between Jedburgh and his own good Border—at the same time taking the opportunity to insert a useful complaint against sundry rival Northumbrian lords whose credit he could do with reducing a little. As thus:

". . . I well perceive your Highness regardeth not the sinister report or rumour surmised against me . . . I assembled your subjects in Northumberland . . . my brother Philip Dacre with 300 men, which burnt and destroyed the town of Rowcastle with all the corns in the same and thereabouts, and won two towers in it and burnt both roof and floors; and Sir Roger Fenwick with 300 men burnt the town of Lanton . . . my brother Sir Christopher Dacre put forth two forays. Sir John Ratcliff with 500 men in one, which burnt Dykeraw with a tower of the same, they laid corn and straw to the door and burnt both roof and floor and so smoked them out. Also burnt the towns of Southdean and Lustruther with a tower in it, and took divers prisoners with much insight and goods . . . burnt the town of Hyndhalghede, likewise the towns of West and East Sawsyde with a peel of lime and stone in it . . ."

That was the sort of thing that bluff Hal Tudor would like to read, and put him in right mood for the next bit.

". . . Sir, I see not the gentlemen of the country in readiness for defence of your borders, for certain of them to whom I had given warning, as my Lord Ogle which

49

promised to come to me, the Constable of Alnwick, and, others, trusting they would have been glad to do your Grace service . . . come not to me at the place appointed, whereby I was not accompanied as I thought to have been . . . Also, please your Grace, it seems it were necessary that your letter of commandment were direct to my Lord of Northumberland and my Lord of Clifford, to cause their tenants to give attendance upon your Warden . . ."

Thomas Dacre, indeed, was almost as puissant with the pen as with the sword. He felt reasonably satisfied with the foregoing, and rightly so.

Meanwhile, other penmanship was practised at Anick Grange—if with a less steady and assured hand. This missive also had to be carefully worded, with tones and overtones of meaning—only, since it was the work of more than one mind, there was considerable argument over certain phrases. For instance, Simon insisted upon the wording ". . . the total sum of 2000 lions in gold money, of which but one half, of 1000 lions, is to be sent by trusty bearer to this place forthwith, the other half to be held until my own person is delivered safe and sound to Stirkshaws, when it shall be handed to my escort, with a safe convoy out of our country." But Abel Ridley deplored this delaying, suspicious and cheese-paring attitude, claiming that all 2000 lions should be handed over right away. Both his daughters, however, supported the prisoner, in that he had to have some safeguard that the bargain would be carried out once the money was paid. It was with a poor grace that the steward conceded the point.

About another item, however, Ridley was adamant. Simon, knowing that other raids on the Scots valleys were projected by Dacre, would have liked to insert some warning of such in his letter, disguising it in some innocent-seeming suggestion that his sister Ailie should sell all the livestock and movable gear and turn it into convenient money, the which she should bestow in some safe place in view of the difficult times that were likely to come. But the steward would allow nothing of this, phrase the warning how he would. Beyond the assurance that Simon was alive, mending in health, and in good hands, no other message than the actual instructions regarding the ransom money were permitted, despite Esther's pleas.

When this letter was finished, to less than the writer's satisfaction as it was, and duly signed, Simon was interested to note that his signet-ring was produced to seal it—and thereupon returned to the capacious pocket from which it had come. No comment was made. The folded and addressed missive was then laid in a cupboard to await the arrival of some wandering friar whom the Prior would send to act as bearer.

Less informative than he would have wished though it was, the sending of this letter lifted a notable load off the prisoner's mind. At least his sister and people would now soon know that he lived, and the measures for his release and return home would be set in train. It was with a growing exasperation, therefore, that Simon learned that no suitable mendicant friar had yet appeared, as day succeeded day. In his helpless and inactive state, this seemed to him to be quite insufferable, a feebleness and folly that amounted to sheer obstruction—and as much against his captors' interests as his own. Surely they could send out and find somebody, some monk or churchman if such it must be, capable of travelling fifty miles through the hills and delivering a letter . . . ?

Marcia Ridley it was who, as recipient of this outburst, sought to explain and reassure—if not to soothe, for soothing was but little in her line. What was the hurry, she asked? Was it not better to wait until a really reliable and suitable messenger could be found, who could cross the wild Debatable Land safely, than to risk some other courier who might never be able to deliver his letter?

"Aye. But surely your Prior could send for such a one?" the patient objected. "So great a man as he . . ."

The girl shook her head. "I think you must be lacking in wit, as well as in patience, Simon Armstrong," she charged him. "What, think you, would be the result if the Lord Prior let it be known that he was seeking especially a courier to consort

51

with the King's enemies across the Border? My Lord Dacre, the Warden, whose minions are everywhere, would soon come to hear of it—and would have something to say, I promise you! And has it escaped your notice, my hasty warrior, that you yourself would be the first to suffer if, in bruiting it abroad that such a messenger was needed, your own presence here was discovered?"

"My presence discovered?" Simon echoed foolishly. "Discovered by whom?"

"By any other than our own folk, and some of the Prior's people. Mary-a-mercy, Simon—do you not realise it that your presence in this house is a secret?"

The man stared. "I do not understand . . ."

"Then time it is that you did, simpleton! My father took a grievous hazard in bringing you here—and takes a greater one in keeping you. It was against the King's express orders. He ordained that no prisoners be taken at yonder battle. Surely you heard of that? Certain Scots who were taken by one knight, it is said, were hanged on my Lord Surrey's orders next day at Newcastle, and their captor punished. The Lord Prior would have had you dispatched the day after you were brought here, and none the wiser, but for our pleadings, and, and . . ." she pulled a face ". . . to be honest, perhaps the gold pieces that you had promised to the Priory were something to the point, also! But there it is. If it should be known abroad that you are here, I fear that more than your patience would be broke, Master Simon—it would be your stiff Scots neck! And ourselves come ill out of it, likewise. My Lord Dacre has a short way with those who counter his orders and the King's will.

Simon drew a hand across his brow. "Then . . . then I am in danger of my life, still? And you, all of you, are in danger through me?"

Marcia shrugged. "So long as you keep this house you are safe—and you will be in no case to do anything else for many a long day! Our own folk are loyal, and such of the Priory people as know will not talk. When you were brought, that day, it was given out merely that my father had helped home a wounded stranger from the battle. None others know that you still are here."

"I see," he said slowly. "So . . . I have even more to thank you for than I had realised."

"Marry—but I think you have! I thank you, sir, for your gallant acknowledgment of it!" She swept one of her mocking curtsies. "Mayhap we shall now see some indulgent response to our little kindnesses, sirrah!" And she ran light but lively finger-tips down the man's arm from shoulder to the back of his hand, lingering there for just a second.

"I . . . ah . . . ummm."

She laughed softly. "I can think of few more fortunate Scots!" she observed. "I hope that you will prove . . . deserving! I think that you will—when you are stronger, eh? The young woman tipped her full red lower lip with a pink tongue. "But . . . I think too, perhaps, that you should not mention what I have told you to my good sister. She has . . . different notions than I have, may be, of what is good for a man!"

Her patient nodded.

"Simon the Silent!" Marcia said. "We can have our secrets too!"

He eyed her thoughtfully. "You will tell me, nevertheless, when the messenger does take my letter?"

"Tcha!" Almost petulantly the girl flung away from his bedside. "Your letter—can you think of naught else? I vow it sounds to me like no sister that concerns you so mightily, back in Tividale! Sisters do not breed so much devotion!"

"My sister it is," he declared. "She is but a child, not yet twenty years. There are but the two of us . . ."

"I am but twenty years myself—and no child!" she jerked, those brown-green eyes smouldering.

"No," he agreed. "No."

It was her sister Esther, however, who told the man, a week later, on the third day of December, that a mendicant friar had come and taken his letter.

53

VI

IT was a great day for Simon Armstrong—his first venture out-of-doors, after all the weary months of confinement to his sick-room. One of his nurses supporting him on either side—though he protested that a stout stick would have served him better—he hobbled out into the sun-filled courtyard of the Grange, amongst the clucking poultry and the cheerful bustle of the farmery. Halting, he blinked in the unaccustomed light, sniffing the excellent vital smells of stable and byre and meadow-hay and midden, and smiled at the cavortings of a young dog that leapt around them barking excitedly. He smiled at all that he saw indeed, more especially at the young women who insisted on leading him, like some aged cripple, to a seat that they had prepared for him in a sunny sheltered corner under an ancient plum-tree, the knobbly branches of which were just beginning to be brushed with green.

And Simon Armstrong was no longer a cripple. He limped heavily, admittedly, his leg still bound within supporting splints of wood, his tall frame was but thinly fleshed even yet, though not actually gaunt now—but he had never been a fleshy man. He was upright, even within the old clothes of Abel Ridley's in which he was clad, over-large and hanging on him as on a scarecrow. Pale he was, but his grey eyes, no more sunken, had a gleam to them, his chin a set to it, and his whole person a bearing that proclaimed him man again. Shaven, his hair trimmed by Esther's shears, his glance eager, he settled himself under the tree, and savoured the scene, the sun, and the stirring scents of spring wafted to him on the mild air.

It was pleasant to sit there, so pleasant that for a little the man forgot his troubles and the shadows that loomed over him. Marcia brought out her embroidery frame to sit beside him; and chattered as she stitched. Esther, with her housekeeperly duties, could not so do, but frequently she came to stand beside them in quiet companionship, or just to smile from over at the house door. Two farmyard cats came to rub and purr about their legs, heedless of the pup's tentative challenges, pigeons preened themselves and strutted and cooed on the thatched roofing around them, and from somewhere farther off the rhythmic creak of millstones sounded as the oxen treaded out their slow measure.

After a harsh and blustering March, with snow lingering long in the Border valleys, it was the first real day of spring. Moreover, it was Simon's twenty-sixth birthday, and this treat had been projected and looked forward to. Now, in the relishing of it, all the long interminable weeks of waiting seemed to fall away from him, the winter of his weakness and worry and frustration to fade like the snow in the sun.

For a time, that is. It was the clatter of hooves that spoiled the illusion, the sound of horsemen riding up the road from Hexham town. And immediately the arranged precautionary action had to be taken. Simon was hustled out of sight, without delay, through the nearest doorway—into the brewhouse actually—while Marcia busied herself with a besom, like any scullion-maid. It proved only to be Abel Ridley himself, with one of his men, returned early from the Priory. But the spell for Simon Armstrong was broken, nevertheless.

Though once more installed on his seat, he remembered again that he was a prisoner—moreover, a prisoner in danger of his life, so that none must know of his presence there. Worse, the worry flooded back on him, the worry that he had lived with these many last long weeks—that there had been no word from Scotland, no response to his letter, no ransom money from Stirkshaws. Four months had passed—more than ample time surely for even the most dilatory and wandersome friar to have reached Upper Teviotdale and delivered his message, for Ailie to have sold sufficient beasts to make up the gold, and for the money to have been brought here.

Day and night the thing had nagged at the man, who had so little else to do but think, growing even as time passed. Had something happened to Ailie? Who could tell what conditions were like now, in devastated Border Scotland? Might not a young innocent girl, protected only by old and done men, have fallen victim to who knew what evil deeds? Might she be ill? Dead, even? Or might it be just that the message had never reached her—that the mendicant had failed them? That—or else that the money had indeed been sent, but had been intercepted, never reached Hexham? Stolen on the way? Or even, maybe, reached grasping hands at the Priory and got no farther? There was so much that could go wrong, such grievous dependence on chance, on people whom he did not know, had no reason to trust. And he was so utterly helpless to remedy anything . . .

Nor was Simon alone in his anxiety, needless to say. Abel Ridley, who had been kindly enough in his way, good humoured, treating his prisoner almost as a favoured guest indeed over Yuletide and its prolonged festivities, and even up till the Lenten fast, had of late grown less and less hearty, less affable, more moody and disgruntled. Less and less he came near his captive; shorter, curter grew his greetings when he saw him. He no longer referred to the delay from Scotland, not by word that is—though a month back he had intimated grimly that the Lord Prior was growing as impatient as he was, and was like to do something about it. Since then he had merely looked his displeasure and doubts. That his daughters showed no hint of corresponding coolness and impatience but on the contrary were only the kinder, more solicitous, was pleasing, a comfort—but did little to allay the anxiety in their charge's mind.

For his own case, apart altogether from his fears for his sister, was serious, and might quickly become desperate. He knew that his only excuse for being alive at all was as a source of ransom. If that should seem to be unforthcoming, then how much was his life worth? Even though, through this long association and the goodwill of his daughters, Ridley himself might not actually move to his hurt, the Prior of Hexham might very well feel no such compunction. At the beginning had he not talked about having him dispatched, according to the royal command? If he esteemed him now as no longer likely to be a source of profit, might he not fulfil his threat—or at least hand him over to Dacre? And Lord Dacre's hatred of Scots was only too well authenticated. He did not doubt but that there would be short shrift for him from the Warden of the Marches.

Though the clear April sun shone, then, and the pigeons cooed, and a fair woman not infrequently touched his knee with hers, and smiled into his eyes, the shadow returned for Simon Armstrong. He smiled back, yes, and was not unaware that he was a man again, even welcomed the awareness—but with only half his attention. The young woman did not fail to note the fact. Nor indeed did her sister, from a little farther off.

They had intended so well for his birthday. Perhaps the fine dinner that Esther had prepared would help . . . ?

It was on his third day of sitting out that it happened. Actually, Simon was not sitting either, perhaps unfortunately, but limping round the duck-pond leaning on a stick and Marcia's firm round arm at the time. The girl was talking, the ducks were quacking and the geese gabbling—and they did not hear the sound of horses until it was too late to take any avoiding action. For this was not the usual clatter of trotting hooves, but the quieter padding of softer ridden palfreys. Turning quickly, they perceived that a group of clerics were approaching, three of them, with four marching armed foot-men behind. The foremost rider sat a pure white beast of great beauty, richly caparisoned.

"The Lord Prior!" Marcia exclaimed. "I . . . we are seen, Simon." She made as though to remove her arm from his, and then thought better of it, pressing his wrist instead.

Her companion nodded, and continued to hobble on round the end of the pond and back towards the courtyard.

The clerical party came pacing in dignified and deliberate fashion, to draw up near the house door. Marcia sank down in a deep curtsey, and so remained. One of the cowherds passing from the byre, doffed bonnet, bobbed awkwardly, and remained rooted to the spot, not raising his eyes. Simon Armstrong bowed briefly.

"God's peace rest upon all who humbly obey Him!" a

sonorous voice said, but peremptorily. A single beringed finger, the jewels thereon flashing in the sun, flicked to convey the blessing. And, not waiting for the two monks behind him to finish their Amens, the voice added, in the same tone, "What means this, daughter?"

Marcia rose. "My lord—we but give Master Armstrong, our guest, the benefits of sun and air, now that he is sufficiently recovered. Just about the yard, here . . ."

"Guest, is it! Prisoner, should it not be?" the Prior said evenly. "And did I not give orders that this man was to be kept close?"

"Yes, my lord—and we do so keep him . . ."

"Tush, girl! I have eyes! And so have others—and there's the mischief."

"But, it was only as far as the duck-pond. None would see him there . . ."

"Sir Prior—it was myself who insisted," Simon put in. "Mistress Marcia would have restrained me. But I was eager to try this leg—the leg that good Father Crispin has so skilfully mended." And his glance slid past the magnificent figure on the white palfrey to one of the more humbly attired monks who sat behind—but who, however kept his glance on the cobbles of the yard.

"Sirrah—you will speak when spoken to!" the Prior snapped. He did not so much as look at Simon, from under his heavy eyelids. He was a massively built man of middle years, square jowled, pale-faced, with the hooked nose and strange hooded eyes that somehow gave him the aspect of a bird of prey—features that once seen would not readily be forgotten. Nor was his apparel less notable. He wore a rich cassock of crimson velvet, gold-buttoned and piped with gold thread, circled with a silken belt with gold tassels, from which hung a bag of finely wrought gold chain-work with jewelled mountings. Thrown over thick shoulders was a hooded gown of purple-figured damask, lined with sable fur and bordered all around with ermine, held with a great golden clasp in which large rubies and sapphires sparkled. On his head was a biretta of purple—

a colour normally reserved for bishops—and around his neck hung, on a gold chain, a large cross also of gold, encrusted with pearls. Prior Anselm of Hexham was a great and proud prelate, a prince of the Church, more powerful and wealthy than many a bishop, with two score of manors and a dozen religious houses under his control. "Where is your father, girl?" he asked, of Marcia.

"He is ridden to Fallowfield to see to the building of the new tannery, my Lord Prior." It was Esther Ridley who answered him, coming from the house door. "In his absence it is I who should have seen that Master Armstrong did not stray beyond the yard. I crave your lordship's pardon." For that calm young woman she was a little breathless. "It will not occur again."

"It will not!" the Prior agreed grimly.

"Will you not honour us—come within for a bite and a sup . . ."

"No, child. Another time, mayhap. What I have to say, since Abel Ridley is from hence, can be said here. It concerns this man, this prisoner Armstrong." The prelate turned his cold hooded eyes on Simon at last. "We have waited long, fellow, for your people to fulfil their part in the terms of your engagement with us. It was an ill-advised business from the first, as I told Master Ridley. I trust no Scots freebooters, godless reprobates and enemies of the King's Grace and of Holy Church. What proof have we that you are what you say, a man of any substance and worth? How can we know that any in your outlandish country will be prepared to pay even one silver penny for your wretched life? How shall we be assured that we have not wasted our time, care and provision on a worthless mosstrooper, deserving only of a rope . . . ?"

"No! No, my lord!" Esther cried. "That is not so, I swear."

"Quiet, child! Mind your place. You may have tricked Abel Ridley, sirrah—but, 'fore God, you will not find it profitable to lie to Holy Church!"

"Sir Prior, I have not lied to any." Simon strove to keep his voice even. "I am as I said, and my estate is ample to provide the sums promised. There has been unexpected delay, I agree.

But I crave your patience . . ."

"Patience, forsooth! For Abel Ridley's sake I have been patient indeed. But the time for such is now overpast."

"I regret to press for it further—but there is so much that could have gone amiss. The money may have been intercepted—on its way here. The messenger might never even have delivered the letter . . ."

"Until now, I have been prepared to consider such a possibility. But yesterday the same mendicant friar who took your message returned through Hexham, on his way to Lanercost. He had been as far as the Abbeys of Dryburgh and Melrose. I had him brought before me. He had much to tell me, much that will be of interest to my Lord Dacre!"

Simon heard Marcia at his side draw a quick breath. Then her hand came to grip his elbow, involuntarily. Not that he required anything such to emphasise the significance of the Prior's words. "He . . . delivered the letter?"

"Yes. And but ten days after leaving Hexham!"

"And . . . he saw my sister? It was to her that he handed the letter, as I said?"

The other nodded briefly. "So he told me. He gave it to a young woman, of your name."

"I thank God for that," Simon said. "Was she well? How did she receive the news? What did she say . . . ?"

"She appeared, the fellow said, to be something overcome," the cleric answered, shrugging. "That was all that he had to tell me. He moved on thereafter, over to Tweeddale, to Melrose and Dryburgh. But the girl, it appears, has been so overcome that she has not seen fit to send your ransom in a score of weeks!"

"M'mmm." The young man pursed his lips. "I cannot understand it. Unless, as I said, the men bringing the gold have suffered attack? Been waylaid . . . ?"

"Would your people be such fools as to send it without proper guard as far as your own bounds?" the Prior demanded. "And between here and the Border, naught is done that the Prior of Hexham hears not of! You would do well to think again, Armstrong—as I have done!"

Simon stared at the man in silence.

"Have a little further patience, my lord," Esther pleaded, then. "Perhaps another message? In case something has gone amiss . . ."

"No, by all the saints! Would you have Holy Church begging from barbarian Scots, and waiting on their pleasure?" the prelate cried. "Not so. I am done with waiting. Master Armstrong has irked my patience long enough—just as he has endangered us all by his presence here, for long enough. And now I find him parading abroad for all the world to see! He thrusts out his weasand, over-eager for the noose, I think! But others are endangered who have given him harbour. For your father's weal, and yours, my daughters, rather than for this man's, I take him now into the custody of the Church. From this present. He shall be moved to the Priory forthwith."

"Oh, no, my lord—no!"

"My good Lord Prior, I crave you . . ."

"Silence! Do you raise your silly women's voices against *my* decision? Enough of talk. As soon as darkness falls, and the thing can be done decently and unobserved, my officers will come for the prisoner. Till then, these guards shall hold him close indoors. Your father to present himself to me, on his return. I commend you to God's mercy and surveillance." That last was cryptic perhaps, if all in the same breath. The one jewelled finger lifted to sketch the sign of the Cross, even as the Prior pulled his palfrey's head around.

Pacing their beasts with quiet unhurried dignity, the clerics rode out of the Grange courtyard, two of the men-at-arms, halberds over their shoulders, still at their heels. The other two formed up on either side of Simon Armstrong.

Mother Church had taken over.

VII

THAT night, Simon found himself in very different circumstances, however enhanced the sacredness of his shelter. He was immured in a small stone cell, some eight feet square, semi-subterranean beneath one of the out-buildings of the great Hexham Priory. Lit only by a tiny barred and unglazed window set high in a bare wall that ran with damp, his quarters were clean, furnished with a stone bench, a single blanket, a pail of fresh water, a slop-pail, a wooden noggin and platter—and nothing else. Whether this repre-sented a punishment cell of the Priory, or merely one of the retreats of the aesthetically religious in more austere days, the present incumbent had no means of knowing. All he knew was that it made singularly poor contrast with his recent comfort-able quarters in Anick Grange. Nor did the soberly garbed serving brother, silent and unforthcoming, who brought him the cold water and dry oaten cakes that constituted his supper, compare favourably with his late nurses.

But unpleasant as were these altered conditions, they were by no means the greatest weight on the man's mind. It was the reason for them that worried him more. Why had the Prior done this? And what would be the next step? He had not been brought here merely because the churchmen had seen him walking beside the duck-pond, and were now protecting him from being observed by any who might inform Dacre—Simon was not so simple as to believe that. The Prior had had his mind made up to remove the prisoner before ever he arrived at Anick Grange—that was obvious. Why? He had come only the day after hearing from this wandering friar, it seemed. Simon had been in no state to seek to escape from Anick. What had this cleric to gain by taking him into his own charge—for surely here was a man who was far from blind to his own interests? Did he intend to hand him over to Dacre, himself—at a price, or to gain goodwill? Or dispose of him summarily, on his own? Or even, by holding him, seek a larger share of the ransom, when and if it came, or indeed, by turning the screw, think to extract a bigger sum from Stirkshaws? The prisoner did not put anything past a man with eyes like Prior Anselm's.

And all that was only one part of his anxiety. Why, if Ailie has his message, had the money not arrived after all these weeks? Did it mean that she was in some way prevented from doing what she would? Under some restraint? Or could she just not raise the money? Had his stock been raided, perhaps, and carried off? Having lost most of her manpower, Ailie might not be able to protect the Stirkshaws flocks and herds. The Elliots had never loved the Armstrongs—might they have taken this opportunity to settle old scores? Though the Elliots must have lost grievously at Flodden, also—he himself had seen three of their leaders fall.

Again, if the money had been sent, in fact, and then stolen on the way to Hexham, he was lost. Stirkshaws could never raise another two thousand gold pieces. But, by all the saints, his people, enfeebled as they might be, would never send so great a treasure ill-guarded? And if what this Prior said was true, he would have known had the bearers ever reached the Northumbrian border. If . . . ! That was the rub. How much trust could be put on this proud churchman's word? Might not the man even have gone the length of having the Teviotdale messengers ambushed secretly, whenever they were across the Border, have taken the money for himself, and declared its non-arrival?

Sombre thoughts for a prisoner shut up alone in a stone cell, day and night—which might account for the uncharitableness, not to say disrespectfulness, of his attitude towards the hierarchy. Solitary confinement can breed strange delusions.

And solitary confinement was Simon's lot. In the first five grim days, apart from the thrice-daily appearances of his uncommunicative gaoler, he saw only a single other face, Father Crispin's the apothecary, and that only twice and briefly. And he was a different man, now, from the benevolent genial friar who had so ably doctored the wounded man and played uncle to the two young women. Quiet, remote, cherubic face schooled to immobility, indifference, he examined and rebound the prisoner's leg, confining his reactions to severe head-shakings and lip-pursings and occasional sighs. Even though Simon sought to detain him, question him, urging him, pleading, even when he perceived that the man would tell him nothing, seeking to hold him if only for human company's sake.

Otherwise only the chiming and jangling of the Priory's great bells, now so close above him, ringing out the Angelus or proclaiming the offices and the hours, served for company and diversion—that, and the occasional chanting of monks heard faintly, and the heart-breakingly free singing of spring birds from some tree near to the high slit that was his window. And the rats.

And then, on the afternoon of the sixth day—though Simon had already lost count of days—his sour turnkey brought him two visitors, the Ridley girls.

They stood in the open doorway, appalled most evidently, staring at the man hunched on the stone bench, and at the dark damp little cell. "Simon!" they cried, as one, as the man started up stiffly, and then came running in to him, amidst a flurry of skirts. "Dear God—how wicked! How terrible! Mercy on us—this is an enormity! Poor Simon—poor, poor man!"

The object of their distress, tongue-tied and awkward after such long silence, stood blinking and shaking his head, gesturing with his hand to disclaim the most of it. While Esther took his arm, urging that he sit down, turning him towards the scanty light that filtered down from up there where the sun was shining, searching his pale unshaven face and biting her red lip, her sister had swung upon the watching monk.

"Shame on you—shame!" Marcia cried. "How is this to treat a sick and helpless man who has done you no hurt? You!—a man of God!"

The serving brother shrugged. "It is the Lord Prior's orders, Mistress. He suffers no hurt here. And comfort of the body works no benefit to the soul . . ."

"Nor does unkindness, and cruel malice!" she flashed back.

"I counsel that you do not so miscall the Godly decisions of the Lord Prior!" the monk warned stiffly.

"No, no, Marcia," Esther put in, looking round. "That will serve nothing. The Prior undoubtedly means well by Master Armstrong—but perhaps he forgets that he is still a sick man. Were he strong and able . . ."

"Father Crispin still attends him," the turnkey declared. "He saw him but yesterday."

"I am well enough," Simon intervened, a little hoarsely. "But I am rejoiced to see you. It is . . . very good."

"You look pale. Ill." Esther turned back to him. "And thin. It is cold in here. Damp. I had no notion that, that . . ."

"That Holy Church was so concerned for the soul of a barbarian Scot!" Simon suggested, finding his tongue. "I wonder that he, that the Prior, permitted you to come?"

"He is gone to Durham, to visit the Bishop." The girl glanced over her cloak's shoulder at the monk, who now stood within the cell doorway. He had turned his back upon them, but very evidently intended to remain there and not leave them alone. Naturally he could hear every word spoken. "The Sub-Prior is . . . is friendly. He thinks that perhaps the Prior would not forbid us bringing you some viands and sweetmeats. Some few things . . ." She had a basket over her arm, and from it she set down on his bench a cold roasted chicken, a slab of cheese, a noggin of cream, some pastries, sugar-coated nuts, apples and a bottle of claret-wine.

"My soul is like to be much endangered, I see!" the recipient commented, mustering a grin. "Perhaps the good brother here will pray for me the harder!"

The monk glanced back into the cell, turned down the corners of his mouth at what he saw, and sniffed audibly.

"We shall bring more, Simon," Marcia said, glaring at the gaoler's back.

"Thank you. You are very kind. But I have not felt greatly hungry . . ."

"But you must have good feeding, to build up your strength."

"No great strength is required of me—in Hexham Priory!" Simon pointed out.

"You are still a sick man. And you look less well than when you left our house."

The captive shook his head. "I am well enough. Only, I take ill out of doing nothing. You . . . there is no word from Stirkshaws? From my sister?"

It was Esther who answered him, shaking her head likewise. "No. I am sorry. Nothing. But perhaps, before very long . . ."

"Can you not send somebody—another messenger? There must be something wrong. Ailie would have sent the gold long ere this. You do not think . . . ? It is not possible that . . . ?" Simon's glance flickered over to the listening monk, and he frowned. He could not voice his suspicions of the Prior before this man. He could not mention any of the dark doubts and fears that were eating him up.

"My father suggested sending another messenger—but the Prior does not think it proper. He . . ." She also looked toward the man at the door. "He sees no profit in it . . ."

"He thinks me a liar! A cheat. That I have not the substance to provide this gold. That is what he thinks," Simon cried. "That—or else he . . ." He stopped, biting his lip. "You—you do not think the same?" he charged, looking from one young woman to the other.

"No, no. Never think it. We know you for a true man, Simon. There has just been some delay, some misunderstanding."

He turned to the other girl, Marcia, who had not spoken. "And you?" he challenged.

She did not raise her eyes to meet his. She looked unhappy. Indeed she had seemed distrait and discomposed throughout, less than her usual assured self. "I care not what your estate is," she said. "Oh, I hate it all! All this . . . this talk of gold. This buying of men's lives!"

"But you yet doubt my word?"

"No. No—I swear it. I said not so . . ."

Esther slipped an arm around her sister. "You must not speak so, Simon," she chided. "Marcia did not mean anything of the like. She thinks only well of you. As I do."

"Yes, yes. I am sorry." The man drew a hand over his brow. "I am foolish. Not myself. It is this being alone, perhaps. If you will forgive me . . . ?"

But despite promptly declared forgiveness, the visit was less successful and satisfactory than it should have been. Marcia did not fully recover her poise, Simon was far from at his best, and Esther, though she did her utmost, could not disperse the feeling of tension, of guardedness, of helplessness that prevailed. And the near presence of the disapproving and listening monk could not but affect them all. So that presently, though it was the last thing that he really desired, Simon was silently urging the girls to be gone—and knowing as he did so that he would be cursing and berating himself therefor afterwards, when the silent loneliness closed down about him once more. Such is man in his folly.

Marcia seemed glad to go—yet turned on the gaoler to lash him with her tongue when he appeared over-eager to get them out and away. Esther's gentle calm did not fail her, though she departed unhappy and perturbed, obviously. But she promised that they would come back again soon, whispering that the Prior was not expected to return for two weeks at least. Simon gripped her arm as she went out, and though he did not say anything, his look was not ineloquent.

Thereafter the cell door clanged heavily, to be succeeded only by the halting dragging sound of Simon's own limping footsteps as he paced round and round his constricted prison. He must have walked a mile or more, bad leg notwithstanding, before finally he sank down upon his bench. Deliberately he refrained still from assaulting the good things in the basket thereon for a considerable time, to appease some obscure challenge in his own nature. When at length he succumbed, it was as well perhaps that there was no one present to behold.

Twice more in the next two dragging weeks the girls came to visit the prisoner. They would have come oftener, they said, but the Sub-Prior would not permit it. He permitted no more baskets of food and wine to be brought, either. A timorous man, he became the less valiant as the time neared for his superior's return, though the young women managed to smuggle in one or two items under their cloaks, to be discreetly transferred beneath Simon's blanket. And each time that they came, they went away less happily. For very clearly the man's physical state was deteriorating in that damp and dismal sunless cell. Each time he was thinner, gaunter, more wan, less steady on his feet. Mentally too, he was showing the signs of his immurement, growing ever more morose, silent, uncertain-tempered, and even suspicious. Their patient was on the down-grade again. He had not been sufficiently recovered to face these rigours. The girls sought out Father Crispin, entreating him; but he would, or could, do little. The Sub-Prior likewise dared not do more than he had done in allowing these visits. Prior Anselm ruled his establishment with a rod of iron—and he was expected back at any time.

How accurately these two subordinates had divined their superior's reactions was demonstrated very clearly two days after the girls' third visit. A message arrived at Anick Grange from the Priory, announcing the Prior's return from Durham, and declaring categorically that no further visits to the prisoner Armstrong would be permitted, nor any sending of victuals.

Simon, in his underground cell, was left uninformed. He waited, and waited. And to his oaten cakes and water was added the unwholesome fruits of bitterness.

VIII

"WE must go to see Prior Anselm," Esther Ridley said. "We must. Something must be done. Before, before it is too late. And there is nothing else that we can do."

"He will not heed us," Marcia declared. "You know that. You know how he will look at us with those eyes. . . . It will avail nothing. Father has tried."

"Father is only a man. And besides he has not seen Simon, does not realise how evil is his case, how great is his need. It may be that the Prior himself does not really realise it. Men have but little sense in these things . . ."

"You think that he will listen to women when he does not heed men?"

"I do not know, Marcia—but we must try."

"He cried out on us not to raise our silly women's voices when he took Simon away."

"Yes. I know. But we must do something. We cannot go on like this."

The two girls were standing in the orchard of the Grange, gazing out over the level cattle-dotted haughlands of the Tyne, towards the towers and pinnacles of Hexham Priory that soared proudly above the climbing grey town on its hill just over a mile away. It was the last day of April, and a week had passed since the Prior's prohibition had come to Anick, a week of anxiety and worry and helpless waiting for the young women, whose thoughts and sympathies were never far from that dungeon beneath the Priory. The brilliant sun-filled days, with the first swallows already darting, the scent of May heavy on the air and the sound of bees loud in the blossoming orchard only added to their distress for the half-buried captive's sake. Simon Armstrong needed that sun and light and kindly strengthening air, needed them almost as direly as he needed an amplitude of good strengthening food, regular ministrations and dry quarters, leaving comfort and company out of it altogether.

"But I tell you, Esther, it will avail nothing. Nothing! Oh, Mary Mother—he will die! I know it. And we can do nothing to aid him . . ." The younger girl's voice broke, and she beat her clenched fist on the ancient moss-grown sundial beside which they stood. "Sweet Lord—have mercy upon him! And upon me!"

Esther turned to search her sister's face. "You . . . you are so fond of him, then, Marcia?" she asked quietly.

"Of course I am! Well you know it. And why not?" the other demanded, her voice rising unsteadily. "Is it so strange? Does he not owe us his life? I am . . ." Marcia's eyes flashed. "Do not stare at me, like that! So kind! So, so sober and sorrowful! You love him yourself! Do you think I do not know it—that I am blind? Do you think that I have not watched you—you, so meek, so careful, so prudent! And all the time you are wanting him—just as I want him! I tell you . . ."

"Marcie! Hush!" Esther's hand reached out to grip her sister's arm, and she glanced quickly around them. They were out of ordinary earshot of the house, but such high-pitched talk might carry in at the open windows. And over at the edge of the kitchen-garden one of the men was working at the bee-hives. "You must not say such things . . ."

"It is the truth. D'you take me for a fool? I've watched how you touched him, held him . . ."

"Be quiet! I'll hear no more of this." Esther part commanded, part pleaded. "Here is no way to talk. You, you are beside yourself."

"Perhaps I am. Perhaps I have reason. You do not know . . ." Marcia stopped suddenly, choking. "I . . . I . . . oh, I am sorry, Esther! I do not know what I say. You must not heed me. But, but . . ." She shook her lovely head, but hid her eyes from her sister, and did not finish.

The other made as though to say something, but stayed herself also. Her colour had heightened, her breathing quickened, but she mastered herself in a moment or two, purposefully resuming her mantle of calm. "Such talk will help neither Simon nor ourselves, Marcie," she said, almost levelly.

Her companion did not answer.

Curiously the elder sister considered the younger. She had been acting strangely for a long time, now—out of character. This past week more especially. Gone the laughing carefree teasing hoyden, on whose shoulders responsibility sat so lightly. She had taken to hiding herself away, to dark brooding, to flashing out in abrupt storms of unprovoked anger. If this, then, was love . . . ? Esther Ridley sighed, a little tremulously.

"You have . . . misread my attentions, Marcie," she said slowly, as though picking her words. "Put any such thoughts from your mind. But let us say no more of it." She took a long breath. "I shall go to the Lord Prior, as I said. This very afternoon. I know there may be no profit in it—only humiliation. But it is what I must do, all I can do. You need not come with me."

"I will come," the younger girl said shortly.

"Very well. Only, I think that I should do the talking, Sister—or most of it!"

Marcia turned, and went swiftly back to the house.

Prior Anselm kept them waiting in the stone corridor outside his private wing of the establishment for a salutary and suitable interval—the best part of an hour, indeed. Resolution had to be continually renewed, in the interim, with every instinct urging the girls to slip quietly back to Anick Grange. And when at length a serving brother came to usher them into the presence, both young women were so impressed by the magnificence of all that they saw as to be almost wholly overcome. It was their first visit to the Prior's own quarters. Passing, almost on tiptoe, through a private oratory with a marble altar, golden vessels and candlesticks, and rich hangings, they were conducted into an inner sanctum appointed with a sumptuousness such as they had neither seen nor imagined. Vivid and colourful tapestries depicting foliage and flowers, hawks and huntsmen, rabbits, squirrels and monkeys covered the walls; a handsome painting of the Virgin and Child hung over the carved stone lintel of a wide fireplace—in which, despite the genial weather, a large fire of logs blazed; rich damask curtains, fastened and tasselled with gold, flanked the windows of stained glass; the floor was of waxed timber, not stone, and furnished with woven patterned rugs and mats, not rushes and skins, and on it were settles, chests, coffers, all of carved wood and provided with a great amplitude of handsome cushions in green velvet, edged with gold. Silverware stood on a great sideboard, reflecting the firelight, and over all hung a splendid brazen chandelier bearing a score of tall white candles. The air was heavy with some sweet perfume. And in a high throne-like chair, well cushioned, sat Prior Anselm, clad in a furred gown worn loosely over, not a cassock, but a crimson velvet doublet of latest design, lined with yellow satin, and hose of Paris black bound at the knee with silken garters and golden tassels.

The great man considered his visitors sternly as, withdrawing their wide eyes from all this splendour with difficulty, they sank down in deep curtseys. "God be with you, my daughters—if so be your coming here is not of idle or frivolous intent!" he said, warningly.

It was as much as Esther could do to find her tongue. "No, it is not. We are . . . we crave your pardon, my Lord Prior," she got out, after a false start, rising up. "Your patience. Please—we know, we understand . . . that you will think us . . . our visit, presumptuous, unsuitable . . ." She had been rehearsing what she must say all that long hour outside, yet now it was but a meaningless jumble in her mind. "We do not do it lightly . . ."

"I hope not!"

"No. I . . . we . . . pray understand, my lord, that we would not trouble you, impose upon you . . ."

"Come, girl—ha' done!" the man said impatiently.

Esther swallowed. The heat in that room made her head swim. "We came to make representations to your lordship on behalf of Master Simon Armstrong," she exclaimed, with a rush.

Those hooded eyes narrowed to the merest slits. "What folly, what impertinence is this, woman?"

But her own articulation of Simon's name had served to restore the girl's wits. The picture of him that his name conjured up in her mind, thin and wan and ill-seeming, in that dark cramped bare cell beneath the ground, so violently contrasted with all the display and grandeur and luxurious profusion here before her, that she knew a great wave of indignation that overcame and vanquished her quaking diffidence and trepidation. But heedfully, for the same sad prisoner's sake, she sought to keep her indignation out of her voice.

"None, my lord, I assure you. No impertinence, at any rate—though of our folly you must be the judge when you have heard us. We come in the name of Christian charity—a duty imposed on us by Holy Church, surely . . ."

"Lord, d'you come prating to *me* of my Christian duty, woman! By the Splendour of Heaven, I'd have you watch your words!"

"My lord, I would not dream of anything so undutiful." A little breathlessly Esther confronted the Church Militant. "But our Lord Christ Himself allowed frail women to seek his aid for those in trouble and dire need. I but humbly do the same. Master Armstrong is in great need of your mercy."

"Tush, girl—I will be the judge of the fellow's needs. Not you."

"Yes, my lord, assuredly. But have you seen Master Armstrong since you returned from Durham?" Almost appalled at her own daring, she bit her lip.

The Prior half-rose from his chair, angrily—and then sank back, his jewelled fingers beating a tattoo on the carven arms. "I see that I must needs read Abel Ridley a lesson on the bringing up of daughters!" he said grimly.

"I crave pardon, my Lord Prior—but I speak thus not only for Master Armstrong's sake. He is much the worse in his person for being prisoned in that cell. He was not sufficiently strong for its rigours. It is dark and damp and cold. Perhaps you have not seen him, visited the place?" She was talking quickly now, racing her words as though she might well not be allowed to finish them. "He is failing seriously in body—and he was a sick man to start with. There will be no ransom, I fear, for a, a dead man!" She looked at the proud cleric directly. "Have you seen him, sir?"

Prior Anselm cleared his throat, and frowned. "I have more to do than dance attendance on rascally Scots—who are the King's enemies, to boot!"

"You have not seen him, then! I was sure that you had not, my lord. I prithee—ask Father Crispin if I am not right about Master Armstrong's health."

Again the Prior frowned. Undoubtedly he would have done much more than that, had not already the apothecary given him a similar report on the prisoner's state—if very differently couched. "Men do not die so easily," he declared. "Besides, no ransom is forthcoming. The fellow has lied to us, cozened us. Your father was a fool to bring him away. He deserves death. He took up arms against King Henry's Grace. Worse, he has deceived and defrauded Holy Church, promising 500 gold pieces which he has not produced, for his worthless life."

Esther heard her sister, silent at her side till this, draw quick breath as though to intervene, to protest. Hurriedly she herself spoke, placatingly. "But, my lord, surely the money may yet come? Is that not why you have kept him here, thus long? In the lawless and grievous state of Scotland, after the wars, it may be hard indeed to sell cattle for gold . . ."

"Only a woman would think that!" the prelate said, contemptuously. "At such a time, gold is cheap and cattle are dear. Filling bellies becomes of greater import than counting gold pieces. And gold will not fill bellies."

"But might not cattle be stolen? Master Armstrong's herds driven off? If there is much lawlessness, many broken men at large . . . ?"

"Then your Master Armstrong is of no service to us," the Prior said flatly, succinctly. "We waste food and time on him."

For a moment Esther was silenced. What could she say to

that? There was no answer, if that was all that Simon's life meant. Desperately she cast about for something to say, to counter that finality. "The messenger? The mendicant?" she got out. "Did he not tell you the style of Simon's, of Master Armstrong's property? This Stirkshaws? Surely he would see something of it, enough to perceive if it was a place of substance?"

The other shrugged. "The place itself he thought fair enough. But that signifies little to the point. It does not establish that this Armstrong is lord of its manor, that what wealth it has is his. Or, if it should indeed be so, that whosoever rules there now will suffer the outpouring of so much gold."

"His sister . . . ?"

"Tush—a chit of a girl! Think you she will be left to do as she pleases? Or if she is, that she will desire to throw away her new-found power, thus? The world wags not so."

"But . . . will you not, at least, send another messenger to discover the truth? To demand the money? Surely it is worth that? A great sum . . ."

"No, I will not, 'fore God! Think you I have no pride, woman? Think you that the Church must go cap in hand to these beggarly Scots, beseeching their wretched few gold pieces? By all the saints—we shall shortly go take what we will! Take not some few paltry coins, but their all! By the King's command. I have it from my Lord Dacre. He comes here next week to discuss the matter. So, will you waste no more of my time, girl?" The Prior rose to his feet, the audience clearly at an end.

"Oh, sir—will you not then, for sweet pity's sake, let Master Armstrong come back to Anick Grange, where we may bring him to strength again? At no cost to you, to the Church . . ."

"Anick Grange is *mine*, child," the Prior cut in, sternly. "Your father is my servant only. All that he has belongs to the Church. The cost of keeping this wretched man has all along been the Church's. You would do well to remember it. Your father, perhaps, overlooked the fact when he claimed so large proportion of this illusory ransom for himself!"

Esther shook her head helplessly. "My lord—at the least,

75

will you not then permit him to be moved to some kindlier place, here in the Priory? Where he may have sun and light. And better feeding . . ."

The prelate raised his hand. "Enough, enough," he commanded. "This is a house for the worship and glory of Almighty God, not for the cosseting of the King's enemies. My people have neither the time nor the duty so to do. Besides, better men than this Scots rogue . . ."

"Then, then you brought him here but to die!" Esther's voice, interrupting, rose uncontrollably. "You would kill him?"

"Silence! You know not what you say, you foolish stiff-necked woman! Were you not your father's daughter, you would suffer dearly for such talk. As it is . . ." The Prior drew himself up, and glanced at the handsome chiming timepiece with the bells, that stood on its own table near by. "It is near time for Compline. You will go now. I will deal with your sinful contumacy later." He had his dignity well in hand again. He reached for a silver bell to ring, to summon a servant.

"No! No, I say! Wait! You will hear *me*. You must—in sweet Christ's name!" That was Marcia, abruptly, almost crazedly, starting forward. "You are all wrong. Deceived. Both of you . . ."

"Marcie—I pray you, be quiet . . ."

"I will not! Not any more. I have been quiet too long. I tell you, you are wrong. It is not as you think. The letter . . ." She gulped. "It did not go. Not the true letter."

"What! Are you beside yourself, wench?" the Prior cried. "Am I to suffer no end to this folly, merciful God!"

"No. Hear me." The younger girl insisted frantically. "The letter that went to Scotland was not Simon's letter. I wrote it. I changed the letters. No gold has been asked for . . ." That ended in a whisper.

"*Deus avertat!*"

Marcia Ridley stood, bosom heaving, gnawing at her lips, hands wringing each other. The Prior and her sister stared at her. The hiss of the logs on the fire, and the ticking of the clock, sounded loudly.

"Marcie!" Esther managed to say, at length. "It is not true! You, you are out of your mind!"

"It is true." The younger girl's voice was level now. Despite the strain to which she was obviously subjecting herself, she spoke in what was almost a dull monotone. "I did not wish that letter, the letter asking for money, to go to Scotland, to this Stirkshaws. I wrote another. To Simon's sister, like the first. I said only that he was a prisoner, that he had been hurt, but was getting well again and that he would come home, one day, when the times were kinder. I said that she was not to worry, that he was in good hands. And that she should look well after his affairs . . ." Her words tailed away.

"Why?" That came from the Prior, like a whip-lash.

Marcia moistened her full lips, and looked at the handsome rug on which she stood. "I did not wish him . . . to go away. To go home . . . yet awhile."

"Mother of God—you, you . . . !" The prelate took a step forward, and for a moment it looked as though he was going actually to strike the girl in his fury. But he controlled himself, in some measure, by an obvious effort, jerking himself around to pace the floor instead. "This is beyond all belief. An affront to God and His Church!" he said. "You evil, scheming, whoring trull! You lying, insolent baggage! You interfering, shameless trollop! You, you harlot!" Pacing, he enunciated the words with individual emphasis, slowly, almost as though savouring them—and all the time he was looking at the young woman sidelong, out of those cold hooded eyes, examining her up and down, closely, comprehensively, as though seeing her really for the first time. "Jezebel!"

"No! Not that. Oh, no!" Esther cried. "She has been foolish, my lord. Headstrong. Misguided, yes. But not . . . nothing of what you say!" She turned. "Oh, Marcie—how could you?"

"Silence!" Prior Anselm exclaimed. He halted directly before Marcia. "Do you realise what you have done, you wicked, wanton woman? You, a mere callow girl, have taken upon yourself to overturn my designs, my orders, my arrangements!

77

You shall suffer for it, I promise you!"

"I have already suffered," the girl said, low-voiced. "What I did, I did of a foolish impulse. I never thought of aught against your lordship. Only that . . ." She stopped, shrugging her shoulders. "I regret it, now. I have been regretting it since I have watched Simon Armstrong suffering. Imprisoned. Growing weaker, sinking—knowing that it was my fault. My doing. That is why I have suffered. Any other suffering, now, for what I have done, I can bear." She raised her head, with a trace of her old spirit. "I have told you this, now, so that *Simon* may not suffer further, for my sin."

"Your sin, yes! Presumptuous overweening sin of the spirit, to gratify the filthy sinful lust of the flesh!" The Prior licked thin lips. "Do not think that talk of false and vicarious suffering for this man, this paramour, shall save you from the just wrath of Holy Church . . ."

"I do not, sir. I only ask that, now that you know the truth, Simon, Master Armstrong, may not suffer further. That you will release him from his cell. That you will aid him back to health . . ."

"Yes. That is the important thing, my lord, is it not?" Esther intervened, a little breathlessly, to help divert the churchman's mind from dwelling on her sister's offence. "The gold! It has not been withheld. They knew naught of the demand. They will send it now, no doubt, if another messenger goes, with another letter . . ."

"The first letter can go," Marcia said quickly. "It is not destroyed. I have it hid. Simon—he need not know. I carefully copied his signature, and borrowed the signet-ring from Father's pocket, to seal it. The messenger knew nothing. If the first letter was to go, now, all would yet be well . . ."

"Be quiet," the Prior snapped. He was frowning—but the frown was of the calculating sort now, and not wholly indicative of righteous ire. His fingers drummed on the high back of his throne-like chair.

"You will send another messenger?" Esther urged. "And, meantime, Master Armstrong must be got well again."

78

"A truce to your prating," the man declared impatiently. He was still frowning. "I do not know if there is time. Dacre will be here next week. He said . . ." The Prior seemed to be speaking to himself, rather than to the two girls. "The raid will be mounted ere I could have the gold back, it may be . . ."

Marcia opened her mouth, but her sister raised a warning hand to stop her, to let the Prior take his own counsel. Self-interest was a more potent ally than any apologies or pleas.

The prelate was counting on his fingers now—presumably days. Then he nodded, as though accepting that there might be just a chance. "There could possibly be time, I think, if God is with us . . ." He looked at his visitors. "This letter—it must be brought to me this night."

"It shall be, my lord," Esther assured him.

"The signet-ring that she talks of, also. I may have to add to the writing. Tell your father to bring it to me."

"Yes. And . . . and will you remove Master Armstrong from his unkindly cell? Give him better quarters and good food . . . ?"

"Tut, woman—the fellow is a prisoner. An enemy. Let us not forget it."

"But, my lord—an ailing one. He has little strength. When we saw him last he was languishing sorely. That cell will kill him. And, and a dead prisoner, sir, will not serve to ransom!"

"No?" The thin lips curled.

Esther swallowed, and clenched her small fists beneath her cloak. "My Lord Prior—only one *half* of the gold will come, until Master Armstrong is delivered safe home. Then the rest. They will not give it, sir, for a corpse!"

"M'mmm." The man touched his chin, pinching it, the gems sparkling as he raised his hand. "I have no soft and dainty quarters available. And he must not be visible when my Lord Dacre and his people come here. They will be quartered here, taking up all my accommodation . . ."

"Then, my lord, let us take him back again to Anick Grange with us. I beseech you! We shall get him well again. I promise you, he shall be kept close. I give you my word that we shall not let him out of the house—I swear it. Let it be as it was before, till he is well once more. None shall see him . . ."

"Save this evil, sinful, fleshly wench! *She* will see him aplenty, I trow! A fine recompense for her shameless infamy!"

"My Lord—if you will let him come back to the Grange, I vow, in the name of the Blessed Virgin herself, that I shall not see him, go near his room!" Marcia cried.

"Your vows! The word of a declared deceiver!"

"I will vouch for her, sir," Esther pleaded. "I will promise you, if you will it, by all that I hold true, that she shall not see him. Nor shall he leave his room."

"Very well," the Prior allowed, but frigidly. "But only because of my Lord Dacre's visit. You will hold to your word, on pain of the fullest rigours of the Church. And think not that is all the penance that this abandoned girl shall make! I shall consider what suitable and condign punishment shall best meet the case. Meantime, she shall appear daily before her priest at Vespers. And on Sundays, at public worship, she shall stand apart from all others, between the outer door and the lectern, taking no part in the service. Nor shall she receive the Chalice. For seven Sundays, at the least. For the rest, she shall hear my pleasure in due course. Now—begone I am already much delayed . . ."

"Yes, sir. And Master Armstrong? We can take him back with us to Anick?"

"Tonight. After you have brought me the letter. And the ring. When it is dark. But I shall have him back when it seems good to me."

"We understand. We thank your lordship." Esther dipped down hurriedly, her anxiety now to be away. Her sister did likewise. "We shall come again, later. Come, Marcie."

Prior Anselm bestowed no blessing on his departing guests.

IX

SO Simon Armstrong came back to Anick Grange, to his old room, back to comfort and care and kindliness. Quite bewildered by the sudden change in his fortunes, he gained no very satisfactory explanation of the causes therefor. Abel Ridley and Esther merely indicated that Lord Dacre was coming on a visit to the Priory to hold a conference on some forthcoming campaign in Scotland, and it was considered best for the prisoner to be out of the way. Because the man was weak and lethargic and dulled in all his reactions, because of his incarceration, he accepted this without overmuch question—even though, at the back of his mind, he wondered.

But the reversion to his former state was so welcome, the care lavished upon him so warm and unstinted, and his need so real, that the entertaining of doubts would have been unnatural as well as unsuitable there and then. With returning strength and fretting idleness such might come to the fore. But that was not yet.

Simon came from Hexham Priory mere skin and bone, a lank, stooping, shambling caricature of a man, constantly suffering fits of trembling and shivers, great-eyed yet blinking owlishly in any light, slow and blurred of speech, unshaven and smelling strongly. But according to Father Crispin, once more in attendance and again the genial physician, there was nothing about him that nourishing feeding, care, time and ordinary warm water would not cure. His leg was actually much improved, and his limping now sprang from stiffness, in the main.

And, after a bad start—for he vomited up most of his fine supper that first night, and thereafter writhed for hours on his clean bed with cramps and pains—Simon proceeded to prove the apothecary right. Each day he showed an improvement. Colour began to come back to his skin, and sparkle to his eyes. He ate a prodigious amount, and though it would be an

81

exaggeration to say that he visibly put on flesh, the fact remains that after only a few days his grievous wasted thinness was nothing like so apparent. For the first five days Esther kept him entirely to his bed, and he slept a great deal. But thereafter he commenced to grow progressively more restless. Soon he could no longer be kept abed. Soon he was spurning his bed altogether. Soon he began to pace his room, as he had paced the so much more constricted cell—and his pace was lengthening. He had an excellent constitution, that young man, and given half a chance it would assert itself. It was doing so, now. He became a considerably less tractable patient for his nurse.

Esther found him more difficult to deal with than heretofore, altogether. Perhaps the fault lay partly in herself. She knew that she was less natural with him, less at ease. She was as attentive, kind, gentle and patient as ever—but her relationship towards him had somehow changed. There was a tension that had not been between them previously; she could not but be aware of it, try to overcome it as she would.

The continued absence of Marcia from the sick-room did not go unnoticed. In answer to the man's questions, Esther could only say that her sister was not very well, and was keeping largely to her own room—which to some extent was true. But when the man could hear the younger girl, in a day or two, about the house and out in the courtyard, such explanations began to wear thin. Demands as to what was wrong with her producing no really satisfactory answer, he came to the not unnatural conclusion that she was offended with him for some reason. Since the last occasion on which he had seen the girl had been back in his cell, constrained in the presence of his gaoler, he imagined that she must still be angry with him because on the first visit he had charged her with doubting his word, of assuming that his claim to the lairdship of Stirkshaws was false. So now he was all contrition, sending messages and pleas and demanding interviews—to Esther's distinct embarrassment.

Just because he had nothing to do, Simon grew the more difficult—and Marcia the more desirable for being unavailable.

82

He was for ever talking about her to her sister, fretfully. As the days passed, Esther came almost to her wits' end to know how to deal with him. Advanced convalescence is nearly always hard on the nurse.

Because of it all, she almost welcomed the other subject that events brought to the fore, as a distraction—sore on the man as it was. Northumbria was agog with talk of a great blow against the Scots, and Hexhamshire was the centre and focus of it—significantly so. The Warden, the Lord Dacre, and his retinue were at the Priory, with sundry lords and knights and esquires from all over the North, discussing the plans for it. This was going to be a major stroke, all accounts said, and no mere localised raid. King Henry was insisting upon it. The Scots had been becoming ever more of a trial instead of being suitably chastened and vanquished after their shattering defeat at Flodden. There had been repeated hit-and-run raids over the Border into the English dales of Coquet and Rede and Tyne and Line, some of them insolent to a degree. They must be taught a resounding lesson—and if possible while the two factions of Queen Margaret, James's widow, and the Duke of Albany, his cousin, were still squabbling as to who should be Regent for the infant King James Fifth. The time was ripe, and Dacre had written to the Privy Council in London that "... there was never so meikle mischief, robbery, spoiling and vengeance in Scotland than there is now, without hope of remedy; which I pray our Lord God to continue".

Nevertheless, Dacre had two difficulties to face. The chiefest men of the North were still holding aloof from him, for reasons of personal enmity and jealousy, intriguing against him to London, and failing to provide the men he desired to carry out the King's commands—the Earls of Northumberland and Clifford, the Lords Ogle and Darcy, and others. He was restricted therefore, for manpower, to his own people, the churchmen—who were usually rivals of the great lords—and the men of the dales, of North and South Tyne, of Rede and Line. So that there must be a scraping of the barrel. And secondly, the Lord Home, the Scottish Warden, was stronger than ever in the

Merse and the East Marches, though out of favour in Edinburgh and deprived of his Chamberlainship. He was said to have a force of two thousand fierce mosstroopers more or less permanently assembled at Hume Castle, ready for dispatch to any part of the Borderline. He it was who had spoiled the last great raid in November; he must not spoil this one. The pity that he had not been killed at Flodden with the rest.

All this Esther came to talk about with her moody chafing charge when she discovered that it took his mind off other matters—even though its effect was apt to be the reverse of soothing. Not that she could have excluded the subject anyway, for her father was full of it, and liked nothing better than to repair to the sick-room of an evening there to expiate upon what they were going to do to the Scots, twinkle in his eye or none. This, informative as it was for the captive, was not calculated to tranquillise him—indeed there were times when Simon all but came to blows with his host—to Abel Ridley's undisguised glee. His daughter felt herself bound to rush indignantly to the aid of her patient rather than of her parent on these occasions—to the enhanced merriment of the latter. The big man had a sense of humour all his own.

But, at least, Simon's growing ire, pugnacity and patriotic resentment indicated advancing physical recovery.

It was on a fine evening of mid-May, exactly two weeks after Simon's return to the Grange, that Abel Ridley came striding into the upstairs room, big with news and obviously in the best of spirits. In his hand he carried his cuirass, the steel breast and back plates of armour, linked with leather girthing. This he flung to the floor at his daughter's feet, where she sat stitching her tapestry, with an echoing clang.

"Work for you, lass!" he cried. "Up, and to it. Leave this idler here, to his own devices. I cannot discover your shiftless sister about—anyhow, she is less skilful with the colours than you are. Let me have the blazon on this thing painted on afresh, back and front, see you—azure and or, the gold saltire on the blue, of our Priory of Hexham. You still have the colours safe kept? We ride tomorrow!"

"Tomorrow . . . ? You, yourself—to the wars again?"

"Marry, yes! Into Scotland. To the Merse. To Coldstream, first. Then to smoke that fox Home out of his hole. Then, heigho—on to fat Lothian! Even Edinburgh itself, maybe, if God wills. Man's work, m'lass!"

"Must you go, Father . . . ?" Esther's voice was unsteady.

" 'Fore God, I must! Think you, anyhow, that I would be left behind? Here is what we should have done long since. Every man is needed—since Clifford and Neville and those other high-born caitiffs are holding back. The Lord Prior is sending 120 men, no less, in three companies under Jem Harndean, the Chief Steward, with myself and Enoch Hall as lieutenants. A goodly array. We shall carry our Priory's banner into the streets of Edinburgh itself, mayhap."

"Mayhap!" Simon Armstrong repeated sourly, slightingly, from the window-seat. "When you have disposed of my Lord Home! And Dacre could not do that with 4000, in November, you'll mind!"

"Tcha!" Ridley snapped his fingers at Simon, and at Lord Home. "The Constables of Alnwick and Berwick will march by the coast, round by Coldinghame, to take Home from the rear. The Constable of Norham will cross Tweed at Ladykirk, and drive straight north by Hutton Ford and Chirnsides. And we, with Dacre himself, will cross at Coldstream, and take him from the west. And that will be the end of your rascally Lord Home, Master Armstrong!"

"The Constable of Norham, I can believe," Simon declared. "Since he is Dacre's own brother. But he has only a hundred or two of men, has he not? Alnwick is the Earl of Northumberland's. Has the proud Percy changed his tune, then? And Berwick is never so keen to turn hand against the Scotland to which she in right belongs—whatever her Constable may say! I wonder if Home is in such danger!"

"They will march, never fear," the older man averred. "It is the King's orders. And with Home out of the way, all the Borders will lie open to us . . ."

"Save for Kerr of Ferniehirst, and Cavers the Sheriff!"

"Sir Philip Dacre and the Fenwicks will deal with them. They will cover our left flank at the Coldstream crossing, and all the way up through the Merse. The Warden is no fool, lad— and this time, he means to make an end!"

Simon compressed his lips. He knew that last to be true, at any rate. He stared out of the window, across the orchards towards Hexham town. It was an ill thing to have to sit here and listen to the plans for harrying and destroying his own people. But what could he do?

Ridley came over, and clapped the younger man's shoulder with his great hand. "Mope not, lad," he said. "You are a deal better off here, I say, than in your sorry Scotland. You should thank us!"

And that was the worst of it—he should indeed thank them. And he did. He had received great kindness in this house. He owed them so much, beyond just for his life. He knew a deep and warm regard, a true fondness for these benefactors of his— even for this great teasing bear of a man, who was now following his daughter out of the room and downstairs, with the cuirass. And in so doing, he felt himself to be a traitor to his country. And a fraud, too, towards these people, with no gold coming out of Scotland. A worthless, useless, helpless fraud.

Sometimes, Simon Armstrong asked himself why he had been so eager for life back there on stricken Flodden Field.

There was great bustle and excitement next day at Anick Grange as the warriors rode away—as indeed there was in all Hexham. For it was here that Lord Dacre assembled the central body of his forces. A brave and gallant-seeming array, they were mustering and forming up all morning and noon-tide, in the haughlands of Tyne below the town, amidst a deal of trumpet-blowing, dashing hither and thither, pennon-flutter-ing and armour-clattering. Simon watched it all, at a mile's distance, from his window—and his heart was sore.

It was late in the afternoon before the great company, fully three thousand strong, moved off, over the Tyne Bridge, and north by east for Sandhoe, Kirkwhelpington and Rothbury, and so to Wooler, to turn the flank of the Cheviots on their way to the Tweed crossing at Coldstream. They had to pass through Anick village on the way. In the forefront, second only to Dacre's own standard, flew proudly the blue and gold banner of Hexham Priory. The Lord Prior himself was riding with them some way towards Wooler, it was said, to assure them of the blessing and authority of Holy Church.

Watching, stem-eyed, the panoply and brave flourish of it all, Simon saw Marcia Ridley, also watching, down at the foot of the orchard. Calling out, he waved to her, the first actual contact he had had with the younger girl since his return from the Priory—though he had seen her, fleetingly and at a distance, more than once. She glanced back and up, half raised her hand, shook her head, and suddenly picked up her skirts and ran, away round behind the hedges of the kitchen-garden.

The man, troubled, frowned and sighed. Esther, when he approached her on the matter, was, for her, strangely evasive and unsure of herself. The man conceived it that they were all beginning to esteem him almost as little as he esteemed himself, as traitor and fraud. Nor did he blame them for that. His morale reached a low ebb that night. He feared too that, now that Dacre was safely out of the way, and moreover Abel Ridley was no longer here to guard his prisoner, the Prior would have him back to his cell. He knew that Esther feared this also.

So, when Father Crispin arrived at the Grange the next fore-noon, Simon was prepared for the worst. But the apothecary was in cheerful, not foreboding, mood, pleasantly excited by all the stir and commotion—indeed, with the unmistakable self-satisfaction of the childlike simple man who has tidings that other people have not got, inside information which he is in a position to hug, if not to impart. He was not concerned about the convalescent's worries at the moment, being obviously full of more important matters—though he did admit that when the Prior returned he probably would order the prisoner back to the Priory. He hoped, kindly enough, that it might not be to the same cell, however . . .

"When will that be?" Simon demanded. "When does he return? How many days? Is he going as far as Wooler with them?"

"He is not." Father Crispin rubbed plump hands together, beaming cherubically. Evidently the question was welcome, just what was required to enable him to put them all right. "He is not going to Wooler. But then, Master Armstrong, neither is my Lord Dacre! No, nor any of them. No, no." The monk chuckled. "Even now, I trow, they will be half-way up North Tynedale at the least. Though whether my Lord Prior will have gone that distance with them, I know not. Possibly he would turn at Bellingham."

"Tynedale!" Simon and Esther cried, in unison. "Bellingham? But that is not the route! That is no road to Coldstream, to the Merse! What do they there? North Tynedale, you said . . . ?"

Father Crispin dropped a knowing eyelid. "Aha, but that is where they are, nevertheless. It was a hoax—a notable hoax. My Lord Dacre is a cunning fox—as the Scots will learn to their cost! The wicked Home has his spies everywhere, they do say, and since he must learn that our forces were assembling, it was necessary that he should be misguided as to their endeavour and destination. So it was spread abroad that the assault was to be upon the Merse and the East Marches—when indeed it was not. No, no, it was not, by Saint Wilfred!"

"Where, then?" Simon demanded, gripping the friar's arm.

"Where indeed but something nearer home, Master Armstrong! To the Middle Marches. To Teviotdale and Ettrick and Yarrow and Upper Tweed. To Hawick and Selkirk and Melrose, no less, and the fat lands . . ."

Slowly Simon rose to his feet, and the friar's voice faltered and died away. "Merciful God—so that is it!" the young man said, as slowly. "The poltroons! The thrice-damned cowards! I see it all. I see your gallant noble Dacre, and his fine Herons and Fenwicks and Fosters. Aye, and Ridleys! They dare not face Home, and armed men—only the helpless women and bairns and dotards that are all that is left to Teviotdale and the rest! Murderers, your fine warriors are to be—woman-harriers, child-killers. The chivalry of Northumbria . . . !"

"No, no, Simon!" Esther cried. "It is not so! My father knew nothing of this—I swear it. He believed that they were going to Coldstream and the Merse. To fight the Lord Home . . ."

"Indeed he did," Father Crispin confirmed. "They all did—save for a few in my lord's confidence. It was necessary that they should, lest Home's spies should hear otherwise."

"But that will not hold them back from the road that they are on, nevertheless!" Simon charged. "They will not refuse to do Dacre's bidding? He dare not send them against the Merse, against the East March lands where there are men, the men who escaped from Flodden! He has to ride against the lands of the Middle March that lost all in the battle, and now lie defenceless. And lest Home comes over to their aid, as he did before, he must be decoyed away, expecting the blow to fall on his own territory—so that Dacre's brave riders shall have none to withstand them save women and children. This is England's great and mighty thrust against the Scots! It is the furtive abject foray of dastards, I say!"

"Marry, but these are hard words!" the apothecary complained, surprised and a little crestfallen. He had never seen his patient like this before. "Is it not said to be a general's plain duty to seek out the enemy where he is the weakest, where he least looks for him? My Lord Dacre but does what a clever campaigner would do . . ."

"What a craven cur would do, say rather! I think that there may be truth in that he played no gallant role at Flodden! I think I see now why my lords of Northumberland and Clifford and the rest will have none of him. They, I take it, do not ride at all? Nor the Constables of Alnwick and Berwick? It was only another lie, to help keep Home waiting in the Merse, while your heroes lay waste fair Teviotdale?"

"They do not ride, no—a plague upon them! But that is not to say . . ."

"Simon—do not distress yourself so," Esther intervened, pleading. "It may not go so ill as you fear. They may never reach your valley, your Stirkshaws. It is far up, beyond Hawick, you said . . ."

"In the name of Heaven—do you think that I am only caring for my own place, woman!" Simon exclaimed. "Think you that is all that counts with me? Think you that I can sit here, and listen to this, this . . . ?" He stopped, at the hurt and pain in the girl's eyes, those same deep brown eyes that had once meant life and hope and strength to him. He turned abruptly away from her, and went pacing up and down his room, limping only slightly, it might have been noticed.

For a little while there was silence in that upper chamber, save for the sound of the man's striding. The young woman and the monk watched him anxiously. When the latter would have spoken, Esther held up her hand warningly.

"I am sorry," Simon said at length, jerkily. "Forgive me. I am not myself, perhaps. You have both been kind to me—so very kind. I owe you . . . everything. But, but I cannot forget my own people. I think it would be better if I was to be alone awhile. If you will grant me that . . . ?"

"Yes. Yes, of course," the girl cried. "Oh, Simon—I am sorry, too. Do not think that I do not understand. I do. I do. There is no blame for you, here—only for ourselves . . ."

"My daughter—you must not say such things."

"Even if they are true, Father? Master Armstrong can have but little good to think of us here in Hexham."

"My trouble is that I have so much!" Simon declared, almost bitterly. "It would be easier, else. But, now—will you go, I pray you? I may be better company later—who knows?"

Father Crispin would have said more, but Esther laid her hand on his arm and urged him towards the door. "The saints bring you to a right understanding with God, my son," he threw back doubtfully over his shoulder, as he went out.

There was nothing doubtful about the answer that the recipient returned, as the door closed quietly behind his visitors.

X

SIMON ARMSTRONG stood still, silent, in the middle of his room, listening. It was dark, save for the faint red glow from the wood ash on the wide hearth. No sound came to his ears, apart from the hoot of owls from the Grange woodlands, and the occasional muted chink of chain from byre or stable. In the house itself all was quiet.

The man had made up his mind, sore as the task had been. He was fully dressed—though the clothing tended to be on the large side for him, being in the main old things of Abel Ridley's; most of his own had been too much slashed, torn and blood-stained to be worth preserving. He even had a bundle in his hand, part of his supper and some fruit tied up in a cloth. Simon Armstrong was on his way.

It had been a grievous decision to take. He hated himself for what he was doing—but he believed that he would have hated himself more for not doing it. He was breaking faith—not actually breaking his word or bond, since he had never directly given these or been asked to do so. But there was no least doubt that the Ridleys relied on him not to attempt any escape. He was a hostage awaiting redemption—and on his own plea. These good people had given him his life, and an infinity of care and attention. He owed them so much—and this was how he was repaying them! Moreover, he knew that Esther had given a pledge to the Prior that he should remain in his room and be available when that proud prelate demanded him again. He was doing something, therefore—or attempting to do it— which could only result in dire trouble and shame for the person he would least wish to hurt in all the world. He could see no glimmer of excuse for what he did—save that he must. And doing it, he was destroying not only others' faith in him but much that had grown to be himself.

But not, in essence, faith in himself. That was at the bottom

91

of it all—his own ultimate self-respect. He could not stay here, in comfort and safety—or even in the Prior's cell, for that matter—when he knew that terror and death was bearing down on his own people, on his own kith and kin, and he had the opportunity at least to attempt to warn them. Whether he could do it, whether he would ever get to Teviotdale, and in time, was not the point. What mattered for him was that he must try, strive with all that was in him, if it was the last thing that he did—as very likely it would be. Otherwise, he had decided in those recent grim dark hours, he could no longer live with himself. He had to choose the lesser evil.

He could not leave any letter of explanation—for he had not dared to ask for paper and quill. All that he could do was to scratch, by the light of a candle, and using the black charred end of a stick from the fire, on the white linen of his bed, the words:

"I am sorry. One day I will come back."

Never had a man left a message less adequate for what he desired to say.

With a sigh, Simon took a last glance round that darkened room. He tiptoed over to the window. He dared not risk the creaking boards of the long landing outside, nor of the stairs, nor the drawing of the bars and unlocking of the heavy outer door below, nor yet the arousing of the house-dog that slept in the great kitchen that opened directly beside the door to the yard. At the window he stooped to pick up the line of bed-covers and blankets knotted together. One end was tied to the post of his massive bed; with infinite care he had wedged this so that it would neither move nor make any noise. The window, as was usual, consisted of two parts. The upper section was glazed and fixed; but the lower was composed merely of two wooden panels that opened, like the doors of a cupboard, inwards. Quietly he opened these, and began to pay out the clumsy knotted line. It was no great length, for the ceilings of the Grange were comparatively low, and there was no more than twelve or thirteen feet to the ground. There was another window directly below, but it gave only into a dairy, the man knew.

The knotted covers made no sound as they were lowered over. Working himself out through the open panels, soundlessly, the man found less easy. The aperture was large enough to thrust head and shoulders out, but to get all of a long body through, and a somewhat stiff body at that, was not simple. Getting one leg over presented no great difficulties; but following it with its neighbour taxed Simon considerably. Eventually he had to push himself out backwards, his stomach resting on the window-sill, his hands on the floor. The general creaking seemed grievously loud in his ears—though nothing to the clatter that resounded as an elbow caught one of the hinged panels and banged it against the wall. The man held his breath, hanging there, half out of the window, waiting, listening. Then, deciding that such was folly, he began to edge over, clutching the blankets.

The descent was comparatively easy—despite the horribly weak feeling of the muscles in his arms and hands. He barked his knuckles on the stone walling twice as he went down, and once, swinging inwards unavoidably at the window embrasure below, he kicked the dairy window slightly. But his footgear was of old soft hide, and made but little sound. His feet touched the grass of the orchard sooner than he had anticipated, indeed, so that he jarred himself a little. Breathing deeply, even over this minor expenditure of energy, the fugitive stood, ears stretched—and hearing only the pounding of his own blood. Then, turning, he set off down through the fruit-trees.

Simon believed that it would be roughly an hour after midnight. He had much to do before sunrise. Three hours only . . .

At the foot of the orchard he turned off, through the kitchen-garden. Though he had never actually been therein, he had observed its general layout from his window. He brushed against bushes and stumbled over various obstacles inevitably, but it did not seem so dark outside as in, nevertheless, and his eyes were quickly adjusting themselves to the night. He worked his way down the hedge, till he found a gap large enough to squeeze through, into the field beyond. This was the Horse Park.

There were at least a score of horses in the park. Mainly they were heavy farm animals, but there were still two or three riding beasts left, despite the demands for mounting the Priory's contingent in Dacre's army.

This matter of providing himself with the necessary mount had occupied Simon's mind not a little. At first, he had been quite decided that he must not steal one from Anick Grange—anywhere but that. Was he not injuring the Ridleys enough without this final touch? But there had been second thoughts. For one thing, since Abel Ridley's stewardship was a wide one, extending over five manors, to go far enough afield to be clear of his lands would entail a great deal of walking—for which the fugitive had neither the time nor the strength. Again, to lift a horse from anywhere else was bound to result in a much wider and more extensive hue and cry; in the absence of their father, the Ridley girls might well put off the announcement of his escape for a little—and that little might be vital for the escaper. And when he was injuring them so sorely anyway, would the purloining of a mere horse hurt them much more?

In the park Simon had little difficulty in finding horses—indeed, it was the horses rather that found him, coming cantering up out of the darkness from all sides, excited apparently at having a visitor at this strange hour. Unfortunately these inquisitive ones seemed all to be the great lumbering draught animals, that, with the oxen, shared the agricultural work of the Priory farms. With these massive brutes circling and wheeling round him in the gloom, the man found it extremely difficult to pick out one of the slighter fleeter beasts—and when at length he did see one, to get anywhere near it in the circus. He hoped anxiously that the pounding of hooves, the snorting and occasional whinnying, was not being heard in the Grange or any of the cot-houses, which lay only two to three hundred yards away.

But eventually, on being all but knocked over from behind, Simon turned to find an animal nosing interestedly at the bundle that he carried in his hand—and rejoiced to see that it was a riding horse—no splendid charger admittedly, but a useful sturdy shaggy mare, deep-chested and broad-hooved. She would not race, but where he was bound she would serve better than a racer. He grabbed her long mane to hold her, and rubbed her velvety muzzle, murmuring words in her ear. She still wanted his bundle.

Though she was not tall, Simon found the getting on to the beast's back quite a tax on his flaccid muscles—he who had been vaulting on to higher backs than this all his days. So much for the long months of idleness.

But at length he was up—and it was quite astonishing how different a man Simon Armstrong immediately felt himself to be for merely bestriding a horse again. The lack of saddle and bridle worried him little. Kicking the mare into motion with his heels, and guiding her with the pressure of his knees, he was away—and for the first time in half a year esteemed himself to be his own master.

The hedge round that park had no gaps large enough to get a horse through—for all the Priory's property was kept in excellent order. Not wishful to use the gate which opened almost directly into the Grange farmstead, Simon trotted his mount round the perimeter of the field, peering at the laid and trimmed hawthorn—and followed by the entire cavalcade of interested and skittish horses. At length, at the far end, he found what he had expected, another gate opening into the rough pasture of the water-meadows bordering the Tyne. He had to dismount to open this—but by using it, closed again, as a mounting-block, he was able to regain his seat without difficulty. Heaving a sigh of relief, he turned the beast's head north by west, and set off at a trot through the shadowy cattle-strewn meadows.

Simon did not know the Hexham area other than in theory. To go blundering on in the dark, relying even on a fairly highly developed sense of direction, was to ask for trouble—and getting lost the least of it. But to follow the great river was different. It came from the direction that he wanted to go. And, fortunately, Anick Grange was on the north bank, so that even when he came to the point where the North and South Tyne parted company, he would be on the right side. It was up the valley of the North Tyne that Father Crispin said Dacre was heading into Scotland secretly, through the lonely empty Cheviots. The windings and twistings of the river might greatly lengthen Simon's journey, of course—but at least in the haughlands of a large river the going was apt to be more level, more free from major obstacles, than elsewhere. Again, there would be no houses and villages in the actual flood-plain. And if there was bound to be wet and marshy ground here and there, at least it had been a sunny dry spring—and undoubtedly there would be cattle-paths along much of it, as there was here.

Shutting all thought of the sleeping house behind him deliberately, resolutely, from his mind, the man rode steadily north-westwards in a series of links and curves and loops, keeping the murmuring river near enough on his left to ensure that he did not go wrong. The feeling of freedom, of space illimitable, and the vastness of the night, became so strong as to make the rider almost a little light-headed.

It was three miles up to the parting of the streams, where the South Tyne swung away due westwards towards Cumberland, with wide meadows all the way on Simon's side save directly opposite Hexham itself, where the bridge crossed. The May night was not so dark that the mare at least had any difficulty in picking her way and avoiding both the resting cud-chewing cattle that lay everywhere and the drainage ditches and stanks and burnlets that scored the level grasslands. The beast seemed well satisfied with this change from her field, and kept up a fairly steady trot for most of the time, even seeking occasionally to break into a canter—a piece of high spirits which Simon had to counter, in the interests of safety, by dragging back on her mane and forelock.

Beyond the fork of the river the haughland narrowed in abruptly, with higher ground coming close to the water, preventing further easy going. Simon knew that the village of Acomb lay somewhere just inland hereabouts. If, by skirting half-right, he could avoid that, and join the north-going road, he ought to be safe enough thereon across the lonely moorland beyond for a few miles. Somewhere along there was the village of Wall, he believed, so that he would have to get down to the riverside again before that, and keep to it till well past the area of the old Roman Wall and the villages of Chollerton and Barrasford. How many others there might be, he did not know, but he believed that after that the country became less populous as the river neared the great hills.

Thus Simon Armstrong rode through the night, turning inland where the flats of the river failed, but always coming back to the haughlands. To do this was not difficult usually, with the entire lie of the land to assist him. He disturbed innumerable cattle, but he saw no single man or any lighted house throughout. He made no impressive mileage, naturally, but by the time that the grey dawn was paling the sky away on his right, he was past Chipchase Castle and some ten miles from Hexham—though by his round-about route he had covered more miles than that. Soon thereafter he came to the first sizeable tributary stream flowing in from the north, and realised that this must be the Rede. That placed him satisfactorily. He knew that he must be now only a couple of miles or so short of Bellingham, the last township of any size in Upper Tynedale. Splashing across the Rede, a little way up from the confluence, the man recognised that it was time that he started to make more particular plans than he had been doing so far. It would be daylight in an hour, the valley was narrowing in—and Bellingham was the place where Father Crispin had considered that the Lord Prior might turn back from accompanying the army.

Where was Dacre's force likely to be, now—how far ahead? Yesterday noon—was it only yesterday?—the apothecary had said that they would be half-way up North Tynedale by then. Though he might not necessarily be right, that comfortable man that was no traveller. A large armed force moved only at

97

the rate of its slowest sections, nearly always much more slowly than moved individual travellers, even when it was a lightly armed and well-horsed Border army. Would they march by night, in order that the surprise of the Scots should be the greater? Perhaps—but they could scarcely travel by day *and* night. It was twenty miles at least from Bellingham on up to the head of the dale at the pass of Deadwater, and the Scottish Border. It was a narrow way, up a winding valley, and a force of three thousand men inevitably would be vastly extended and strung out. He did not see that they could have got much further than Deadwater yet.

Beyond that, over the watershed, there was a few miles of desolate empty Upper Liddesdale, and then the long narrow climb up through savage hills to the high pass of the Note o' the Gate, and down to Rule Water at Bonchester—a difficult dozen miles more. Thereafter Teviotdale would lie open to them, with Hawick and Jedburgh each only eight miles or so further. How long would it take Dacre to get that far?

A lot would depend on how much devastation he wrought on the way. And whether he kept his array in one great body or split it up into several distinct forays, harrying the different valleys of Liddel and Rule and Jed and Oxnam and Slitrig and Borthwick, as well as the main dales of Teviot and Tweed. That is what he probably would do, lest the men of these valleys, such as still lived, gathered behind him, between him and home. If he was now at or near Deadwater, then it would take him all day to reach Bonchester and the Rule, surely. So that the attack on defenceless Teviotdale itself could not begin till the morrow, at the earliest.

He, Simon Armstrong, had a day and a night, then, twenty-four hours, in which to try to achieve a warning of some sort for his people. Could he do it? Was it remotely possible? He did not know, he did not know at all. But what he did know was that he must make the attempt.

What he must attempt, of course, was to cross the Cheviots, not by roads and tracks and valleys and passes, but the direct way, straight across the hills and the mosses. To do so success-

98

fully would be to halve the length of the journey to Teviotdale—as the crow flies, a high-flying crow—by making the string to Dacre's bow, by following only one side of a triangle while the normal route followed two.

Hillman and mosstrooper as he was, the prospect daunted Simon even as he accepted its challenge. Between this valley of the Tyne and that other valley of Teviot, twenty-five miles to the north, lay as grim a barrier of sheer territorial hostility as was to be found in the two kingdoms south of the Highland Line—not a mountain range or a succession of ranges, but an inchoate jumbled infinity of tall, massive, hump-backed summits rearing out of a high and terribly waterlogged tableland that was criss-crossed in every direction by an endless confusion of clefts and ravines. It was a fearsome directionless place, a desert of high old heather, difficult tussock-grass, quaking green bogs and slimy black peat-hags, with water lying and gurgling and glinting everywhere. Up there was a succession of lofty extensive moors, remote and treacherous, isolating the great summits of Peel Fell, Carter Fell and Catcleuch Shin—Highfield Moor, Comb Moor, Burngrange Moor, Emblehope Moor, Blakehope Moor, East and West Kielder Moors, Kielderhead Moor and the rest, all at an average altitude of around 1500 feet, identical, trackless, a womb of waters, birthplace of mist and cloud, breeding-ground of storms. It was no place for men, even strong and vigorous men—and certainly not for a man weakened and enfeebled and tending to light-headedness. Simon, knowing it, told himself that it was his mount that would expend the energy; he would only sit still and direct.

He decided that the sooner that he started the better—especially as Bellingham just ahead fell to be avoided anyway. The great hills were now looming blackly out of the mirk on his right, inimical, monstrous. Turning his mare's head almost due north, he put her to the first of the long grassy braesides. And though he refused to admit it to himself, already the man was feeling tired and weak.

As the new day grew and the stripling sun mounted over the

crouching mist-wreathed land, so man and horse mounted up and up through the endless sheep-strewn foothills towards the far and ever-receding skyline.

XI

THE mare was game, and blessedly sure-footed. Short-legged and stocky, she climbed with a steady unhurried pacing. On broken ground and the soft uncertainty of the mosses her broad splayed-out hooves seemed to feel their way instinctively. Simon had cause to congratulate himself on his choice of mount, at any rate.

For all that, he knew that, even at this early stage, he was not averaging much more than five miles in the hour—and five very crooked and unprofitable miles at that. And this southern foothill area was, he was well aware, nothing to the grim conditions of the high tableland towards which he was slowly and painstakingly mounting.

It was this thought that eventually, after perhaps a couple of hours of it, began more and more to turn Simon's face westwards, out of due north. His own strength, feeble as it was, he was managing to harbour fairly well. But his mount, though showing little sign of distress as yet, obviously was going to be tired before very long. He was not going to be able to face the main mass of the Cheviot barrier without resting her, and sufficiently—that was apparent. The wearing nature of the terrain, especially its soddenness, was even harder on horseflesh than he had imagined it. And he had no time for resting, even brief and inadequate resting. His mind, therefore, began to turn on the possibility of winning himself a fresh horse before that major assault began.

This, of course, was out of the question—save in one direction. These hills were empty, in the main—as well they might be. But Simon knew that the twin small dales of Tarset and Turret thrust deep into this great landmass somewhere not very much farther to the west. And these valleys were populated, after a thin and scattered fashion. Had he not told Abel Ridley, away back on that first day, that he had far-out Armstrong

101

relatives in Tarsetdale? It was years since he had been hereabouts, but he recollected that while the Turret, the nearer easternmost valley, petered out in empty solitary mosses, the Tarset thrust deep into the hills to end in a sort of high wide amphitheatre, at Emblehope, from which tributary streams fanned out like the spokes of a wheel. And at this Emblehope was a small peel-tower and farmery. Certainly there would be horses there, hill-bred horses. At a guess, it would not be more than four or five miles west of his present position.

And so Simon turned his mare's head westwards towards a long ridge that should give him a field of view. In due course, from its windy crest he looked down over a vast sprawl of the broken foothill country—but right below him was a recognisable valley with a sizeable stream that flowed out of a welter of peat-hags a mile or two to the north. That would be Turret, for sure. Beyond another broad and lumpish hog's-back of ridge he could make out the dip of a still wider and deeper groove that only could be the Tarset. It looked no more than three miles or so farther. Slantwise down into the first valley, Simon set his mare.

The losing of all this height, and the consequent climbing out on the other side, was a trial and a weariness—especially when the second ridge proved to be only an intermediate one with still another shallow valley to cross, with another hill, before that larger dip that he had seen. Angrily Simon thrust this sense of weariness and lassitude from him—from his mind, at least. That was a luxury that he could by no means afford, with his main task still lying ahead of him.

At last he was astride this farther eminence, and gazing down into the long trough of the Tarset Water. He could make out four buildings below him, but all to the left, to the south of him. The two nearer were peel-towers, less than a mile apart—though one of them appeared to be in ruins; the other two seemed just to be farmsteads. But there was no amphitheatre. Presumably Emblehope was higher up, to his right. He rode along the ridge for half a mile till a bend in the valley opened out for him the great hollow that he sought, with its

102

grey stone tower and steading, two or three cot-houses, and small rough fields dwarfed in the midst. A lonely place to live, Emblehope. There were beasts agraze in one of the fields—horses, and milk-kine for the house. Ordinary cattle-beasts, stirks, littered the hillsides around. So far, so good.

Simon did not ride directly down to that little community in the dale. He was unarmed, penniless, curiously dressed and riding a horse with neither saddle nor bridle. While it was just possible that the folk down there might be prepared to allow him to make temporary exchange of this mare for a fresh horse, without too many questions asked, it was not probable. Anybody wanting a fresh horse there and then in all likelihood would be making for or coming out of Scotland—and as such highly suspicious. These were difficult times, and people living in this wild and forlorn spot, so near to the Border, so liable to the attentions of reivers from the north, would be apt to strike first and enquire afterwards, in sheer self-protection. The fugitive dare take no unnecessary chances.

Keeping well back on high ground, he worked along northwards till actually beyond his goal a little, till he found a fair-sized burn tumbling down into the great hollow, and scoring a wedge-shaped ravine for itself all the way down, in which stunted birch and rowans had found precarious foothold. Dismounting, the man led his mount down this, as down a stairway—and very promptly knew that he was a deal better man on horseback than on foot. Unsteadily he progressed, stumbling more frequently than even the steep route warranted, till he was down at the valley floor, perhaps a quarter of a mile above the little square peel-tower on its knoll. He would have been hidden, thus far, save from very alert and watching eyes indeed.

There was nobody out and about, in view. Blue peat-smoke rose from the single chimney of the tower and from the only cot-house visible from here. The field with the beasts in it lay across the rushing sparkling river—a stream of about a score of feet in width, but shallow, and lined with a fringe of alder trees on both banks. Simon hoped that the Tarset, or whatever this uppermost reach was called, would remain shallow for two or three hundred yards more at least.

He moved into the bed of this little burn, actually into the water, to go stumbling and slithering over the last fifty or so yards of level ground to where it joined the main stream, still leading the mare. This gave him the only cover that he could gain. The water was cold on his legs and feet, but invigorating. At the river, he waded out into midstream, and so continued down towards the tower, splashing and floundering unsteadily, the water about his knees most of the time. The banks were three or four feet high and, with the alder trees above them, he thought that his approach ought to be screened in the main. The river-bed consisted of solid basalt slabs overlaid with drifts of large rounded pebbles, and though he slipped and staggered continuously and would have fallen had he not had the mare's clutched mane to support him, there were no deep pools or pot-holes in this level stretch. Every few yards the man caught glimpses of the square tower on its knoll, but thankfully saw no sign of movement thereat.

At length he was down opposite the field that contained the horses. There were five of them, amongst the half-dozen milk cows, penned in behind a stone dyke. That wall came to within a score of yards of his riverside—but unfortunately it stood solid and substantial, though dry-stone, and the only gate into the field opened only a few yards from the tower itself.

Simon cursed. Within the enclosure were some excellent horses, especially one, a big raw-boned long-legged grey that looked both fast and a stayer. But how to get a beast out without going right up under the walls of the peel itself? Must he just risk a dash, mounted, to the gate, open it, ride in, seek to corner the grey, transfer himself to its back, and dash out again? What chance had he of doing all that without the folk in the tower hearing and coming out to intercept? Surely they must hear the hooves. If he was caught inside the field, he was trapped—at least, he might scramble over the wall himself, but not with a horse. And that would be the end of him. Might it be better to leave the mare and creep out on foot, under cover of the wall, and so get the gate open without the noise? But that would entail him having to catch the grey, or one of the others, dismounted—not always a swift or simple task, with spirited beasts. No, he couldn't risk that—the thought of himself chasing unwilling horses round and round that little field under the very walls of their owner's tower was just not to be contemplated. He would have to be mounted to capture the other horse in a hurry. He might combine the two approaches though, creep up on foot, get the gate quietly opened, come back for the mare, and ride in fast? The only other solution that occurred to him was to try to demolish the wall itself at this end, to make a gap to ride through. But that would take a lot of time. And some of those stones were very large—small boulders; Simon doubted whether he had the physical strength for it. Anyway, he could scarcely risk working away there in the open, in broad daylight, demolishing the laird's wall!

No—there was nothing for it but the obvious straightforward attack. He could only hope that most of the fighting-men of Emblehope were away with Dacre on his raid.

Shrugging to himself, Simon led the patient mare on through the water for another hundred yards or so, his heart in his mouth lest at any moment somebody should appear, spot him and raise the alarm. He had to halt before he was actually level with the tower, because the alders faded out here and the bank of the stream itself offered insufficient cover. At the second-last of the trees he tied a hank of the mare's mane to a bough and climbed dripping up the bank. The field wall was no more than twenty yards away, the tower itself seventy or eighty. Fortunately the bulk of the latter, with its steading, now hid the cot-houses from view entirely.

As he crouched, a little dizzily, before making his dash, Simon asked himself whether this was all worth it? Whether he should not just have carried on with the mare, tired as she now was? But he had no real doubts about the answer; that short-legged mare would never take him right across the grim terrain that he had to traverse, in time. She would do it

105

eventually, yes—but not in time for him to bring warning to the people of Teviotdale. And that was the whole reason for his effort. Time was all-important. He must have a fresh horse—and a longer-strided one, if possible.

Taking a deep breath, the man started his run for the wall, bent double—a breathless business at best. Though he tripped once and went down on one knee, he made it, panting. Still no sign or sound of people. Under the shelter of the dyke he crept along to the corner of the field. There he peered round. He was only some thirty yards from the peel. It was four storeys high, the top one a gabled garret within a parapet walk. On this face it had only two windows and a slit at ground level. That last would be merely into the dark vaulted basement. Both windows were very small, for defensive reasons, and provided with arrow-holes beneath. Fortunately the door would be round at the other side, opening on to the steading, as was usual.

From this corner the field wall ran at right angles, rising with the lift of the land; the gateway was some thirty yards up, directly across from the tower. Should he creep up the side, in view of the peel, or climb over the dyke and so get behind it? The latter would shorten the trial—but would be more notice-able. He decided on the former.

It was a miserable furtive performance, creeping, bent low up there, under the windows of the place. Seldom had the man felt so vulnerable. He still crouched, so that at least he would have the background of walling. Every moment he expected to hear a shout, a challenge. He could hear movement—he thought from the steading behind the tower. The clank of pails, it sounded like . . .

At last Simon was at the gate. It was a roughly made thing of untrimmed timber, held shut to a stob by a loop of rope. It was the work only of a moment to unhitch the rope. Standing up, he picked up the gate, lifting it bodily, soundlessly, and carrying it right round on its rope hinges, to lay it against the wall. The beasts in the field regarded this operation interest-edly. Two of the horses even began to move towards him. That was all right—so long as they did not whinny, or get into any excitement that would draw attention to the situation . . .

Simon crept back down the wall again. It did not seem quite so long, this time. Once round the corner, he breathed more freely—though deeply, almost panting. All this stooping was bad.

The crouching rush across the open greensward to the riverside set him almost choking. Unsteadily he untied the mare, and from the height of the bank got on her broad back without difficulty. Kicking her forward, he coaxed her up out of the water. Now for it!

He did not make a headlong dash for the gate, though every instinct urged him to do so. It was noise that was most likely to betray him, and the sound of casually walking hooves might just pass unnoticed when there were horses in the field anyway. Feeling both foolish and conspicuous, he rode quietly out from the alders to the corner, to the open gateway.

Two horses were standing quite close now, ears cocked forward—but unfortunately not the raw-boned grey. And that was quite obviously the best horse there. It was out in the middle, cropping the grass unconcernedly. Simon glanced over his shoulder at the tower windows. No faces showed thereat. He urged the mare forward, into the field.

He frowned as the two horses in front of him plunged away to one side, throwing up their heels playfully. Keeping his mount to a walk, sore as it was to do so, he moved out into mid-field. The grey was taking notice now. The remaining pair of horses were approaching from the farther end. The original two were weaving to and fro in foolish fashion just behind him. Their hooves made a highly evident thudding.

Simon, biting his lip, asked himself whether he was being a fool? Should he just seek to grab one of these, and get away while the going was good? Was it worth it, trying to catch the best horse? His brain told him that it was, whatever instinct said. It would carry him fastest and farthest—and he was going to need that. Moreover, if he was pursued from here, he would doubly benefit his position by himself having taken

107

the best animal . . .

The field was small, no more than three or four acres. It looked as though the grey was going to allow the newcomer to ride right up to it. But with only a yard or two separating them, it suddenly tossed its head and pranced round, mane and tail streaming, to trot off towards the far corner of the walling. Muttering, Simon followed, also at a trot.

He tried to corner the grey in an angle of the dyke. But the creature preferred its freedom, and escaped him. The mare was tired and a little sluggish in her reactions for this sort of thing. Simon halted her, and holding out his hand towards the suspicious grey, spoke low-voiced, coaxingly, soothingly—though feeling anything but soothed himself. Two of the other horses had come up alongside the grey now, intrigued by these tactics. None moved forward.

Slowly again Simon walked the mare towards them. They did not let him nearer than a dozen yards before they were off again, shaking the earth with their going, towards the opposite top corner of the field.

Desperately Simon turned to look back. Still no sign of men about the tower. But the six milk cows had congregated in a bunch just behind him, staring with heavy interest. With a swift decision the man wheeled his mount round behind them, and began to drive them, in a lumbering udder-swinging trot, after the horses.

This time he was successful. The grey, leading the way, found itself hemmed in amongst a clutter of eight other animals within the angle of the wall. Using his mount skilfully, and the stupid bewilderment of the cows to block movement and escape, Simon managed to get the entire group penned tightly into the corner, the grey restless but trapped in the midst. Working his mare in towards it, the man leaned suddenly over the back of a cow, and grasped a handful of the grey's mane.

What happened then was never very clear in his mind. As the grey sidled and the cow plunged, and Simon was in process of being dragged off the mare's back, a shout from behind jerked his head round. One man was standing within the open gateway, gesticulating, and another was coming running round the side of the tower. Action may at times be involuntary, instinctive, but none the less effective in such circumstances, while the mind is preoccupied with action two or three steps ahead. Somehow, having thrown himself bodily across the ridged back of the intervening black-and-white cow, Simon found himself roughly astride the grey horse, without having touched the ground, clinging on tenaciously as the brute reared. Then, twisting its head round by the forelock, his heels drumming on its flanks, he drove it plunging down the field, scattering the other beasts right and left.

The two men in the gateway were staring, and both shouting, one brandishing a stick. Simon did not require to think up his programme with any nicety; he had no choice. Straight for the gateway he thundered, right hand flailing at the grey's haunch, heels digging, crouching low over the beast's outstretched neck. Too late one of the men thought of shutting the gate; leaning back against the wall as it was, it had to be lifted and carried round in a full half-circle. The fellow, a heavy clumsy man, did not seem to like having his back turned to the oncoming horseman in the process, and so made a poor stumbling job of it. Realising that he was not going to be in time, he dropped the thing half-way and lumbered outside after his fellow. A third man, with a woman, appeared from behind the peel.

Then, yelling defiance, Simon was pounding down upon them. In the gap of the gateway itself he dragged back and round on the grey's head with all his available strength, so that the brute slithered and then caracoled, its forelegs up pawing the air, the men in the way leaping back from lashing hooves. Simon directed a side kick with his own foot at the individual with the stick, who had it raised to strike. The blow fell short in consequence, grazing Simon's hip and the horse's rump— which in turn made the animal plunge and sidestep wildly. The rider was all but thrown off, but managed to retain his seat by hanging round the brute's neck. The fellow who had dropped the gate made a grab at him, but Simon spared one arm from

109

his clinging to swing a backhanded swipe which he felt strike home. Then the horse was past.

The third man, with the woman, was older than the other two, and better dressed—probably the owner of the establishment. Naturally enough he was wearing no sword there and then, but he had a dirk at his belt. His features convulsed with rage, he whipped the dagger out of its sheath, and hurled it at the horseman with all his strength.

Elderly the man may have been, but his eye was not dim or his arm weak. The knife came streaking at Simon, the steel flashing wickedly in the sunlight, and had not the younger man thrown himself flat along the grey's neck, undoubtedly he would have been struck. As it was, the wind of the weapon's passing distinctly fanned Simon's neck.

The grey, in a wild canter, made as though to swing right-handed round the corner of the tower and down the valley. Its rider had to drag at the creature's head savagely, leftwards, to get it pulled round to face upstream. But once it was facing in the right direction, the man had no complaints to make as to its going. A few slaps and urgings and it had stretched its long legs into a flat raking gallop. Along the streamside it pounded, the great hills to the north beckoning.

When, after three or four glances backwards, Simon still saw no sign of pursuit, he heaved a sigh of relief. Pursuit there would be, some attempt to follow him, he had no doubt. But neither had he much fear as to the result. He bestrode the best mount there, and he had a good start. The other horses were excited, and might take a little time to catch, on foot. These men, not being actually desperate, might well delay a little longer in order to put on saddles and bridles.

Ahead, the amphitheatre was entered by three distinct valleys. Simon decided to take the central one, that pointed roughly north-west, as likely to serve him best. As he began to mount towards it, looking back he saw two horsemen spur out from the vicinity of Emblehope Tower in his wake. Then a third, and later a fourth. But he had nearly a mile's start. He should be all right. The only risk lay in their superior knowledge of the ground. The fugitive settled down to steady hard riding.

Soon the valley had opened its jaws to engulf him.

XII

AFTER half an hour of it, and his last glimpse of the pursuers amongst the winding valleys showing them to be still farther outdistanced, Simon Armstrong let himself relax somewhat. Not entirely, of course—for he had felt reaction setting in for some time, and he had to fight against it, consciously, deliberately. Unaware of the fact at the time, in all the excitement, he had called drastically upon all his poor reserves of strength—and to good purpose undoubtedly. But now the reckoning fell to be paid. Dizzy, limp, sick and trembling, he could only hope and strive to pay it in as small and gradual instalments as possible. That, and keep the grey going at a sufficiently vigorous pace.

His route, perhaps, should have concerned him more than it did. But by keeping the sun at his back, he was heading approximately northwards. And he knew the general Cheviot formation well enough to be satisfied that such a course must bring him out on to the great central watershed eventually, somewhere at least within sight of the soaring twin-peaked summit of Oh Me Edge. And once he could view that readily identifiable crest, he could find his way—so long as mist and cloud did not descend to blot out the landmarks. He thanked God that it was a sunny, breezy day of high clouds.

It must have been around noon that the grey brought him at length up out of the hollows and valleys and on to a long high ridge that was really a series of linked hump-backed summits running north-east and south-west. Behind him the land sank away in a vast succession of thrusting shoulders and rolling moors to the green dale of Tyne, rising again beyond to the far horizons of Wark Forest. But ahead all was a brown chaos, a lofty, spreading, jumbled desolation of heather and blaeberry and peat and russet deer-hair grass, streaked with the black of the moss-hags, dotted with grey outcropping rock.

Water lay everywhere in that sombre infinity, not sparkling and dancing, but still, sullen, glooming in the smile of the sun. And out of it all heaved hummocks and ridges and eminences innumerable, featureless, identical—all, that is, save a jagged stony double-toothed tor rising high and lonely only two or three miles to the north. Oh Me Edge, whose distinctive outline had been the saving of men uncounted since men sought to cross that untamed engulfing wilderness—when men could see it. Half-left, therefore, many miles away—eight or nine at least, even as the crow would fly—seen through and above a series of gaps amongst the hillocks, the long remote blue crest that bounded sight to the north-west must be Peel Fell. Across its mighty head ran the Borderline, and out of its sprawling northern flanks Jed Water was born. Scotland. That was where he must make for. Let him reach the Kielder Stone on its high north shoulder and he would know his ground. Was that too much to ask? Could he hold out that far? He would, and therefore could, the Lord willing . . .

Not lingering on the skyline for fear of observation, he rode on into the watershed.

It would be a great weariness and entirely profitless to seek to chronicle Simon Armstrong's journeyings and wanderings through that brooding nightmare of a place. He could maintain neither consistent pace nor direction. Three-quarters of his time was spent not in progressing but in deviating, in avoiding, getting round tarns and meres, steering clear of bogs and mosses and deep unexpected ravines, encircling hillocks and bare basalt spines, casting about, seeking viewpoints and lines and landmarks. While he was still up on East Kielder Moor he at least could follow a general trend of direction; but once he had to descend into the unlooked-for network of deep waterlogged valleys thereafter, he had only the southerly position of the sun to guide and place him. Maddeningly he was forced to ride with it first on this hand, then on that, frequently in his face even—and so seldom directly at his back. When he eventually again won out on to the higher ground of what might be either West Kielder or Kielderhead

113

Moor, it was to discover that he could no longer discern either the beckoning ridge of Peel Fell ahead nor the twin fangs of Oh Me Edge behind, because of intervening lesser summits. He could only blunder on in what he prayed was approximately the right direction.

By late afternoon he knew that he was lost. The multitude of streams and burnlets, which should have guided him by the direction of their flow, seemed to run all ways. There was no system to the lie of the land. One rounded hill was no different from its neighbour—and when wearily he set the horse to climb to the top of one, it was to perceive therefrom nothing to lead him in any of its fellows. A long, low, level ceiling of cloud had swallowed the sun. He had been going round in half-circles all day, inevitably—he might well be completing the circles now.

Even with a fine and stout-hearted horse, it was spirit only that kept the man going, moving, seeking ever to work north-wards, when every physical inch of him cried to let him be still, to rest, to lie on the soft inviting ground and forget. Only the stubborn, dour, unyielding spirit of him—sustained it may be by sheer pride and a sullen anger in tune with the terrain against which he fought—kept him going on and on. Or was it round and round? He did not know. He could only hope. And keep the grey moving, slumped heavily on its back.

It was a voice out of the past that spoke the word that saved him, eventually—the faraway past. In a dazed state, half-asleep, eyes swimming in a red haze of weakness and fatigue, Simon gradually became aware, as grey evening settled on the land, that his mount's pace was easier, smoother, more steady. Shaking muzzy head, he peered about him—and was aston-ished to find that they were on a road. Green, grass-grown and rush-dotted it was, pitted and broken down—but a road, for all that, distinct and continuing. Much too wide for any mere path or track, it maintained an even twelve feet at least, with cuttings into the bank here and there, which, though semi-collapsed and overgrown, were obviously artificial. Looking ahead, the man could see it stretching away, amazingly straight

114

considering the territory, following the valley that he was in on a terrace above the burn, and then, where the valley twisted, striking right on, away up the flank of a long hill. Looking back, he saw it reaching away behind him till it dipped out of sight over a drop in the terrain. Seen from itself, it was the plainest, clearest feature of the landscape; but obviously, from any distance off, even a few yards, and from almost any angle, it would be practically invisible even if looked for. Simon's father had told him, long ago, that there was a Roman road crossing the great welter of these hills somewhere, linking the Wheel Causeway and the main military road, Dere Street, that ran from the Wall up Redesdale into Scotland. This must be part of that link.

Thankfully the weary man urged his mount along it, even putting the beast to a trot. As far as he could guess, the road was heading in an approximately northerly direction. That was good enough for Simon Armstrong.

It was quite amazing the difference made by that green highway, in pace, in ease and, most of all, in morale. It drove ahead through the wilderness with a certainty, a directness and a purpose that was the best possible tonic for the exhausted traveller. The surface too was remarkably good, and though washed away here and there, and otherwise broken, there was never the least faltering or doubt as to its route—a tribute indeed to those long-dead engineers of Rome. Wherever it chose to cross into Scotland, its aid was infinitely to be preferred to any blind struggle across country—even if it was known in which direction to struggle.

In the event, and much sooner than Simon could have thought possible, he found his road lifting up to a great rounded shoulder of hill, which offered him the view that he wanted. Vague and indistinct as were the hills now, there was no doubting the position. Peel Fell reared its lofty crest no more than a couple of miles away to the left, westwards, across the dip of a wide but shallowing valley. The road itself climbed directly on over what was clearly a major outlier of Carter Fell, the central of the three great summits of this section of the

115

Cheviot range. Praising his Maker, Simon pressed on along it.

In little over a mile farther he drew up on the crest of the ridge, the ultimate ridge, the spine of the land, the Border. Before him Scotland spread, dark, shadowy—but his own land. Almost overcome with emotion, Simon sat his grey there, staring, blinking, swallowing. He had done it. After all these months, he was back in his own country, in his beloved land, on the soil that he had feared that he would never see again. He could admit that to himself, now . . .

And then a more practical, more urgent consideration than this emotional preoccupation possessed him, and he peered northwards with a more intent eye. And the level blanket of the oncoming night that enfolded it all, lifted his heart by its very unbroken obscurity. No fires blazed yet in the Middle Marches, no red glare of destruction yet lit up the threatened land. Dacre's army had not yet managed to begin its fell work, then. He was in time! His effort was not in vain!

Delaying no longer, Simon rode on, downhill now.

The road took him down, in the deepening twilight, by the side of a rapidly growing burn which, he decided, must be one of the principal headwaters of the Jed. On his left the tall and recognisable peaks of Dand's Pike and Carlin's Tooth loomed blackly. Down there, only four or five miles ahead, would lie Southdean, and the peel-towers of Dykeraw and Lustruther. And then the man recollected—these had all been destroyed in Dacre's last raid, in November, Ridley had said. Hotly, almost petulantly, the tired man cursed. If this land was already wasted, empty, who was he to tell, who to find to warn? Was he never to gain rest? Must he go on riding, riding, seeking men?

The surface of the old road was more broken on this north side of the watershed, no doubt due to the fiercer weathering and the steeper descent; and, with the increasing darkness, the grey had to pick its way more deliberately. Whatever his irritation and vexation, Simon could only let the brute take its own time. He dare not seek to rush it. Yet every minute now counted, he recognised all too clearly. For once it was fully dark, he might well pass within a few yards of houses, unseeing. And once men were abed, his warning would be wasted. If he had to ride on, all the way to Bedrule, or Jedburgh . . . !

It was with a great lift of the heart, then, that much sooner than he had expected he saw a yellow light gleaming in the little valley ahead of him. Then, as something heaved away lumberingly on his right, he realised that there were cattle on the hill around him. Soon he could see that the light shone from a small square building, half-tower, half-farmhouse, that crouched amongst outbuildings under a black bulk of hill just a little way across the stream. Over to it he splashed.

As Simon rode up, a dog began to bark madly. Then a door was flung open, and he glimpsed two men outlined in the glow of a lamp. There were shouts. Simon tried to shout back, tried desperately—but he could nowise raise his voice high enough to carry above the noise of that damnable dog. Time and again he tried, brokenly, gaspingly, to declare himself, to say what had to be said. But he could not make himself heard. He could not even hear himself. Sagging on the grey's back, he mouthed and mumbled, from lips that were both stiff and slack at the same time, into the crazy din—and knew a mortification beyond all words. He had to get down, to come near to them, to speak to the men. Away from the hellish barking. As though it was a major effort, he got his leg over, and slid off the horse. Touching the ground, his limbs buckled under him. He sank down on his knees, and would have fallen flat had he not still clutched the grey's mane, dragging the beast's head down. The yellow lamp seemed to dance and cavort around him.

And then strong hands were reaching out to him, lifting him up, supporting him. And good Scots voices were speaking. And, glory be to the saints, the dog's barking ended in a strangled yelp, as a boot-toe met its ribs.

"The English . . . !" Simon panted. "Dacre! They are coming. Over . . . the Note o' the Gate. Now. In their thousands. Dacre's army. Quick! Haste you—get the beacons lit. The balefires. It is the Middle March . . . not the Merse! A trick . . ."

"Eh? Dacre? Man—what is't? Whae'n Goad's name are you?"

"I'm Armstrong of Stirkshaws. I've come . . . from Hexham. But . . . but haste you. Get the beacons burning, I say . . . before the men are sleeping. Warn Teviotdale. And Jedburgh. It is to destroy them that he marches . . . Dacre. The English. Lord—d'you hear me? You have beacons set?"

"Aye, we have. But this is nae cheat, man—nae covin?"

"God in Heaven—why should I cheat you?" Simon wagged his head helplessly, supported between the two men. He found the greatest difficulty in controlling any part of himself, including his lips and his tongue. "I am Simon Armstrong, of Stirkshaws on Borthwick Water," he got out, thickly. "I was a prisoner. Since Flodden Field. I fought with Drumlanrig. Ridden from Hexham. Through the hills. By Kielderhead. English in front of me . . . up Tynedale. Coming by Liddesdale . . . Note o' the Gate . . . three thousand . . ." He choked, swayed, and could say no more.

But he had said enough. "Tam," one of his supporters cried. "Awa' up wi' you, and light Millmoor Rig. Cry on Jocky to light Charlie's Knowe. Off wi' you." The voice was upraised. "Wife! Meg—oot here, wumman! Here's a man near foun'ered. See's him inside . . ."

Simon was dimly aware of being more than half-carried indoors, into light and warmth, of women's care and concern, of fiery spirits being forced between his lips, of being laid on a box-bed in an alcove, and being pressed to eat. He did not want to eat. He wanted only to sleep. But before he might sleep, he must warn them, warn everybody. He kept trying to tell them, to impress upon them the terrible need and urgency . . .

Sometime later, that he might sleep in peace, kind arms upheld him again, guiding him outside into the night, and pointing there. And, dazed and heavy-eyed, but glad, Simon was able to perceive the flickering red plumes of flame that crowned the black bulk, not only of two neighbouring hills, but of many, pinpoints of light stretching far away to east and west. The balefires were lighting up, all along the Middle March, linking up, warning Jed and Rule and Teviot and Tweed and Borthwick and Ettrick and Yarrow—a whole land. Whatever happened now, the Middle March would not be taken entirely by surprise.

Satisfied, Simon Armstrong suffered himself to be conveyed back to his couch.

XIII

IT was high noon next day before Simon came to himself. He found that he was in the modest tower-house of Mark Kerr of Blackburnhead, just a mile up from that burn's junction with Jed Water. The master of the house was not present—indeed there were only his comfortable wife and strapping daughter about the place, Kerr, his sons and his male adherents being all out on the hill. They had been out since well before dawn, rounding up the cattle from amongst the foothills and driving them up to a hiding-place safe from marauding English bands, in a deep beef-tub high on the side of Carter Fell. The same thing would be going on, thanks to the balefires' warning, all along the March. The eldest son had been sent hot-foot down Jed, to carry the news that Simon had brought, to the scattered communities there, to Jedburgh itself. The young-est, a mere stripling, was sitting up on a knoll of the green hill of Millmoor Rig, above the house, keeping watch over the upheaved landscape to south and west. Already, apparently, he had descended far enough, twice, excitedly to announce that great smokes were rising from the direction of Hardlee and Wauchope.

The news and the hour put Simon in a fret to be off again. He felt well and strong, he assured the women—and even though that was an exaggeration, he was greatly rested and refreshed, and indeed felt better by far than he could have believed to be possible any time during the day before. And ravenously hungry.

This last requirement he took time to satisfy, at his hostess's urgent persuasion—since anything else would have been folly. Then, mumbling his thanks from a full mouth, he was pushing outside, seeking his horse. He should have been on his way long ere this. If the English were burning as far north as the Wauchope already, then it was high time that he reached

Borthwick Water and his own place. To the women's charges that he should take a care as to how he rode, he nodded and waved. He would have liked to have seen and thanked Mark Kerr—but must put first things first.

Simon rode down the burn to its confluence with the Jed, and then on down the river to Southdean. A sorry sight the place made, church and houses still black, roofless and gaunt since the November raid. The same applied to the neighbouring tower of Dykeraw and to the hamlet of Lustruther. The new season's green that was beginning to burgeon everywhere could not wholly disguise the charred desolation of burnt steadings, barns, and corn and hay stacks, cast down walls and broken gear. The white skeletons of beasts, picked clean, still strewed the area. Some small attempt at rebuilding had been made here and there, but lack of manpower, after Flodden, prevented any real restoration.

From hereabouts, looking southwards and westwards, Simon could see, beyond the grassy ridges of the Wolflee hills, the growing darkening columns of smoke that rose from three or four points, to converge and coalesce into a single sullen pall, blowing towards him on the south-westerly breeze. It was hard to say just how far away that was, but presumably it came from the valleys of the Wauchope and Lurgies Burns. He wondered how far north Dacre's outriders might have got beyond the areas actually being burned. It was important that he should not run into them. Would they have reached Bonchester yet?

He left the Jed Water and rode almost due westwards, through the green rolling foothill country. The larks were carolling above him, untroubled by the acrid smell that was already beginning to tinge the air. A thin veil of smoke had now covered the midday sun.

Simon decided not to risk the south side of Bonchester Hill. Safer to the north, though longer. He passed one or two farmsteads up here that were not burned. But they were deserted, nevertheless, of men and beasts—though only very recently, obviously, peat fires still smouldering on their hearths, an occasional cat or barn-door fowl being alone in possession.

This undoubtedly was the result of the beacons' warning. These scattered remote places could not be defended; their folk had fled to more populous centres, driving their herds with them. Many had been busy while he slept.

Rounding the lofty shoulder of the grassy pinnacle of hill, the man looked out over the Rule valley and down to the village of Bonchester Brig directly below him. So far, Rule Water seemed to be secure, uninvaded. At least, no smoke of burning rose, no troops of horsemen rode its fair reaches. Indeed, no sign of stir or life showed anywhere, from up here. Simon rode down to the village huddled around the hump-backed bridge under the hill.

It was as a place of the dead. The houses stood empty, even though the blue peat-reek still lifted above many of the thatches. Somewhere an outhouse door banged occasionally in the breeze— a dull and unchancy sound. A dog snarled at the intruder from behind a gable-end, and then bolted, its tail between its legs. A single cock crowed, with untimely shrillness—and the day was the lonelier for its cry. No other sound, save the murmur of the river, broke the unnatural silence. The Turnbulls had gone. Though this was as it should be, the sign that his efforts at warning had been in time, Simon could not but feel uneasy, troubled. He was glad to ride out of the place. He was glad, too, for the excuse to cross himself as he passed the church. The feeling was strong on him that he ought not to be there.

He could have turned southwards here, to follow the Rule down to Teviot. But his own valley of Borthwick lay still some ten miles to the west, and home called strongly. So he headed the grey directly thitherwards. He would cut across the commons behind the Kirkton of Cavers, this side of tall Ruberslaw, past Adderstonelee, across the Slitrig valley, and so over by Branxholm to Stirkshaws in its own quiet glen. And he prayed that still it would be quiet when he reached it. It was a tiring business, riding against the grain of the land, crossing all the multitude of streams, great and small, that drained northwards from the mighty watershed of the Cheviots, up and down, in and out of a score of valleys, and across the shaggy heathery slopes between—with always that ominous dark pall of smoke growing, spreading, filling the sky to the south. Simon saw no man in all those miles—though there were still many cattle grazing on the commons. The lonely place of Adderstonelee, the only farm that he actually touched, greeted him with blank eyes and every sign of hurried departure.

He was crossing the steep deep valley of the rushing Slitrig Water before he heard the sound of human voices. He was just trotting over the drove road in the winding floor of the glen before fording the peat-brown waters when a hail jerked his head sharply to the left, southwards. Half a dozen horsemen had appeared from amongst willows at a bend in the valley some two hundred yards away. One glance was enough for Simon. It was not the morions, breastplates, lances and the rest that upset him—it was the miscellaneous gear that hung about their saddle-bows and draped the led horses that they towed. Spoil, plunder, again. It could be only the English.

Simon's open hand slapped down hard on the grey's rump as he set her straight at the water.

Without actually reasoning it out with himself, the man's decision had been immediate. He could have raced on down the drove road, in the direction of Hawick. This was a good horse, and less heavily laden than these others, for he was neither armoured nor saddled with booty; he might well have outdistanced any pursuit. But these men were not necessarily the first of the English outriders on this road. There could be others ahead. Clearly they must have come from Liddesdale by the pass at Shankend. He could ride into a trap. He preferred the open hill—even though it reduced his pace and delayed his flight. Those scouting riders of Dacre's were unlikely to be archers.

He could not be particular as to where he entered the swift-flowing Slitrig. Fortunately the river's very speed meant that its pebbles and boulders were scoured clean and not weed-grown, and so were not slimy—otherwise the grey would surely have gone down. As it was, the beast floundered, splashing mightily, water up to its middle, plunging, hooves slipping

123

amongst the ledges and rounded stones. But there was no great width to cross, and in a desperate few moments the brute was over, and clambering out on the rocky bank, streaming water.

Above the rushing noise of the river, Simon could hear the drumming of hooves and the yells of men, as the riders came galloping down the valley. But his instinctive decision had been the right one. Before he was half-way up the steep braeside of tussocks and bare red earth that rose for a hundred feet or so above the stream, the chase had halted, and only shouting and abuse was following the fugitive. They would have chased him down the road; but a single unarmed, unequipped, and poorly dressed refugee represented nothing worth going to any trouble over. Undoubtedly there would be infinitely more profitable pickings down the valley.

On the lip of the trough Simon, looking back, shook his clenched fist at the invaders below, and set off through the last belt of low grassy hills and knowes to the next dale, that of the lovely Borthwick Water.

It was mid-afternoon when its laird made his so long delayed homecoming to the pleasant fertile place of Stirkshaws. Set in its own alcove to the north of the main glen, it was like an emerald lying in the bosom of the swelling hills, a fair demesne of tilth and birchwood and pasture flanking a little reedy loch. On a promontory that thrust into the loch, the tower stood, separate from its farmery and cottages, its gardens and orchards. Though in an excellent defensible position and strongly built, the tower was not just the square peel, as at Emblehope and Blackburnhead, so common in the Border-land, but of a tall L-shaped structure that doubled the accommodation, with a corbelled-out parapet all round the wallhead, at fourth-floor level, and a dormered garret within the stone-tiled roof. Plain it was, yes, with no gesture towards ornamentation; but sturdy, substantial and, as towers went, commodious. And its lands rose in rolling waves around it to the summits of the enclosing hills.

Simon's throat constricted more than a little at the sight of it all. How long his forbears had been settled here he did not know—though legend had it that they had come not so very long after their ancestor, Earl Fairbairn Siward of the Strong Arm, the Norseman, had stormed north to use his terrible sword to place Malcolm Canmore on the throne of Scotland, a full five hundred years before. Such length of tenure might err a little on the safe side, but certain it was that no one had ever heard of any other than Armstrongs in Stirkshaws. Not so many days ago Simon had wondered whether he was to be the last of them.

Thankfully then, but still very much aware of the shadow that hung over his fair heritage, as over all this land, he rode into it, eyes busy. He noted that there were fewer cattle and sheep than he had been wont to see grazing on the surrounding slopes; that only about half the ploughing had been completed, even though it was now mid-May; that a winter's spate had washed away the bridge spanning one of the outflows from the loch—and only a couple of planks had been set up to replace it; that gaps in the stone-walling around the fields had not been built up, but merely filled with heaps of brushwood. But smoke still rose from the tower chimneys, and from holes in the thatches of the half-dozen cot-houses; the creak of the waterwheel still came from the mill buildings at the burn's outflow from the loch; a man, old and bent admittedly, but still a man, was slowly leading a pair of oxen into the steading; and ducks and geese still swam and plowtered around the little promontory on which the tower stood. It might all have been so very much worse, the man recognised. With the haunting unchanging voice of the cuckoo echoing from the encompassing hillsides, Simon rode, dirty, dishevelled, saddleless, and dressed in other men's clothes, up to his own doorstep.

It was not the homecoming that the man had visualised, nevertheless. Ailie, his sister, was from home—gone to Hawick to sell beasts for his ransom, apparently. Old Janet, who kept the house, threw her voluminous apron over her grey head at sight of him, and burst into tears. Abby, the kitchen-maid, took incipient hysterics, swearing that he was a ghost and no man, and that she had known that he was dead all along. The few other old men and boys that remained to the place were gone with Ailie, herding the cattle. It remained only for Simon to go to tell the wives of Wattie's Dod and the others the manner in which they had become widows—no happy task.

Moreover, all the while that he was talking to his folk, cleaning himself up, changing into clothes of his own, resisting attempts to have him put to bed, and pecking at the enormous quantities of food thrust before him, Simon's glance was apt to lift away southwards above the enclosing barrier of the Teviothead hills. The sun had worked well into the west now, so that the thing was not quite so obvious; but even at this range, and above all those intervening ridges, the brown pall of smoke was beginning to show.

Simon heard with astonishment that a couple of monkish messengers had arrived at Stirkshaws only four days previously, with his letter asking for the ransom money—four days, not four months and more. Yes, a letter *had* come earlier, back at Yuletide it had been, old Janet agreed—but that one had only said that Master Simon was alive, though wounded, and held prisoner somewhere by the English. Aye, and there had been a great praising of God and thankfulness, for these same tidings, as of one back from the dead—though Abby here had not believed it, holding it all only as a trick of the cruel deceitful English . . . No, no—there had been no word of money then, Janet swore. Only the plain word of his living. And glad enough they were, at that, the good Lord knew! It had made a new lass of Mistress Ailie. Yes—only this self-same week had come the two mendicant friars, with word to send the gold, much gold. Indeed, yes—Mistress Ailie had got it for them, had sent it back with them. How much Janet did not know—but all she could lay her hands on. She had borrowed from their uncle at Milsington, and from Drumlanrig's widow, in the Black Tower of Hawick. And now she was away in with the beasts to sell, to pay them back . . .

Simon, beyond deciding that the old woman had got everything mixed, could make neither head nor tail of all this. He must see his sister. She was not intending to come home to Stirkshaws that night, it seemed, but staying in Hawick to complete the sale of the cattle in the morning. And in the unsettled state of the land, and the rumours that were rife after the beacons' blaze of last night, she was safer there . . .

Despite the protests of the women, Simon, clad and armed as himself again, on a fresh horse, rode out of the secluded sanctuary of Stirkshaws as the evening spilled violet shadows into all the valleys and hollows of that tumbled land, to turn down the brawling Borthwick Water, eastwards. He did so with a great reluctance, admittedly, feeling tired and heavy—but he had felt a deal worse than this not so very long ago.

XIV

HAWICK lay some five miles to the east, deep amongst its thrusting hill-shoulders, and Simon approached the town with the darkening, by way of the confluence of Borthwick and Teviot, and the Coble Pool. As he rode, he could by no means banish from his mind that last time that he had come this way, nine long months ago. Then he had ridden, brave and confident, with six stout lads at his horse's heels, to meet Drumlanrig before his Black Tower of Hawick, proudly armed, well mounted, high of heart. The road to Hawick, that August day, had been throng indeed with such as he and his, a gallant company drawn at the royal command from all the branching valleys of the Middle March—every man between 16 and 60 years who could bear arms, for 40 days' service with his liege lord King James. And none had come riding back; not one—save eventually only himself. At Stirkshaws he had learned the whole fell truth. As far as Teviotdale and Hawick were concerned, there had been no survivors, no fleeing fugitives, no stragglers, no limping wounded. Stubborn Scottish pride and King Henry Tudor's grim orders between them had combined utterly and entirely to reap a land of its able-bodied manpower. And not only Teviotdale, apparently—to Selkirk, it was said, only one man, the Town Clerk, returned. Only the very remote upland cleuchs and valleys, which had not been worth summoning to the Standard, retained a few grown men—as at Blackburnhead above Jed Water. Simon had been luckier than he knew when he had stumbled upon that lonely household. The rest of the chain of beacons had been lit perforce by boys and women and greybeards.

Changed conditions were impressed upon the lone rider before ever he entered the town. High-pitched, youthful and not very steady voices challenged him from behind a barrier of tree-trunks and rubble, a good quarter-mile in front of the

128

West Port at Myreslawgreen—and he had some difficulty in establishing his identity with the four youngsters who crouched there in the shadows, armed with swords and lances too big for them by far. After considerable excited discussion, the smallest of them, a lad who could have been no more than fourteen years old, was deputed to conduct the traveller into the town. Bearing a sword almost as tall as himself over his shoulder—and having to use both hands to get it there—this warrior led the way at the horse's head. He chattered ceaselessly as they went, informing that the bloody English who were thought to be converging on Hawick from south and east, were assured of a warm welcome.

At the gate in the walls there was another guard to win past, even less mature than the other—though it might be that some of the boys here were only admiring onlookers. Thereafter, Simon's progress through the narrow dark streets was slow indeed, for the people had pulled the straw and reed thatching from the roofs of their houses and heaped and spread it on the roadways and lanes, to be fired when the invaders arrived— a drastic step, but likely to be fairly effective; it was difficult enough to move through these littered and choked alleys now—what it would be like when the stuff was burning and smoking could be left to the imagination.

Along the Common Vennel, Simon, leading his horse, came at length to the Howegate, where his widowed Aunt Bridget dwelt under the shadow of St. Mary's High Church. Here was where his sister Ailie would be staying overnight in the town, for certain.

His aunt, the elderly and somewhat feather-brained relict of a former bailie and corn-miller of the burgh, greeted him with much relief—though tinged almost, it seemed, with a touch of suspicion. The latter appeared to query just what her nephew had been up to in his long absence, upsetting them all; the former, intense satisfaction that there would now be no need to squander the family's hard-won resources in amassing gold pieces to send to the insufferable English. Simon omitted meantime to explore these matters with the old lady, demanding

129

only the whereabouts of his sister. He was informed that she had been there, yes, and would be coming back presently—but meanwhile she was over at the house of that upstart none-account cattle-dealer, Andrew Cessford, who, being the only member of the Council who had not ridden off to Flodden, now perforce foisted himself on to long-suffering Hawick as its senior bailie and chief magistrate. A sprung-up, two-faced, time-serving nobody, with whom her late revered husband, God rest his soul, would not so much as have passed the time of day . . .

Simon took himself off forthwith for Bailie Cessford's house in the Cross Wynd.

"Sim! Sim! *Sim!*" Ailie Armstrong cried, rushing across the not over-clean straw of the Bailie's floor, to hurl herself into her brother's arms. "Is't yourself, Sim, my dear? Really and truly you? Yourself—alive and well? At last—at long long last? Oh, Sim—I am so glad, so happy. Dear God—to see you again, after all this time. You are real—it is no dream? It is truly you, Sim? Say it is true, lad! Yes, oh yes. Oh, but my dear—you are thin, waeful thin and poorly! There's nothing to you, at all." Her hand came up to stroke his unshaven cheeks. "You are sick, ill, starved—a done man. Och, the devils—the wicked English devils! They have made an old man of you, Sim . . ."

"Hey, hey, Sister—not so fast!" Simon only just managed to get it out, what with the vehemence of his young sister's arms around his neck and the choking effects of his own emotion "It is none so bad as all that, surely? Am I such a sight? So ill-favoured? And what about *you*, lass? There, now—unhand me, will you, and let me have a look at yourself, girl." Gently he disentangled her arms, and held her from him. "Och, my—but you are older too, lassie! 'Fore God, you are a woman now, Ailie—no bit of a girl any more. A woman grown—and a bonny one!"

The girl blinked away the tears from shining eyes—an auburn-haired, blue-eyed, finer-featured edition of himself, with the same long Armstrong face, all the better for being scarcely so stubbornly chinned. "No, no . . . I mean, yes. I am not. But you . . . och, Sim—Mary Mother be praised for the sight of you, wae as you are! But how got you here? Where are you from? I cannot believe it. Only two or three days agone, the friars told me that you were a prisoner in Hexham. Was it false? How came you to Hawick . . . ?"

"Over the hill, just, lass," he told her. "A prisoner I was. And, and it may be, I am still, in a fashion. You see . . ." He shrugged, and let that go. "It is a long story, that will keep. But . . ." He glanced beyond her to the man who stood by the table across the untidy stuffy room. "We forget our manners. The Bailie . . ."

Andrew Cessford was eyeing him keenly from shrewd foxy eyes. He was a small stunted man, with a stoop that was all but an incipient hunchback, and an over-large head—a sorry physical specimen to represent the proud and ancient burgh of Hawick—though, by his glance, noways lacking in intelligence. "Aye, aye—hech aye, Stirkshaws," he said, in a creaking voice. "Here's a right surprise, is't no'—a right amaze. Dod, aye—a man returned frae the deid! Goad kens hoo ye got here, Laird—I dinna. But . . . a'weel, welcome tae Ha'ick, for a' that."

Simon sensed no great welcome there nevertheless. Even in the flickering lamplight, the little man's eyes were calculating, searching. "I thank you," he nodded briefly. "I am thankful to be back."

"Ooh, aye. Aye. Nae doot. But hoo came ye here, Stirkshaws, frae Hexham—wi' a' the English bands in between? Hoo won ye tae Ha'ick . . . just noo?"

"Over the hill, as I said. From Tynedale, over by Emblehope, and Kielderhead, to Carter Fell and the Jed. By the mosses and the heather . . ."

"Say ye so? Aye. Ihmhm." The other was pinching his already pointed chin. "Just that."

Simon's heavy eyes widened. Could he be believing his ears? Was that suspicion in the fellow's voice? Was this manikin suspecting him, *him*, Simon Armstrong of Stirkshaws? And of

131

suspecting him, *him*, Simon Armstrong of Stirkshaws? And of what? "You sound . . . almost doubtful, sirrah?" he said, his own voice rasping harsher than he knew.

"Me? Na, na—wha's Andra Cessford tae doot the word o' the braw Laird o' Stirkshaws? Goad forbid! It's just that the times are chancy, unco chancy, Maister Airmstrang—an' it's a strangelike thing tae reappear frae the grave, as ye might say, at the selfsame moment as Dacre's damned English reach oor doorsteps! A coincidence, as ye might say . . ."

"My God—are you saying . . . are you suggesting that, that I have been sent here? By the English! That I am a traitor?" Simon cried. "For, if you are, by all the Powers of Heaven . . . !" The younger man's hand clapped down on the hilt of the sword that once again hung at his hip.

"Guidsakes! Mercy on us, man—wha said onything o' the sort?" Bailie Cessford jinked quickly farther round behind his table. "Ye're ower quick. Far ower quick . . ."

"Pay no heed to him, Sim," Ailie's hand was on her brother's arm, urgent pleading in her voice. "Let him be. Do not fret yourself over him. Let us away from here. We do not need him now, anyway . . ."

"I mislike his manner of speech," Simon declared, breathing hard. "Hawick is in ill case if this is the voice of her!"

"Ha'ick is in damnedest danger, man," Cessford gave back swiftly, tensely. "Ha'ick has tae fecht for her life! Hawick canna afford tae tak' ony chances. We're like tae be beleagured here, Stirkshaws—an' we maun clear oor feet an' oor sword-airms!" The little man seemed to grow in stature as he spoke, however incongruous his talk of sword-arms. "Ae single English spy could cost us dear. We ken they're no' far off. We ken they're making for Ha'ick. We ken they're ower the hills intae Slitrig frae Larriston, an' doon Teviot at Lanton an' the Spittal. There's even a cry they've been seen up at Teviotheed, at Coltherdscleuch . . ."

"I saw them myself, nearer than that, at Coliforthill in Slitrig, as I came through," Simon interrupted. "I had to run for it. But these were only outriders, I think—scouts. The main

132

many miles behind."

"Aye. But they'll be here, Laird, afore lang—maybe this night. We'll be at handstrokes wi' them, the baistards! Maybe there'll be nae Ha'ick by the morn's morn! But there'll be a wheen less Englishry, tae, by the Lord Goad!"

"You'll fight, then?"

"While there's ae blaw o' breath in ae single callant or dotard or wumman in this toon, Stirkshaws!" Andrew Cessford cried, his squeaky voice cracking. He brought down his clenched fist hard on his table.

Despite himself, Simon could not but admire the spirit of this misshapen runt of a man. Just as he admired the spirit of the youngsters guarding the town's approaches, and the house-wives who tore off their roofing to help fight the invader—little faith as he could raise in the efficacy of any of it all to save Hawick. Knowing the temper and quality of Dacre's men that were approaching along the valleys of Slitrig and Teviot, he knew also a great wave of pity for this town and all within it, a wave strong enough to drown the personal pride injured by Cessford's suspicions. He did not trust himself to say anything.

Ailie's hand was on her brother's arm. "Come, Sim," she urged. "Let us be away home. There is nothing to keep us here, now. No need for more bickering with Master Cessford over the cattle. We do not need the gold, now . . ."

"Mistress, did I no' tell ye—it's as ill a time to sell beasts as ony I've ken't in a' my days," the bailie declared. "Wha can tell if your herd willna be a' Dacre's beasts by the morn! It's no' tae be expected that . . ."

"Then your money also will be all Lord Dacre's by then, in that case!" the girl returned, with spirit. "But it matters not, now that my brother is safe back . . ."

"H'rr'mmm." Simon cleared his throat. "I would not say that . . . I fear that the gold still will be needed, Sis," he mentioned. "It is not all just so simple as that."

"But why? You are escaped, Sim—so what need is there for ransom money?"

"I . . . I have still a debt to pay, lass. My word to redeem, after a fashion."

"Ha!" That was Cessford, swiftly. "Your word . . . tae the English! A debt tae pay, hey? Save's a'—here is strange talk, Stirkshaws! Aye—strange right eneuch! Ye'll be in touch wi' the enemy yet, then? Eh, man? Is that it? An' here's you slipping in tae Ha'ick nae mair'n a skip ahead o' Dacre! You'll no' deny it's queerlike, Laird—queerlike!"

Simon took a deep breath, clenching his fists tightly. "Not so strange, Bailie," he declared, seeking to keep his voice and his temper even. "It is no accident that I have arrived only a little ahead of the English—since I came expressly to warn you. I broke my faith with my captors, to whom I had pledged ransom, when I heard of Dacre's raid—that he was going to fall upon Teviotdale—to escape and warn the country. Dacre had set out before I could get away. So it is small wonder that I was only just in time."

"Man, man—d'ye tell me that! A' that!" It was clear that Cessford did not believe a word of it. "Is't no' a peety, then, that we were gi'en the warning by the beacons last night? After a' your steer an' swink!"

"It was my news set the first beacon ablaze, at Blackburnhead on Jed Water. I got the word to Mark Kerr there, who lit it."

"Ooh, aye. Is that so? Weel, noo." The older man was pinching his chin again. "Tell me, noo, Laird—if ye came ower by Carter an' Jed, hoo comes it ye were seeing the Englishry up Slitrig?"

Simon frowned. "I came the shortest way to Stirkshaws from Blackburnhead—by Rule Water and across the commons behind Cavers. When the balefires were lit, I had done my task. The March was warned. I made for home . . ."

"And that is where we'll be making for, now, Sim," his sister intervened. "Here's enough of talk. We can leave the cattle in Hawick tonight. It's home for you, and your own bed . . ."

"I fear ye canna dae that, lassie," Bailie Cessford declared, flatly. "Naebody's leaving Ha'ick this night. Naebody. No' if he was the Archangel Gabriel!"

"You cannot do that! You cannot keep us here . . ."

"Can I no'? I'm Chief Magistrate o' this burgh, Mistress, I'd hae ye mind, an' I can dae mair'n that!" the little man cried.

"But why?"

"Because Ha'ick's in deidly danger, an' naebody's tae be let oot that the English could lay their bluidy hauns on, tae force tae their will maybe. Tae guide them in. The walls are weak an' broke eneuch. The gates will stay shut. Aye." Cessford drew breath. "Och, an' it's for your ain guid, Mistress. The English could be in Borthwick Watter by noo. You an' the Laird'll be fine at your Auntie's. Ye were for biding there, onyway, ye said, before . . ."

"But it is different now. Do you not see . . ."

Simon Armstrong was feeling desperately weary now, in spirit as well as in body. Suddenly he had reached breaking point. "Come, Ailie," he interrupted harshly. "Have done. Let us away from here. Leave him. I'm tired. We'll get back to the Howegate. Come." He swung round, a little unsteadily—and the girl, quick to see it, clutched his arm to support him. In the doorway he looked back—and he did not know just what a death's-head he presented to the bailie. "My sword . . . is at Hawick's service . . . when needed, Cessford," he muttered.

"Ooh, aye. I'ph'mmm. I'll mind that, Stirkshaws." The other nodded, and watched them out, narrow-eyed.

Simon was less than satisfactory company that night, offering sister and aunt but little information and enlightenment on all that they wanted to know. But Ailie at least was patient, understanding, restraining her questioning, urgent for his well-being. She would have had him in bed and cosseted forthwith. But the man would not hear of it. This was no night for men to be between sheets, in Hawick. A corner of a settle, before the fire, for him. And once therein, his eyes stayed open barely long enough for him to finish a bowl of hot spirits. Ailie draped a plaid about his hunched shoulders, and then settled herself on the sheepskin at his feet, leaning against his knees.

It was long before she slept—and even then but lightly. From the noise outside, it seemed that there was little sleeping achieved in Hawick that night. A group of armed callants, mere lads, had taken up their stance just outside her aunt's door. Was this just a coincidence, she wondered, or did it represent the practical outcome of Bailie Cessford's suspicions? Was it a guard over them? Whatever it was, she wished that excited young voices would moderate themselves, for Simon's sake.

Her brother did not stir in his corner, however, as the long hours went past—though now and again he muttered a name in his sleep. It was not Ailie Armstrong's name.

XV

THE clatter and shouting and uproar in the streets of Hawick some two hours before the dawn that May night, however, might well have wakened the dead. Suddenly shattering the lull that had settled with the chill small hours, young voices yelled, women skirled and pleaded, armour clanked and horses' hooves stamped and rang on the cobbles. Starting up, Simon threw the plaid from him, all but fell over his sister, and groped his way to the window, to fling open the shutters. Were the English come, then, indeed?

Nothing definite could be made out from there. Nobody answered his shouts of enquiry. Buckling on his sword, but still in his hosen soles, Simon went padding downstairs, out through the pend, and into the thatch-strewn street.

Three or four boys and a group of shawled women stood near by, talking loudly—indeed, carrying on long-range conversations with the many other women who seemed to stand at every house-door and pend-mouth. Simon could just distinguish, amongst the babble, reference to Hornshole, Wattie Somebody-or-Other, Trow Mill, Denholm, and, of course, the devilish and damnable English. He pushed forward, over the straw and reeds, demanding information.

At sight of him the youngsters grew still more excited, waving and shooing him back as though he had been a refractory barn-door fowl. A lance was poked awkwardly and vaguely in his direction, a dagger brandished half-heartedly, and a long rusty sword tugged some way out of its sheath. The man ignored all this, waving the gestures aside with his hand.

"What's to do?" he questioned them. "Is there an attack on the town? Where are the English?"

A variety of answers replied to that, simultaneously, incomprehensibly.

"Quiet!" Simon rapped out, and pointed to what seemed

137

to be the oldest of the youths, a fair-haired lad as tall as himself but so slim and slender that the steel corselet that he wore, made for a grown man, looked grotesque, with room enough inside for another two of him. "You!" he said. "Tell me what you know."

"You . . . you're Laird Airmstrang, are you no'?" the boy said hoarsely. "You're no' tae be oot. You're tae bide in the hoose. The Bailie said . . ."

"Never mind what the Bailie said," Simon snapped. "I'm a soldier, not a cattle-dealer. I want to know what is being done for the safety of this town?" Which may not have been very fair or helpful to the authority of Hawick's much-tried temporary Chief Magistrate.

Left in no doubt as to the authority of the voice, the youth swallowed. "Aye, but . . . och, sir—will you no' going back? Intae the hoose. It's no' us that's saying it. It's the Bailie. He doesna trust you. He says you're maybe in the English pay . . ."

"I'm not interested in your Bailie, boy. I'm Simon Armstrong of Stirkshaws, and I want to know where are the English now?"

"They're at Hornshole, Maister," one of the smaller boys cried. "They're campit in the haugh there . . ."

"They're bedded doon at Hornshole, aye. Bluidy hundreds o' them!"

"Denholm's burned! The fowk are a' deid . . ."

"No' a' o' them. They're in Denholm Dean, wi' the cattle."

"Wee Wattie Wilson, frae Ashybank, seen them. The damned English. He says they came up frae Denholm. The whole o' Tividale's blazing . . ."

"They're no' three mile awa' . . ."

The women were joining in now, all speaking at once, an incoherent flood of information, conjecture, imprecation and alarm. Simon's hand sliced down in a fierce but eloquent cutting motion. "Quiet!" he bawled. "One of you, speak. You!" And again he pointed at the fair-haired youth.

He did not achieve any quiet and lucid account of the situation, of course, even then, but he did manage to piece together enough to gain a fairly vivid picture of what had transpired that night. It seemed that a herd-boy, Wattie Wilson by name, had arrived in Hawick a little while back with the news that a large band of English raiders were encamped at the bend of the Teviot only three miles downstream. Wattie, orphaned at Flodden like the rest, belonged to the farm of Ashybank, near Denholm, a mile farther on, but was now staying for safety's sake in the town with his widowed mother. Their black-and white cow, Jintie—details, however irrelevant, made the picture only the more graphic—had strayed away from the town common, and Wattie, guessing it to have wandered off home to Ashybank, had gone seeking it that late afternoon. It had been a long search, but he had run it to earth at last in the deep secluded wooded cleft of Denholm Dean, that thrust from the main valley up into the foothills of Ruberslaw. And he had found not only Jintie there, but many another beast also, together with some of their owners—the survivors from the fair village of Denholm, those who had managed to get away in time, before their houses went up in flames, their fellows died and their women were ravished. Horrified and terror-stricken at what he heard, young Wattie had hidden there with the others—for it was known that the raiders were working their way up Teviot, making for Hawick—till concern for his mother, who would be worrying about him, at last drove the boy out, to make for the town in the dark. And slipping discreetly over the high ground, above the river at Hornshole, he had seen the glow of the many cooking-fires in the shadowy haugh below, and, though desperately frightened, had crept nearer, to peer down into the pit of it.

The River Teviot here made a loop that enclosed a level semi-circular area of greensward on the south side, with a gorge ahead, spanned by a high bridge, and steep banks behind, the whole forming a natural enclosure where cattle might be penned without herding and fear of them straying. And since the English raiders had collected a deal of cattle, as well as other booty *en route*, they had apparently decided that this was an excellent place to halt overnight, after their labours,

139

and to leave Hawick till daylight. So there the enemy lay, according to Wattie, asleep around their fires, in their scores, their hundreds maybe, and with not much to be seen in the way of guards and sentries, evidently—as who was to blame them, with the country practically swept clean of fighting-men to oppose them. Wattie had seen and noted—and come running all the way back to Hawick, to yell his news to his young colleagues sleepily guarding the East Gate.

So now also, Simon was further informed, they were going to sally out and meet the enemy. They would fall upon them in the darkness, while they were disorganised and heavy with sleep. They would smite them hip and thigh. They would so. Teribus ye Teri Odin! Hawick for ever!

"Who will do this? Who is to do the smiting?" Simon wondered. "Not Bailie Cessford!"

"Guidsakes, no! Him!" There was a hoot. "We'll dae't oorsels. Oor ainsels. Us yins. The callants."

"Aye, will we! Goad, aye!"

"Up, the callants! We'll gie them something tae tak back tae England!"

"Andy Turnbull says we've got them coopit! Andy says hit them noo. When they're tired—no' wait till the morn for them tae attack us, when they're fresh. Aye, an' he's right . . ."

"Andy's the boy—hech, aye!"

"Who is this?" Simon demanded. "This Andy? Andy Turnbull, did you say? Is he one of the Council?"

"Him? Goad, no! Andy's yin o' us. A callant. A right bonny fighter, tae. His faither was Pate Turnbull, the skinner. He's deid. So's his brither Davie. Kill't in the war."

"Andy's a' right, Maister. You should see him at the swording . . . !"

"Aye, lads. That is fine. I admire your spirit. But this is serious—man's work. You are going out against trained soldiers. See you—where is this Andy? I must see him. I am trained to arms myself, you see . . ."

"Na, na—you canna dae that, Laird. You'll hae tae see the Bailie. It's no' for us . . ."

140

The fair-headed boy stopped, as a hail came echoing down the narrow street, from the direction of the Kirkstyle. All heads turned thitherwards.

"Come o-o-an! A' o' yous! Come o-o-o-an! Andy says every callant's tae come," the caller shouted shrilly. "Tae the Tower Knowe. Noo."

As a gabble broke out around him, the tow-headed young leader with them cried back, "We canna. The Bailie said we'd tae bide here. Tae watch this man . . ."

"Tae hell wi' the Bailie!" resounded down the Howegate to them, forcefully. "Come oan!"

Apparently these sentiments coincided exactly with those of the youthful guard, for without another scruple three of them turned and went running up the street, leaping and dodging amongst the thatching. The fourth, of the fair hair, looked after them, glanced at Simon, and then, shrugging shoulders within his oversize corselet, set off after the others long-strided. The women's chatter rose to a crescendo.

Simon almost followed the boys himself, then realised that he was devoid of footgear. He hurried back to the house. Ailie was in the pend-mouth, watching. He threw her a few brief words of explanation as he ran up the stairway, weariness forgotten. He paid no heed to her urgings about not involving himself in needless danger—just as almost the entire masculine youth of Hawick that night was equally heedless of women's pleas and warnings. But he at least was campaigner enough to grab a chunk of cheese and a portion of oaten loaf from the table, to stuff into his pockets, on his way to stride down the stairs again. Ailie was at his heels, still.

But down in the little yard to which the pend led, at the back of the house, where he looked to find his horse stabled, he was disappointed. The beast was gone. More of Bailie Cessford's precautions, undoubtedly. Cursing, he hurried out into the street, and set off down the Howegate on foot. Lifting up her skirts, amongst all the litter and debris, Ailie ran half a pace behind him.

It was no great distance to the Tower Knowe, above the level

141

haugh of the Sandbed where Slitrig joined Teviot, and where the endless refrain of rushing waters hymned Drumlanrig's Black Tower of Hawick, soaring high amongst the huddle of lesser buildings. But tonight the tumult of the rivers was drowned in a greater hubbub. The open space in front of the Tower was a seething mass of people and animals. Everybody seemed to be shouting, dogs barked and horses whinnied and snorted. Boys of all ages predominated, but there were a few old men, cripples, and the like, and a great many women and girls. Simon did not glimpse a single able-bodied man such as himself. A few torches flared redly, but did little to dispel either the darkness or the general confusion. Youngsters dragging unhandy lances and long swords through the press added to the chaos, tripping and stumbling and almost tearfully demanding passage, amongst the orders, instructions, demands and cursings, and the cries of the women. Some small proportion of the lads were mounted, and they did better—though many of the riders looked the more absurdly small. Here, surely, was the strangest army that ever assembled in all broad Scotland.

Simon pushed his way hither and thither through the throng, seeking the leaders, this Andy Turnbull in particular, Ailie clinging to his sword-belt. He asked many people as to which was Turnbull, and got much pointing but little profit out of his enquiries. He recognised his own horse, in passing—but did not seek to challenge its eager dancing-eyed rider. Near the base of the Tower itself he caught a glimpse of Bailie Cessford and one or two other elderly men, who looked ill-suited to the task of defending a town however stout their spirit—and from these he sheered off heedfully. He was despairing of ever being able to speak to anybody who could influence the course of events when the continued blowing of a forester's horn from somewhere over near the Tower doorway gradually quelled the general noise. A couple of torches raised high, in the same direction, served to illuminate the individual who was winding the horn lustily, a well-built stocky youth of around sixteen years, wearing a leather cuirass and a huge helmet that seemed to rest wholly upon his ears. He stopped blowing, to shout instead.

"A' them that's coming, this side here!" he bawled into the comparative lull. "Them that's no' coming, awa' doon the hill there. Tae the Sandbed. Come oan—the lot o' yous! Weemin an' lasses—git oot o' the road! Armed callants this wey . . ."

"Aye, aye, Andy."

"Here we come. Guid for you, Andy."

"Teribus ye Teri Odin!"

"Doon wi' the English!"

"Hud your tongues! Hud your tongues, will ye!" young Turnbull roared. His voice at least was bull-like. "Them wi' horses, tae me. Them on fut, ower the side there. Come oan . . ."

In the general movement of coming and going consequent upon these instructions, Simon was able to force his way over to the loudly directing Andy. In dire risk of being ridden down by horsemen inexperienced in marshalling at close quarters, he worked to the lad's side—and Ailie also, perforce, since she by no means would be shaken off. The horses of the two torch-bearers, who closely flanked Turnbull on either side, were a nuisance. But at last he was near enough to shout up to the callants' leader—and when his shouts failed to outdo the boy's own, to reach out and grasp and shake his knee.

"See you here—I am Armstrong of Stirkshaws," he cried, as the youngster looked down. "I can help you. I know about this fashion of fighting. You must listen . . ."

"Guid for you," the youth acceded, briefly. "Get yoursel' a horse, an' come oan."

"Yes. But . . . there's more than that. I say that there is more than that!" Andy Turnbull was back at his own shouting again. "See, man—at this Hornshole place. I know it. It's a trap, if properly sprung. But it could trap you, too. Are you heeding me, boy?"

"Och, aye. I hear ye. But I'm busy, see. You come along, Maister. Ye can tell me on the wey . . ."

"But . . . oh, very well. I'll do that." Simon saw that was

143

indeed all that he *could* do, then. He turned, to seek some youngster that he could profitably unhorse—and looked straight into the angry contorted face of Andrew Cessford, torch in hand.

"Damnation! I thocht it was you, Stirkshaws," the little man yelled. "Here's nae place for sic as you! Awa' back tae the Howegate wi' you. I tell't ye . . ."

"Here is the place for me, fool!" Simon gave back wrathfully. "Damn it—I believe that I am the only soldier here! And if ever Hawick needed soldiers, it is this night. I am riding with these callants . . ."

"No you're no'! That's the last thing ye'll dae—d'ye hear?" The Bailie raised the torch, to gesture with it, almost in Simon's face. "Hud him, boys! Tak a hud o' him. It's Stirkshaws—new come frae the English!"

There was a rush at Simon from all sides. A score of hands, young and old, seized him—and because his sister was still clutching him, Ailie also. He was pushed and tugged and buffeted. His sword was dragged from him, out of its scabbard. His every instinct was to fight back, to resist and struggle. But he told himself to wait, to hold back, for the time being. This was not the moment—with all these impetuous hot-headed boys about him, unaccustomed naked steel in their eager hands. And Ailie involved. Moreover, any altercation, any internal disagreement now, might well upset and spoil the whole spirit of this brave but forlorn venture. For Hawick's sake he must wait. Allow himself to be held, meantime. But for Hawick's sake there was still something that he might do.

Suffering the grasping and rough handling, he raised his voice to its utmost pitch. "Turnbull," he cried, above the din. "Heed this, at least. Send a band round the back. By Cavers Dean. To attack from their rear. And another band by the north bank of Teviot. And the cattle, stampede them through the English, if you can. You understand? Use fire, tinder . . ."

That was as much as he could enunciate, over and through the hubbub. His voice broke. Whether it had been heeded, or even heard, he could not tell. The callant Turnbull was already wheeling his big roan about, his mounted supporters jockeying around him, the horde of those on foot surging into motion, swords and lances and staves held high, waved, shaken.

A great shout uplifted. "Teribus! Te-e-eribus! Teribus ye Teri Odin!" The ancient stirring warcry of Hawick lifted high-pitched and quavering a little, but vehement and resolute and fierce as ever it had been rendered. And to its barbaric age-old chant the entire company of the callants streamed away along the street towards the East Gate. Those that had been grasping Simon relinquished their hold and ran to join their fellows. Only a few, old and frail, remained around the Bailie and his Council. The womenfolk came pushing back from the Sandbed, some taking up the chant, some shouting encouragement, others warning, some wailing and keening, few with dry eyes.

And so they watched them go, the youth of Hawick—boys as young as eleven and twelve, since there was no holding them back, none older than sixteen. How many there were it was impossible to say; there might have been thirty or forty mounted, but those on foot hugely outnumbered them. Two hundred men had followed Douglas of Drumlanrig eastwards out of the town nine months before—an equal number of their sons, even their grandsons, may have followed Andy Turnbull that night. And how different a cavalcade they made, from the bravely equipped banner-bearing gallant array that rode to answer King James's summons; now the majority were ragged, bare-foot, armed as variously and incongruously as the minority were horsed, with no pennon or standard other than their own high courage and tense resolve.

Simon Armstrong's own eyes were not entirely clear as he watched them go, and Ailie sobbed openly at his shoulder.

Andrew Cessford, presently, was shouting some sort of instructions to the crowd of women, as to manning the gates, and being ready to fire the thatching if a beacon was lit on the parapet of the Tower as signal. The little man's squeaky voice was inadequate for the task, but he kept on with it, seeking to penetrate the noise. Simon perceived that the two or three old men who still held him did so now in token only—and anyhow, he could have knocked them over with ease. Ailie had been let free altogether. Folk had other things to think about there and then.

Catching his sister's eye significantly, in the flickering torch-light, Simon nodded. Then abruptly jerking both arms forward and up and round, he broke free of those feeble grips, and leaping backwards, turned and plunged into the throng of women, Ailie at his back. None sought to restrain them—as far as they could gather, none sought to chase them either. They pushed their way through, hurrying back towards the Howegate.

When they were clear of the press, Simon said, panting, "I've got to get a horse, Ailie. Somehow. Where is yours?"

"It was in Aunt Bridget's stable, where we put your own. But it is gone now, also."

"Then we must hunt for one. Anywhere. Come."

"Must you, Sim . . . ?"

"God help me—you know that I must, girl!"

XVI

SIMON, panting, halted at the summit of the long rise and looked back towards the darkened town. The valley wherein Hawick lay was the darkest area of the entire landscape indeed, for all to south and east some reflection of the ruddy glow of burning villages and farm towns and stackyards still stained the night sky. It was brightest directly ahead of him, here, down Teviotdale; that would be the villages of Denholm-on-the-Green, five miles away. And Hornshole haugh and bridge lay two miles nearer. No sound reached him on the still night air.

Simon was almost half an hour behind the callants. Search as he would, he had been unable to find a horse; probably indeed the callants had not left one mount in all Hawick that night. He had wasted precious time in his seeking, before finally giving it up, leaving Ailie with hurried assurances, and making for the eastern extremities of the town. He had avoided the gates, since they were manned—if only by women—but had found little difficulty in making his exit through walls which were only too frequently faulty and broken-down. He had not been challenged—as he might well have been had he been mounted. It did not say a lot for the town's hopes of defence.

He was on the track of Turnbull and his callants—but whether he would be in time, now, to affect the issue in any way, was highly doubtful. All might well be over before he could reach the scene of conflict—even if anybody would pay any attention to him and his advice. But he had to make the attempt. He had no doubts about that. At least, if the worst came to the worst, and what he feared eventuated, he could strike one blow for Hawick and Scotland before dying with the rest—if somebody would give him a sword!

Simon slanted down towards the winding Teviot, through

147

the whinny knowes and grassy slopes, all deserted of their accustomed cattle now, reaching the river near Bucklands. There was a ford here, and if Turnbull had done what he had suggested, a band of his boys should have been sent across here to seek to menace the enemy's northern flank. The man investigated the approaches to the ford, found horse-droppings that were still warm, and presently, peering, managed to distinguish fresh tracks, some barefooted, in a muddy patch at the waterside. Satisfied in some small measure at least, he hurried downstream. Andy Turnbull was using his head to that extent.

Hornshole lay less than a mile ahead. Still no sound of any clash reached him. Cutting the corners of the river's windings, Simon hurried on, eyes and ears urgent. Had the boys sent a party to the right, up through the knolls, to come down Cavers Dean behind Hornshole? Would they have the sense to wait, to time their attempt properly, so that any flanking parties were able to get into position? Would they, in their excitement, keep their approach reasonably silent? Laddies they were, just laddies, headstrong and impetuous. Old heads were never set upon young shoulders. Would God that most of those young heads remained on their shoulders after this night!

Simon reached Trow Mill, deserted now and forlorn, within a mere quarter-mile of Hornshole Bridge. It would be dawn very soon; almost he could imagine a lightening to the east already—though the fluctuating glow of distant fires made it difficult to be sure. A deal of new horse-droppings littered the greensward beside the dark mill buildings. This could only mean that the band had waited here for some little time—presumably while scouts crept forward to investigate the enemy's position. Again a welcome indication of forethought.

Thereafter Simon had to leave the river bank on his left, where it rose to the high bluffs flanking the narrows over which the arched stone bridge was thrown, almost above a gorge. His heart in his mouth, he climbed, setting his booted feet with the utmost care so as not to break twigs or otherwise betray his going. Not a sound, save for the noise of the river itself, came from ahead of him. It was uncanny. The semi-circular green

148

haugh of Hornshole opened directly beyond the bridge and the little gorge—not two hundred yards in front of him now. If what the boy Wattie had said was true, a large party of English raiders lay no more than an arrow-shot from him—and still nearer presumably, on the tree-clad knowes, were all the noisy youngsters of Hawick. Yet no hint of the presence of men broke the night's hush. From somewhere in the waterside reeds behind, a mallard quacked sleepily, and then, from in front, at no distance, a bullock lowed restlessly. That was all. Simon would have expected to hear at least, the mailed clanking of a sentry pacing the stone bridge on his left, if not the excited stir of the callants. Had the English moved back? Retired? Or had the boys all gone round behind, by Cavers Dean, to attack from the rear? Surely not, when they had obviously waited at Trow Mill, only a little way back . . .

And then, just as Simon began to edge forward once more, almost on tiptoe, a sound, two sounds, froze him in his tracks, lifted the hairs at the back of his head, and sent a shiver through him. The first, clear, metallic, decisive in the hush, was the swift screak of steel—a sword being whipped out of its scabbard. And following immediately upon it, high, thin, falsetto, piercing the night with an unchancy weird cry that ended in a choking sob, "Tee-e-e-eribus! Tee-e-e-eribus!"

And promptly the answer came, bellowed and screamed from scores of dry young throats, "Ye Teri Odin! Ye Teri Odin! Ha'ick! Ha'ick!"

The night seemed to burst wide open in sound and movement, as, just a little way ahead of the man, the crouching callants obviously hurled themselves down the steep slope into the shadowy haugh, in a chaos of thudding hooves, clanking clashing steel, and frenzied yelling.

Simon went running forward.

To describe coherently the Battle of Hornshole would be beyond the tongue or the pen of any man—since there was nothing coherent about it. It was indeed no battle at all, but a massacre, with neither manoeuvre nor system nor any

149

sequence to delineate. Simon Armstrong certainly, the only on-looker at that bloody nightmarish holocaust, found no words then or after to report it. He stood on the crest of the bank, and stared down, rooted still in horror, seeking and yet not seeking, to pierce the grim obscurity of the dark, of the mist-filled haugh, of the terrible confusion, of the yelling screaming pandemonium.

Certain circumstances fall to be recorded, however, for any general appreciation of what approximately transpired. Firstly, undoubtedly the Englishmen were ill served by their sentries—since it is almost inconceivable that seasoned campaigners would have omitted entirely to set a watch of some sort, even in territory which experience had so far shown to be devoid almost wholly of organised resistance. But sentries can sleep, or be drunken—and from the quantities of looted liquor that survived in that haugh in the morning, much might be surmised. At any rate, there was no warning given.

Again, the fact that the large number of stolen cattle had been herded and penned at the west end of the haugh, nearest to Hawick, was very relevant. For by accident or design it was these brutes which took the first impact of the callants' crazy downhill charge, and in consequence stampeded off eastwards through the sleeping ranks of the raiders, in high-tailed thundering frenzy, scattering the dully glowing embers of the camp-fires, trampling and bellowing. And no sleeper, befuddled or sober, is at his acutest when thus awakened. Indeed, it is to be doubted whether many of the English ever realised that it was an attack, an assault by armed assailants, and not merely a charge of distracted livestock, before cold steel was thrusting and flailing and smiting at them, and the outlandish names of Thor and Odin were being yelled in their ears. If even Lord Dacre's veterans failed to react with suitable swiftness and decision to this rude awakening—probably, in perhaps the majority of cases failed to react at all, in time—it may be that there was excuse enough. A large proportion of the Northumbrians, at any rate died in their blankets.

As irresistible as a flood of Teviot itself, and quite as

furiously impersonal, the host of the callants stormed down upon the unsuspecting encampment, their front ranks not so much in the wake of the cattle as in the midst of them. No finesse, no tactics, no generalship, no swordsmanship even, was employed or attempted. The thing was wholly of impulse, fiercely elemental, entirely and wholeheartedly and terribly destructive. Possessed by one mass emotion, vengeance—to avenge their dead fathers and brothers, their harried savaged land and burning villages, and to save their mothers and sisters, the youth of Hawick hurled itself down into Hornshole. And in the few minutes that sufficed for the business, it is likely that scarcely one of those who smote and hacked, consciously and sensibly realised that he was killing living men.

Tirelessly, gulping and sobbing and shouting, their swords and whingers whirling and beating, axes and clubs cleaving and battering, daggers stabbing and lances thrusting, the boys poured across the meadow, trampling on and stumbling over their victims, slipping and falling, but always plunging on again, arms unflagging. Men slain by the first ranks were slain again and again by those who followed. There was no real resistance, organised or individual. Those of the English at the east end of the haugh, wakened by the uproar in time at least to gain their feet before death was upon them, found themselves dodging and leaping away from snorting pawing terrified cattle, rather than reaching for arms and armour—and in consequence were wholly unprepared for the onslaught of steel that followed so closely.

Coming to the closed eastern end of the semicircle of haugh, the cattle, faced by the abrupt barrier of the enclosing high tree-clad bank, largely swung away to their left, to plunge headlong into the river, many breaking legs and backs in the process. Two or three fleeing men followed them—with a few leaping yelling boys at their heels. But the great majority of the attackers, finding nothing more to smite in front of them, instinctively, almost blindly, turned about and went hewing and hacking back again over the killing ground—this time slipping and falling still more frequently on the blood-soaked grass. If

151

any of the unfortunate sleepers retained any life in them after the first onset, they certainly did not survive the second. By the time that the fierce tide of the callants had ebbed back to its starting-place at the foot of the western bank, whereon Simon Armstrong still stood transfixed, no single Englishman still breathed on the grassy sward that had been green before.

For a strange few moments thereafter there was comparative quiet in that haugh of Hornshole, after the indescribable bedlam that had shattered the dawn previously. Only a panting, gasping, gulping sound rose from the crowd of youngsters, shot through with a sort of whimpering, to compete with the bellowing and urgent lowing of injured cattle from the river. And then the reaction set in—a varied one. Shouts and yells of triumph resounded, verging on hysteria. Some lads leapt and danced and embraced each other—but as many were violently sick. Some few came running up the hill and past Simon, unseeing, desperate only to get away from that ghastly scene of carnage. Some crouched down, heads between their hands, trembling, while others boasted and babbled in tense high voices. Few there were who dared to look often or for long directly at the littered haugh. The wan and sickly light of dawn, the smell of blood, lack of sleep, the sudden cessation of tension and furious action releasing the strain on overwrought nerves— all had their effect. The price of victory fell to be paid—and would go on being paid, undoubtedly, for a long time to come. Yet, as far as the watcher could see, no single one of the callants had fallen—though many were variously cut and bruised, largely probably by each other's weapons.

Some of the older and tougher lads, Andy Turnbull prominent amongst them, with a strange mixture of bravado and reluctance, moved over to spoil the vanquished, as tradition required, beckoning, almost beseeching more of their number to accompany them. But few indeed, even of these, did not avert their eyes from the fallen. Some of the corpses still twitched, inevitably. Whatever the intention, there was no robbing of the slain, no actual touching and handling of the so bloodily dead. But where there were little heaps and piles of weapons and armour laid aside the night before—and most of the raiders had died unaccoutred and empty-handed—such were pounced upon eagerly by the boys, and waved and brandished in triumph. A greater number, with less stomach for such close contact now, rushed to take their pick of the horses, which, restive and frightened, still were hobbled and penned at the bottom end of the meadow. Practically all would be able to ride back to Hawick that morning, however barefoot and ragged.

Simon was coming pacing slowly down the slope, deciding that he had better gain a mount for himself—his own if possible, which should be amongst the throng of the callants' beasts—when a great shout halted him. Out in the middle of the haugh, Andy Turnbull had found and raised high a flag, a handsome silken pennant. And even in the pale light of a May dawn, there was no mistaking the blazon of it, as the callant waved it back and forth in jubilation; on a blue background was imposed a golden cross, saltirewise. It was the banner of Hexham Priory.

Ignored in the excitement, Simon watched the callants, now joined by the detachments that had been sent round by Cavers and the northern bank, form up and stream away westwards. At their head rode Andy Turnbull again, on the finest horse that he could find, the Hexham flag fluttering bravely on its lance above him. He had found a helmet, gold inlaid too, that fitted him better than the great thing that he had tossed away in the first rush. Behind, a chattering, cheering, strung-out crowd, the youngsters jostled and curvetted on their new-won steeds, not one of them without some item of booty, some piece of captured armour or clothing, some token of victory—to make up for the white strained faces and weary bodies that were never for a moment allowed to droop. Without a backward glance into Hornshole they rode away—and it would be a strange thing indeed if Hawick and the Borderland did not make a ballad, an epic, a saga, out of what they had achieved that night that would live as long as songs were sung and men loved freedom.

Simon had his own horse again. It had been with the Cavers Dean party, and the youth who had ridden it was better content with a captured grey that, though a poorer brute, was now his own, and glorious. As the boys disappeared over the tree-clad rise, he turned and led his beast out into the stricken haugh. He had to do what must be done.

Alone now amongst the dead, the man moved up and down the ranks of the slain, searching, peering, probing—and did not love his task. So very clear in his mind was that other similar scene, nine months old . . . These were the Hexham people, sure enough, most of them wearing the Priory's blue and gold livery. In his quest he identified no fewer than four of the servants from Anick Grange itself, two of whom had escorted him from Flodden Field. Also Jem Harndean, the Chief Steward, who had commanded the ill-fated company. But of the one man for whom he sought, Abel Ridley, he found no trace. Straightening up at length, his back sore from long bending, Simon stared down Teviot, heavy eyes blinking, towards where the sun was at its rising. He was not there—Ridley was not there.

Looking distastefully at his blood-smeared hands, Simon moved down, slow-footed now, to the riverside, to wash them in the clear water—and to wish that he could wash the pictures of ugly and ignoble death that were etched upon his inward eye as readily. And crouching there, dabbling his hands, he suddenly perceived that there were more bodies lying further downstream a little way, under the cornice of the bank. These must have been those men, sleeping at the bottom end of the haugh, who had managed to make a run for it in the wake of the stampeding cattle—men either more wide-awake or more quick-witted than their fellows. But scarcely more fortunate, nevertheless—for there they lay only a few yards nearer safety than the rest, trapped between the high red-earth bank and the rushing Teviot. Some lay actually in the shallows of the river itself, one half-across a dead bullock that had broken its neck in its plunge over the bank. And even from a distance Simon could see that one of the figures was that of a very big man with a dark beard.

Hurrying thitherwards, Simon lowered himself down the slippery bank. Sliding, he fetched up against one of the recumbent figures that lay half-in half-out of the water. A faint groan rose from the body. Stooping swiftly, he turned the blood-clotted head gently. The eyelids flickered slightly. There was life here—the first that he had detected in all that shambles. Carefully he drew the man up from the river—and saw by the great stain of darker red on the soil underneath how desperately this Englishman was wounded. He would never survive, that was clear.

Leaving him, he moved over towards the bearded man. There was no doubt—it was Abel Ridley. He lay in a peculiar position, part asprawl over the spreading twisting roots of a riverside tree—but face down, and giving the impression that he had drawn himself up there by his own efforts. His booted feet trailed in the water. To get at him, Simon had to step over still another body—and this man's back stirred just sufficiently to reveal that he still breathed. Hope burgeoned in Simon Armstrong. These people, obviously, once cut down, had been left, forgotten, not hacked over and over in the callants' mad frenzy, like the others. Ridley might be alive, also?

Reaching the man who had been his captor, his gaoler and his saviour, Simon bent over him. At first he feared him dead, so inertly did he hang, so horrible the bloody gash at his neck. Then he sensed warmth and life in the body, and pushing a hand beneath, inserted it under the steel breastplate—and felt the heart to beat within. Thankfully he straightened up. The account was not yet quite closed. The debt that he had to pay might still be redeemed.

Getting Ridley lifted off his root and up on to the grass at the top of the bank taxed Simon's powers to the utmost—for his strength was by no means fully restored, and the big man was no light weight. Moreover, he was concerned to see that he handled the other as gently as might be, lest he reopen the neck wound, which had congealed meantime in its own blood.

155

And he knew not what other injuries the man might suffer. Panting and sweating and straining, he worked away, lifting, tugging and inserting himself underneath the great sprawling body to hoist it up on his own back and shoulders. At last he had it up on to the level sward—and had to lie beside his fallen benefactor thereafter for a little, gasping.

Inspection presently revealed a further two wounds on Abel Ridley—a sword thrust through the left upper arm, and a heavy blow, probably from some sort of club, on the back of the head. The steward must have slept in his breastplate, prudent man always, unlike most of his fellows—but presumably he had been unable to grab his helmet as he ran. The neck wound was the worst, undoubtedly, but the younger man adjudged none of them mortal—if Ridley had not lost too much blood already. He was wholly unconscious and suffering from concussion also, almost certainly.

Simon, with plenty of dead men's clothing available for bandaging, bound up Ridley's wounds as best he could. He unstrapped and threw away the breastplate emblazoned with the cross of Hexham Priory, and tore off any portions of the steward's livery that might be recognised—for safety's sake. Then, though anxious to be off, concerned now lest he be discovered at this aiding of the hated enemy, he moved over to have a look at the other survivors. Not that he could do much for them, if anything . . .

He found the first man, the one that he had dragged from the river, already dead. The second, lacking his cuirass, had been run through the chest, but the heart had been missed; whether the lung was damaged, Simon could not tell, though the breathing was very laboured. At a loss to know what to do for the unfortunate man, to know whether it was kinder to seek to prolong his life at all, in the circumstances, he nevertheless bared the gaping wound, tied a pad of cloth firmly over it, and drew the fellow up until he was sitting slumped with his back against the same roots that Ridley had lain over; at least, thus positioned, any blood or fluid in the lungs would be less apt to fill his throat and choke him. He filled a helmet with river water to leave close beside the man—and could think of nothing more to do.

Deliberately, weakly perhaps, he did not look around for any more injured men to succour. He was going to have his hands full, as it was. He fetched his horse, quickly recognised that he could by no means hoist Ridley on to its back unaided, pondered for a little, and then led the beast along and down the low bank to the water's level. Working back, splashing occasionally in the shallows, he sought and eventually found a place where the bank was sufficiently undercut and sheer to allow the horse to stand under it, its back only a little lower than the bank's grassy top. It meant dragging Ridley the score or so of yards—but that was less difficult than trying to hoist him bodily.

There followed the problem of getting the inert man safely down to the horse's back without him falling or sliding off into the river. At length, by using two blankets knotted together as a sort of sling, Simon was able to ease the steward gradually over the lip of the bank, and to lower him the foot or so to the beast's broad haunches. There was a nasty moment when a small section of the turf cornice crumbled away under the strain, and the consequent sagging of the heavy burden all but pulled Simon's arms out of their sockets. But by a mercy he held fast, the blankets did not slip—and equally fortunate, the horse stood reasonably still. It was a blessing too, that Ridley was so limp that his body folded, to droop across the animal's withers, head and shoulders hanging down on one side, legs and feet down the other. Even so, Simon had to leap down hurriedly, to adjust the balance, or his charge would have slid off feet first. Leaning thereafter against the brute's warm flank, the younger man panted, trembling, and prayed for greater strength and vigour. Prior to last September, he had always taken adequate and even lusty muscular and physical strength for granted.

He used the blankets to tie Ridley as firmly as he might over the horse's back—and made a clumsy job of it.

Along the river's edge he led the beast, until he could urge

157

it up the bank again. Then, with a last look over that terrible haugh, none the better now for the dispersing mists of night and the slanting golden brilliance of the stripling sun, he turned his face westwards, and, plodding at his mount's head, climbed stiffly, heavily, up the hill and away from it all.

The larks were trilling with uncaring joy as he went.

XVII

SIMON crossed Hornshole Bridge immediately. He would be safer on the north side of Teviot, less populous, more broken and heavily wooded than the south. His aim was to convey himself and his burden to Stirkshaws as nearly unobserved as was possible. He would seek to do it by cutting back through the low grassy gorse-covered hills of the Stirches and Harden districts, avoiding Hawick altogether, and coming down on to his own ground from the north. That would entail a walk of seven or eight rough miles at least.

Simon was under no illusions as to the risks and dangers of the task with which he was saddling himself now. In the circumstances and mood prevailing in invaded Teviotdale, any man found befriending one of the hated invaders was likely to be unpopular if not considered to be something of a traitor. And if that man was already suspect, indeed publicly accused of treasonable activities—so much the worse. And he did not wish to bring down further trouble upon Ailie and his people at Stirkshaws, who had had trouble enough of late. Again, he was equally in danger from the English invaders themselves. How far they had progressed was a matter for guesswork— but he knew that Dacre had intended penetrating as far as Ettrick and Yarrow and Upper Tweed. Therefore it was possible that parties might already have passed behind Hawick and be athwart his route. If they were not even now attacking Hawick.

The man's glance lifted frequently half-leftwards up the valley, towards the town, as he plodded on. He could not actually see the place, because of the green shoulders of the foothills. But no ominous cloud of smoke rose above its position—as yet. Even yesterday's great murky pall, from farther south, had dispersed in the night, and the fresh morning air was clear and clean. Long might it remain so.

Simon wondered what scenes might Hawick be witnessing now, with its victorious callants home, declaring their triumph? Youth would be quite beside itself; mothers would be next to crazy with relief; the whole town would be in a ferment of pride and gratitude—and the fact that the threat from other quarters would be by no means lifted would be apt only to add urgency to this wonderful first deliverance. Simon would have liked to have witnessed, to have taken part in it all, he who had witnessed that grim and dreadful prologue thereto. He would gladly have paid his tribute, with the rest, to those boys and what they had achieved, proud of the blow that they had struck for Scotland—though sorry indeed that such as they had had to strike it. But Hawick was not for him, yet awhile. He had much to achieve himself before he could set foot on its cobbles once more, head held high.

Simon Armstrong's heart held no bitterness over his reception in the old grey town—not even over Bailie Andrew Cessford's attitude. Looked at calmly, in the candid light of morning, he could not find it in himself to blame the little man. Under great stress and strain, and quite unfitted surely in stature, physical and mental, for the task thrust upon him, the Bailie had his excuses. Simon's appearance, just then, might well have seemed suspicious in the extreme. For months it had been accepted, sorrowfully, that there had been no survivors from terrible Flodden. How was it that this one man had escaped—nursed back to health by the same English who had so notoriously killed all wounded and taken no prisoners, on their king's express orders? And to appear just when Dacre's riders were on their doorsteps would look very much as though they had brought him with them—a hostage to be used for ulterior ends. Especially when he had admitted that he still owed a debt in England, a debt which he intended to pay—and which implied that he was still in some sort of communication with the enemy. No, he could not really blame Cessford, angry as it had made him to be accused of treachery. And, if his present activities became known, would not suspicions seem to be thoroughly confirmed by facts? Loyalties can be less simply straightforward, Simon perceived, than he himself a while ago could have envisaged.

So the man chose his route well—if less than kindly to his tired frame—keeping heedfully to the woods and unfrequented hillsides, avoiding populated valleys, farmsteads and the haunts of men. Was he not quite used to such furtive progress by now? And in due course, some three weary hours later, unobserved as far as he could tell, and having seen no sign of any English bands, he led his burdened horse quietly down a rift in the hillside behind his own hidden glen, and past the lochan to the grey tower of Stirkshaws.

Ailie Armstrong, of course, was still shut up in Hawick, but other willing and gentle hands helped him to get his unconscious charge down off the horse and into the tower. Sizing up the situation promptly, and not to be deceived about her master's own state of fatigue, old Janet and her muscular if excitable coadjutor Abby took vehement charge. Simon, assured that the wounded man, whoever he was, would be properly looked after, was practically driven to bed, hustled and shooed to bed, food and drink being as good as thrust down his throat in the process. He was to sleep and sleep. That was an order, not advice or suggestion—an order that every inch of the man was aching to obey. He need not worry—the iron yett would be bolted shut, the great inner oaken door locked and barred, and any seeking body—save only Mistress Ailie herself, if she returned from Hawick—would have to pull Stirkshaws Tower apart stone by stone to win inside that day. With such assurances, and the information that no ravening English had yet been seen in Borthwick Water, Simon was content. Divesting himself only of his outer gear and boots, he collapsed on his own bed—and did not recollect his head touching the pillow of feathers.

The night was closing down again over the hills outside the small iron-grilled window of his upper room when at last Simon awoke to find a candle flickering near by and Ailie sitting quietly at his bedside. It was good to waken thus, naturally, of his own accord, in his own place and with his

161

sister there at his side—the best awakening that he had known for many a day. He savoured the peace of it for a moment or two. But not for long—for, as the troubles and problems that still beset him came flooding back to his mind, unbidden, he knew an emotion that had to be banished swiftly. He was suddenly and wistfully sorry for himself, sorry for poor hard-used misunderstood bone-weary and never-let-be Sim Armstrong. Poor, poor Sim!

"Well, Sis," he said, more forcefully and emphatically than he knew, startling the girl out of her long day-dream. "I seem to spend my time with you sleeping like a hog! A boorish troublesome brother you have, eh?"

"Oh, Sim!" Impulsively she reached out to grasp his arm, his hand. "I am glad! Glad to see you lying there, in your own bed . . . after so long. So long, long! Sleep on, Sim, dear. Close your eyes again. It is nearly night-time, anyhow . . ."

"Not so, lass. A man, even a poor sort of a man, something knocked about and fushionless, has more to do than sleep, in this day of our good Lord!" There was the self-pity trying to speak, again. "I have slept the sun around, as it is, it seems."

"But you need it. You look as though you should sleep for days and days," his sister cried. "You look an old man, Sim, so different . . ."

"Tut—what way is that to welcome your brother home!" he protested. "An old man, am I!" He sat up—and found himself stiff and sore to a degree. "So you are back from Hawick. They let you out, then?"

"Oh, yes. Nobody is heeding, anymore. Hawick is like a mad place! Everybody is in the streets. There is singing and dancing and laughing. The callants are riding high. It was wonderful, was it not? A notable victory. You reached them in time, Sim—you were there?"

"I was there, yes—though I had no hand in the battle."

"I asked some of them, had they seen you. I was afraid. I feared that you might have been hurt, dead even, when you did not come back with them. But it seems that none, from Hawick were killed—not one. Only the English. And none said

162

that they had seen you. Even Andy Turnbull . . ."

"Those lads were in a state to see nothing but glory and waving banners and prizes won splendidly," Simon told her. "As well, too, if that was what they saw, the picture that they took away from Hornshole! For there were other things to see that were less fair!" He waved a hand, as though to dismiss that other picture from contemplation, if not from his own inward eye. "But they still keep watch and ward in the town? They have not forgotten the danger from otherwhere . . . ?"

"No—oh, no. The guard is still kept. Indeed, all is warlike and ready. The callants strut the streets with two swords apiece! They long for the English to come now, I swear! They will be sore disappointed if there is no attack on the town!"

"It is a good spirit, at the least. It may serve Hawick well, if it comes to blows. Though I fear . . ." He stopped, keeping his fears to himself. "Is there no word of the main English array yet, then? No other bands closing in on the town from other airts? That Hexham company could not be all that was making for Hawick?"

"I do not know," the girl said. "There is much talk. Many rumours. It is said that they have been seen behind Cavers. And up Slitrig. And up at the head of our own Borthwick Water. Jedworth too has seen fighting—though they say that my Lord Warden Home has come to their rescue there. Indeed, some have it that Home's riders have won a victory far to the north—in the Forest of Ettrick, near to Selkirk. But how that could be, I know not . . ."

"Say you so? All that? Selkirk. Jeddart. Cavers. Borthwickhead. And, moreover, Hornshole and Denholm—the Lower Teviot." Simon tapped the areas off on the side of his bed, thoughtfully. "Either rumour lies with a busy tongue—or Dacre has mightily dispersed his forces. If these reports speak truth, then his people are scattered wide over the whole face of the Middle March. He can have no large array left to strike any heavy blow. Against Hawick, or otherwhere. Yet Dacre is an able soldier, if a hard man. Why has he broke up his force thus?"

Naturally Ailie could not tell him that. "There would be

more spoil to win that way, would there not?" was the best that she could suggest.

"There would, yes—but it was not for spoil that Dacre marched, this time. It was on his King Henry's orders—a major stroke against the Scots. While the bickering over the Regency goes on between the Queen and Albany, and the nation is divided, and weakened after Flodden Field. This was to be no mere reiving and raiding. So something has gone wrong, I think—something a deal bigger than Hornshole. And I believe that you have told me, lass, what it is! If Home has already reached as far west as Jeddart, not to say Selkirk—then he was not deceived. He was not held down in his East March, in the Merse, as was intended by Dacre's stratagems and the threats of a thrust up from Berwick. Perhaps Berwick did not march? Perhaps Home guessed, or was informed, that the real threat was to Teviotdale and the Middle March—and risked all to move his men westwards, away from his own territory? Perhaps, even, my own warning, the beacons' message, reached east to Hume Castle in time to establish his guess? Who knows? It could be. 'Twas said in Hexham that Lord Home has three thousand lances held at a day's mustering, in Lothian and the Merse. If that is so, and they were moved in time into the Middle March here, then our canny Thomas Dacre would likely not hazard a major clash with them, but disperse his companies far and wide, to wreak what damage they could and find their own way home to Northumberland. He has run from Home before—he fears him, manifestly. It could be that."

"I know not," Ailie said. "Such matters are beyond my ken. But, if so, is it good—or ill?"

"Good, in the main, surely. Good for Hawick, for Scotland. Though many outlying small places may suffer instead, at the hands of these bands. And it would add a deal to my own difficulties—that is certain."

"Yours, Sim? But how should that be? Are you not snug in your own tower? Safe. Do you fear that these bands will attack us here, in our own hidden glen?"

"No. That is not my fear, lass," he assured her. "I think that

164

they could find easier pickings than Stirkshaws. Nor would they smoke you out of this tower easily. Snug enough you will be, yes. But not me, lass. I must be out of here this night."

"Sim! No! What are you saying?" Ailie cried. "Why? Where? You cannot go away again. So soon. You are weak, tired . . ."

"I must, Ailie," he said, gently. "I am sorry. But it is the thing that I must do."

"It is that man! To do with that wounded man that you have brought here—whoever he is?"

"Yes. That is so."

"Who is he? Why have you brought him? He is . . . an Englishman, is he not?"

"An Englishman, yes. An enemy . . . and a friend!"

"How can that be? Oh, Sim—what are you doing? What folly is this? He is . . . from Hornshole? One of the raiders? Bloody men who massacred and burned and raped and looted! Denholm and Lanton and Bedrule and Minto—all are dead places now, they say, blackened, women and children and old men slain, butchered. And you bring one of the butchers here, to Stirkshaws!"

"A friend I said, girl, nevertheless. War is war . . ."

"And succouring your country's enemies—is that war? Oh, Sim—think well what you do! What if he was found here, at Stirkshaws? If the word got abroad that you had him here? Think what could happen to us all—to himself, for that matter."

"And there you have it!" Simon exclaimed, grimly. "That is why he must go this very night. I may have been seen, bringing him here—though I was careful. But who can tell? Some of our own people, even, might talk. In the state that Teviotdale is in now, his life would not be worth a plack. Nor mine, either. He must be got away forthwith. Back to his own place. I told you that I owed a debt, did I not? It was not only in gold pieces. That man, Abel Ridley, is my debt—his life for mine. He saved my life at Flodden, as I must seek to save his now. You understand, girl? He took great hazards for me—the same hazards that I must now take. Oh, I know that there was gold in it, to begin with—the ransom. But that is the least

165

of it. He and his household cherished me, for months, nursed me back from the borders of death itself—against the commands of Dacre and King Henry. Is that not enough for you? And, Ailie—there are those who will wait, at Hexham, for Abel Ridley, as fearfully as you waited here, for me! Would you have them desolate?"

"I . . . no. No. I am sorry, Sim. I did not know. I did not understand." Desolate herself, the girl shook her head. "You must do . . . what you judge is right. But, oh Sim—need you take him so far? All that way? Could we not hide him somewhere, near at hand? Out of the house. Find someone to tend him. Until all this is overpast. Until you are strong again, yourself . . ."

"And have them wait, at Hexham, not knowing? Thinking him dead?"

"I had to wait," she said flatly. "Thinking you dead. For months. Empty, endless, weary months."

He touched her hand, nodding. "I know. I am sorry. It is the thing that most troubled me. But . . . there is one there . . . who I would not wish to suffer. As you had to suffer."

"Yes. I thought that was the way of it." She tried to keep her voice level, even. "But . . . an Englishwoman, Sim?"

"An Englishwoman, yes." That was harshly said.

There was a moment or two of silence, eloquent silence. The man broke it.

"What will be, will be—and I look and hope for little good of it, little joy, God knows! But I know what I have to do, here and now, nevertheless. I intend to be on the slopes of Carter Fell before the sun rises tomorrow morning. And I must travel the soft way, the way kindest to a sorely injured man."

"But he is not fit to travel by any way, kind or not . . ."

"He is fitter to travel than to wait here to be found and slain! Or to die of his wounds. He needs a physician or an apothecary. We dare bring none such to him here. At his home, the skilful ones who brought me back to health may do the same for him. A cunning monk and, and . . ." He stopped, and levered himself off the bed, albeit stiffly. "I have thought it all

166

out, as I rode here with him, Ailie. God willing, I shall have him home in two nights. Better that, hurt as he is, than to hold him here. He is a strong man, and so long as I can keep the bleeding from starting again, I think that he will survive the journey. That head wound should hold him palsied for long—and best so. Tied on a litter slung between two horses . . ."

"I shall come with you then, Sim. To aid you with him."

"That you shall not, lass! I am better alone, besides. These English raiders will be abroad, many of them probably returning home to Northumberland in small parties, wide scattered. How think you they would treat a woman, if we met with them? Myself, I can pass for one of themselves, mayhap, taking home a wounded comrade. But with a woman . . . ! No, girl—you are best here, keeping Stirkshaws for me, till I return again."

"Till you return again," she repeated dully, heavily. "If you return again! Oh, Sim—have you not done enough, hazarded enough? Is there no better way . . . ?"

"No," he said, gently but finally. "This is my road—my Roman road. Straight and clear ahead. I must take it. You would not have me hating myself, knowing myself an ingrate?"

"No. No, not that."

"Then come you away downstairs, lassie—for we have much to do, and little enough time for it. Such a sleeper as I am!"

XVIII

SIMON ARMSTRONG, partings behind him, paced his mount into the gloom of the night, eastwards. At his heels walked two more horses, hitched close together, with a litter of sorts tied between them, on which was strapped the unconscious person of Abel Ridley, swaddled in plaids and covers like a mummy. Because of that burden he did not hurry the animals as he would have liked to do. Ridley's wounds had been very firmly bound up, padded with sphagnum moss as dressing and absorbent—but the less jerking and jolting that they had to suffer the better. The time might well come when Simon would be forced to a trot, a canter, even a gallop—but until that was essential, he must take hold of his patience and go gently. Moreover, he must hold to roads and tracks if he could, in order to keep the litter on as even a keel as possible—a grievous handicap for a fugitive as anxious to avoid his own people as he was Dacre's bands. It meant that he could not take the shortest and most direct routes, either. It was close on midnight, and there was a faint chill smirr of rain on the night air.

Borthwick Water was behind him, and he was riding down Teviot, with Hawick just ahead. But where the Wilton Burn came in, a track branched off towards the village of Wilton on its hillside, which enabled him to pass Hawick town by the left. The village he avoided also, by skirting round behind it by the Sillerbithall path, having to climb fairly steeply. Thus he was able to reach the Minto road at Howdenburn. So far so good. He had gone unchallenged, and had seen no soul abroad.

The next four or five miles were but sparsely populated. The scattered hillfoot farm towns and mill-places were all discreetly and noticeably drawn in on themselves, shuttered and barred against the threats of the night. Only a dog barked here and there at his passing, and a horse would whinny over a hedge at its kind, and even pace with them a little way, companionably, to the limits of its field. But presently, as the dale began to widen again, even such manifestations began to fade. Soon there were no dogs to bark, no horses to whinny, no cattle to stir and puff amongst the shadows, and the farm-places and cot-houses, though growing more frequent now, while as dark and silent as ever, wore a different air about them, somehow. All were empty, deserted.

Long before the traveller reached Minto, crouching beneath the dark mass of its twin shapely breasts of hill, the scent of burning was tainting the damp night air. The evil smell grew steadily stronger, even though the wind was from behind him, and its staleness made it none the less ominous, baleful.

Suddenly Simon's horse reared and shied, refusing to pass something that lay darkly on the track ahead. Dismounting, the man stooped to investigate. It was a sprawled body. Dead. A woman, her skirts over her head, stiff and cold. His lips moving, Simon forced himself to rearrange her clothing, and then dragged her to the grass bank at the roadside. She had been pregnant. He laid her gently, face downwards, where the vile sword-work would not show. He was wearing a plain morion and breastplate again, as being less likely to attract attention in the circumstances, and he doffed the headpiece now, for a few brief moments. There was nothing else that he could well do. Remounting, he took up the reins of the led horses again, and moved on, set-faced.

He passed a burned-out cottage a couple of hundred yards farther on. Another body seemed to be lying across the charred threshold. This time the man did not dismount nor halt. He merely raised a hand to sketch the sign of the Cross, and rode on.

The horses had an upsetting uneasy time of it thereafter, constantly sidling and shying and plunging at what they saw and sensed and smelled. Minto village and its environs was a shambles, no single building unburned. Bodies lay everywhere, anywhere, as they had fallen, men, women and children. Household goods and furnishings were scattered abroad and smashed. The feathers of poultry drifted before the night wind. Somewhere, some distance off, a dog was howling endlessly, inconsolably—a sound that further set the horses in a fret. Simon turned them aside, downhill, and rode away from it all, his mind in a whirl of violent emotion. But he still retained some control, some discipline—and he deliberately did not allow himself to associate the wounded helpless man behind him with the raiders who had done these things. In all his stress of mind he had to cling to something. What he clung to was that which had saved him before from the horror of great darkness, a gentle, strong, encouraging, reassuring presence, that had dawned as a tiny beacon of sanity and warmth and had grown to be just Woman, constant, upholding. He held that image before him resolutely, and rode on, due southwards now.

Crossing Teviot by a hump-backed bridge, he approached Denholm-on-the-Green. This was a much larger village than Minto, and he was prepared for what he must see. Denholm had been destroyed by the Hexham party the evening before Hornshole. At least, then, vengeance had been gained for this shattered place.

Yet Denholm did not seem to Simon as grievous a scene as Minto had done—not that he sought to probe its horrors closely. Its fair wide green, with its aspect of space, helped in this, of course, especially at night; but there seemed to be fewer bodies about here, less concentrated chaos and havoc. Many of the inhabitants had managed to escape in time to Denholm Dean's secret shelter, according to Wee Wattie Wilson. No soul moved therein now, at all events.

Simon pressed straight across, and uphill beyond the village, heading over a shoulder of green hill towards the deep-cut valley of the Rule Water. Obviously he was now proceeding directly along the route that the invaders had come, for every farm-place that he passed was ravished and destroyed, every stackyard burned, every cottage pillaged and cast down.

The Turnbull country had suffered sorely. Bedrule village lay as stricken as had Minto, even its ancient semi-subterranean

170

kirk a smouldering ruin. The nearby Turnbull castle had not saved it. Simon did not turn aside to see whether the castle itself, glooming dark on its eminence above the rushing Rule, had fallen or no. Here, only a score of years previously, when Simon was a lad, no fewer than two hundred Turnbulls, with halters already round their necks, had been brought before King James, as a consequence of their unruly habits; some of those not executed there and then undoubtedly had recently ridden out to die with the same James and their chief at Flodden. Leaving the harried blood-stained Rule valley above the still-smoking place of Ruletownhead, Simon led his nervous pacing beasts along the track that climbed up through the moorlands to Southdean, back where he had come only forty hours before—forty hours that might have been almost as many days to the man. It had taken him four of those hours to come thus far from Stirkshaws, now, and already he fancied that there was some faint lightening of the mirk over above the lower lands about Jed Water, to the east. It was still raining, and the day would be slow of dawning—for which Simon was thankful. He had to pass the tower of Blackburnhead in another three miles or so—and he did not want Mark Kerr and his people to be asking any questions. Hospitable and grateful they might be—but his present mission would take a deal of explaining.

Actually, it was only a little lighter when he passed the lonely little tower on its knoll across the rushing stream on his right, and no light nor sign of life showed about its square black bulk. Nor did that noisy dog bark. With a sigh of relief Simon left it behind.

He was plodding up that Roman road, now, climbing ever more steeply.

It took him an hour to reach the long heathery summit ridge of Carter Fell, high amongst level grey cloud. By then the sun should have been well and truly risen, but only the faintest lightening of the heavy pall of swirling mist indicated the fact up here on the roof of the land. The man had no quarrel with the cloud and mist, chill and inimical as it might seem. So long as it did not grow so dense as to hide from him the line of his Roman causeway, he was content that it should hide himself beneath its shroud.

He turned to consider the man at his back. Abel Ridley lay utterly motionless, as one dead. Backing his mount, Simon leaned over the back of one of the led horses to peer, and then to insert his hand under the plaiding which so thoroughly enfolded the wounded steward. And he nodded to himself. The body was warm, and the heart beat steadily, strongly.

It was a strange unreal progress that the two men made thereafter, pacing out into that vast lofty wilderness of the Cheviot watershed, steadily, unhurriedly, silently, almost blindly. There was no vista, no sense of the boundless wastes that surrounded them, of quaking bogs and towering summits and plunging valleys. Though that ancient forgotten road was only visible for perhaps fifty or sixty yards ahead, in the cloud, it ran straight and true, unswerving, mile after mile, green and moss-grown and pitted and scored, but never faltering, cunningly engineered, timeless, indestructible. Simon had only to follow it faithfully, trustingly, and it would take him far—right to Upper Tynedale, he imagined. It was not the sort of road that would die out on a man; its builders had been men who knew their minds.

Time counted for little on that curious spectral journey. There was no incident, no milestones, no prospect, no feature stood out, nothing to hold the attention or distract the mind. The road reached endlessly through a void, either gradually climbing or gradually sinking—that was all. On its soft but enduring surface the horses' hooves made little sound.

Presently Simon nodded and slept. The animals paced on, wise enough to esteem a clear path in that savage terrain when one offered.

It was the brightness of sunlight troubling his lidded eyes that eventually roused Simon to take notice of changing conditions. He had been vaguely aware of the sun for some time— but he was nowise prepared for its height in the sky when at length he sat up, stiffly, to gaze around him. Though not exactly overhead, it was not so far off it that it could lack more than a couple of hours to noon. Could he have been dozing thus for four hours? It hardly seemed possible—but in his state of chronic weariness it might be so.

Where was he now, then? The beasts were still walking, stolidly, deliberately. Presumably they had never halted—he imagined that he would have been aware of it, and wakened, if they had. Even at only two miles to the hour, that would have taken them far across this ten-mile-wide desolation. The cloud had cleared now, and visibility was fair—but he did not know where he was, save that he was still on the undeviating cause-way, and still amongst the hills and moss-hags. But, half-right and reaching on forward, there seemed to be a distinct sinking in the ground level, a dipping away into a deeper and wider valley than that of any mere hill stream. Could that be the Tyne, then, already? If it was, it behoved him to start using his wits again.

Dacre's host had entered Scotland by way of Upper Tynedale and Liddesdale, and while some might find their way home by other routes, it must be expected that many would seek to return that way. Whether any might be likely to be riding down Tyne this morning would depend on circumstances of which Simon had no sure knowledge. He could only make a series of guesses, based on the rumours which Ailie had brought him. But if, indeed, Dacre's invasion had gone awry, owing to the unexpectedly early intervention of Home's hard-hitting forces, and in consequence had broken up into a series of hit-and-run raids, wide scattered, then it was almost certain that these small bands would have been instructed to find their own way home to Northumberland after striking their blows—and, if he knew anything of Borderers, on either side of the line, that homeward retiral would begin just as soon as each man had collected sufficient booty to handle, with no dangerous hanging about or delay thereafter. Which could mean that bands could be streaming home now, on various routes through the hills—and this way might well be a favourite.

Should he lie up, then, here in the hills, through the day, to avoid any encounter with such, waiting for nightfall again before risking the road down Tyne? It might be wise, for his own and the beasts' sake. He was carrying food and fodder for the horses with him. The creatures had been going steadily for the best part of twelve hours—and though not going hard for any of it, they must be tired. For himself, the thought of throwing himself down into the heather there, to sleep in the smile of the sun, to sleep and sleep—that would be bliss indeed. But what about the silent corpse-like figure at his back? What about Abel Ridley? Might not every hour count with him? Every hour that he was denied skilled attention and proper nursing might mean the difference between life and death to the man. There could be no choice in the matter, really. He must not consider fatigue, his own or the horses', nor the risk of clashing with English riders. He must keep going, as long as the horseflesh would hold out. He was paying a debt, was he not?

Flanking a wide shoulder of hill, he noted, away below his road near the side of a sizeable stream, the green mounds and enclosures of what obviously had been an ancient fortified camp—not Roman, since it was insufficiently rectangular and orderly. He had heard of a British camp at Kielder, which returning reivers had found a useful collecting point for the penning of stolen cattle from the lower lands. If that was it, and that stream was the Kielder, then he was only a mile or so from its junction with the Tyne.

Soon this turning sinking hillside revealed his assessment to be correct. The vale of the North Tyne, wide only by comparison, opened before him. The causeway slanted down into it. For better or for worse, he was committed. The alternative, to seek to remain on high ground, working his way south-eastwards over the rough broken hillsides, was not to be considered, for the sake of the man behind him.

Just before he reached the floor of the Tyne valley, with its road and its river, he halted, dismounted, sore and stiff, and watered the horses at a burnside, feeding them with oats. For half an hour perhaps he let them crop the sweet grass, and sought to refresh and reinvigorate his own jaded self by splashing the cold water over his face and head. Then, lest he sink again into the sleep which ever beckoned, he mounted again and was on his way. He reckoned that he had between twenty-five and thirty miles of the Tyne between him and Hexham. The fact that there was a beaten track all the way was both comforting and the reverse. Along that road were many villages, much people to get past.

Simon said farewell to his Roman causeway with regret.

For the first mile or two down Tynedale Simon's head was not infrequently turned over his shoulder, looking apprehensively for trouble, in the shape of bands of returning raiders who might overtake him. But, after a little, as none materialised, his head began to droop again, chin on breastplate, frequently as he sought to jerk it up. The more lively motion of trotting would have kept him awake, but the slow pacing that he must keep to for Ridley's sake was a soporific in itself. And his eyes were as heavy as his head.

In the event, the dreaded encounter, when it did take place, was the reverse of what the man had anticipated. He was the overtaker, slow as was his progress, not the overtaken. And his entire attitude and position was subtly altered by the fact inevitably. Approaching the hamlet of Thorneyburn, and rounding one of the many sharp bends of the road and the river, Simon was very abruptly and successfully roused into full wakefulness. Only a few hundred yards ahead of him was a large herd of cattle. It was plodding away from him, westwards, in a cloud of steam—and it was plodding still more slowly than was he.

Simon reined up, cursing. He ought to have thought of this. Those who were droving harried cattle home must inevitably go very slowly as the beasts grew tired. These men, coming all the way round by Note o' the Gate and Liddesdale, would probably have been in the saddle all night, as he had. They blocked the narrow roadway, the cattle spreading out right and left, reaching to the waterside on one hand and a little way up the rising ground to the other. There was no getting past them without highly obvious hill-climbing. Yet to lag behind and wait would not serve him, with probably faster folk coming on at his back. And such loitering might serve notice of death on Abel Ridley—for this weary shuffling herd was not making much more than a mile in the hour, by the look of it.

Then, as he debated the matter, biting his lip, one of the herders, turning his mount to head off a straggler, faced towards him—and most evidently saw him. Simon shrugged to himself. He could no longer hang back—that would arouse suspicions immediately. He could only move onwards at his own speed, and hope for the best.

It took him all too short a time to come up with the drovers. But on doing so, Simon was relieved to find that they paid practically no attention to him. Quite obviously they were as tired as he was himself, if not more so. There were seven of them here at the tail of the herd, heavily armed, rough-looking characters in nondescript jacks and helmets on which no heraldic distinctions were blazoned—and only the one, a mere youth, showed any liveliness at all. Three were frankly asleep, and the others nearly so, their mounts' heads drooping as low as their masters' did. The led horses at their backs were heaped high with the pathetic plenishings of Scottish homes. Clearly these men belonged to the entourage of no great lord or knight, and, having looked after their own interests adequately so far, would be apt to be little concerned with matters abstract or political until they were safely home.

"Ho, there, friend!" the youth greeted, as Simon came up. "Is it a corpse you've got there? Marry—is that the best you could win out o' the accursed Scots!"

"My master it is," Simon returned, seeking to make his voice as broadly Northumbrian as he knew how. "He is sore wounded. I must bring him home if he is to live."

"Wounded? Did you ha' to fight, then? The more fools you!"

"Aye." Simon was non-committal. "You ha' done yourselves

passing well, lad?"

"By the saints we have! The pity that we could not carry more away. But we had notable sport, see you! Aye, man—notable!" The lad's voice cracked, and he sniggered. He was patently dead-tired and living on his nerves now, a corner of his slack mouth twitching continually. "Oh, aye—sport, man. The women . . . ! Hey! Hey, there. Whoa!" Suddenly he was shouting, as a heavy stirk broke away from the others and sought to lumber back whence it had come. Spurring his reluctant horse, he went to deal with it.

Riding on at the funereal pace of the herd, Simon found the lack-lustre eyes of the man nearest considering him. But not really interestedly. He nodded, and the fellow nodded back, and then let his head sink forward on his chest again. The Scot noted that over his saddle-bow, amongst other things which included a corked jar of liquor, this man had a woman's furred gown hanging. He wondered where that had come from. Certainly no farm or cot-house.

The youth came back. "I ha' to do all the herding, sink them!" he complained. "Where are you from, friend? We are from Allendale."

For only a moment Simon hesitated. He decided that probably little was to be gained by prevarication. "Hexham," he declared. Allendale was far enough away for it to be improbable that any of these people would know Hexham men individually. "This—my master—is one o' the Priory stewards. The Lord Prior will have a deal to say if I do not bring him home while there still is life in him! Can you not make a way for me, lad, through the press o' your beef?"

"Mother o' God—I ha' plenty to do without that!" the youth objected sourly. "Push your own way, man."

Since that was manifestly impossible advice to follow, with his horse-litter to cope with, through the densely packed herd—and clearly no help could be looked for from the remainder of the party, as much drunken as exhausted, perhaps—Simon had to summon what patience he could, and droop along with the rest. He noted that there had been no reaction to his mention

177

of Hexham. These people, then, could not have heard of the disaster that had befallen the Hexham contingent at Hornshole.

The youth had lost interest in Simon, now. It was not long before the latter's chin was down again, sagging like the rest. The pace was even more sleep-enticing than before.

For how long he continued thus, Simon did not know. But presently he was aroused by a great clatter and shouting. A large party, much less patient than he had been, had come up at their backs, unencumbered with cattle, and making their requirements known with no uncertain voice.

"God's death—get these devil-damned brutes out of my way, fools!" a haughty richly armoured man was crying. "Out of the path of a Grey!"

"A Grey! A Grey!" men-at-arms at his sides called. "Way for Sir Thomas the Grey!"

The herders roused themselves sufficiently to draw aside, and to curse—though not too evidently. But they made no attempt to clear a passage through the thronging cattle.

Riders of the impatient newcomer's party, not waiting to see the results of their lord's commands, drove their foam-spattered mounts forward, blood-stained swords out, to belabour the rearmost bullocks with the flats of them, shouting and smiting, to clear a way. It was a large well-accoutred company of perhaps a hundred, the white lion on red of the Greys of Chillingham painted on their cuirasses, as it was embroidered on the pennon that fluttered just behind their leader. Though hung about with a certain amount of booty, this band was carrying nothing that would delay it; moreover, these men had not met only with sport on their sally, obviously, for some few of them wore bloody bandages, and some had lost lances and headpieces. It looked as though the Greys had had to fight for their gains—perhaps encountered some of Lord Home's forces. Simon would much have liked to question them—but decided that he could not risk it.

Not that he allowed himself to dwell on that aspect of the situation. He was having to make hasty decisions. These people were entirely ignoring him, intent only on getting on their way.

178

They were managing to force a passage through the herd, too, by dint of much exertion, whacking, and noise. Behind his busy henchmen, Sir Thomas Grey was following closely through the press, his company stringing out in single file at his heels. If he, Simon, attached himself to the end of that column, he probably could get through too. Was that advisable? So long as he stayed with these Allendale herders and their cattle, he reckoned that he was safe; he would be taken for one of their party. Not so with Grey's troop; he could never keep up with them, anyway. So he would be alone again. But safety, here, meant intolerable delay, progress only at a snail's pace. He owed Ridley better than that. And by his experience to date, it looked as though Dacre's returning forces were unlikely to trouble their heads over such as himself. Unless he was actually known and recognised, nobody was likely to see anything suspicious in a single man leading home a wounded companion from a less than successful raid. And, fortunately or otherwise, most of those that could have known or recognised him were safely dead in the haugh at Hornshole.

So, watching his opportunity, Simon manoeuvred himself and his two led horses quickly in behind the last of Grey's men, before the tide of steaming protesting cattle flowed back again to block the way. Beating about him with the third sword that he had had to take to himself, he forced his way through, almost choked by the stink of the unhappy brutes. And then he was out in front, where three more of the Allendale ruffians were leading the herd after a fashion. They paid no attention to himself. Already Grey's company, without waiting to re-form in any sort of ranks, were streaming away down the road after their lord.

At his own sedate pace Simon Armstrong followed them.

And that was the pattern of his progress, with minor detailed differences, for the remainder of the journey down Tynedale. Simon overtook no fewer than four more herds of Scots cattle, was able to win past two of them on his own, at Bellingham village and where the ground levelled out at the confluence of Rede and Tyne, and had to wait at the tails of the other two for more potent travellers to clear a way for him. There was no lack of these; in large numbers and small, variously burdened and tempered, a great proportion of Dacre's host came beating down that long road that day. None seemed to see in him anything suspicious, few so much as gave him a glance in passing.

Nevertheless, when evening found him at Chollerford, only some five miles from his destination, Simon decided that to risk a closer approach to Hexham, save under cover of darkness, would be folly. He had now reached an area where danger was only too apparent. Accordingly, he drew aside into a wood on the east bank of the river, near Brunton, hobbled his horses, to lie up until darkness. As far as he could tell, Abel Ridley had not stirred throughout the long day. Simon, his back against a tree-trunk, fell asleep as soon as he sank down.

It was later than he had intended when he awoke, much later, and quite dark. As he started up, there was a groaning sound from the litter between the two patient hobbled horses—probably it was that which had awakened him. Lurching dazedly over, he peered at the figure strapped so tightly in the litter. He could just perceive that the eyelids flickered slightly. Ridley was not conscious yet—but undoubtedly the grip of the concussion was beginning to slacken. Haste now seemed the more vital. Simon blamed himself for this last unnecessary delay.

Mounting forthwith, he followed the river down by that selfsame route that he had used in the reverse direction those few nights ago—only *four* nights ago, when he came to count it up, barely credible as it seemed. Skirting the villages of Wall and Acomb, he came to the great haugh below Hexham town on its hill, and turned thankfully up, unchallenged, through the cattle-strewn meadows in the direction of Anick Grange.

Strong emotions surged within the man as he approached the dark huddle of buildings amongst their tall trees. Mixed emotions they were, and some in conflict with others. But Simon did not analyse them. A warm gladness to be there, in sight of the place, triumphed over the others, anyhow.

No light showed anywhere about the Grange. Cautiously, heedfully, as silently as he might, Simon paced his beasts towards the house. He thought that if he left the horses beside the duck-pond for the moment, and went forward on foot, he might manage to make his presence known quietly, discreetly, without too much commotion and alarm. Unfortunately, as he was about to dismount, a dog came bounding out from the stable side of the courtyard, barking furiously, to leap and snap around the horses' feet, yelping its excited tocsin. It took only a moment or two for the clamour to be taken up by another dog inside the house itself. Cursing the whole tribe of canines, Simon urged his horses onwards. Nothing was to be gained by any furtive approach now.

As the iron-shod hooves clattered on the cobbles of the yard, the wooden shutters of one of the upper windows was thrown open, and a woman's voice called out—a young woman's voice.

"Who is there? What's to do? Who comes? Father—is it you . . . ?"

Simon, sitting his mount, cleared his throat. "No. It is . . . yes, it *is* Abel Ridley. Your father, yes, Marcia. But . . ."

"Simon! Simon Armstrong! You . . . you have come back!" The voice rose swiftly, joyfully, exultantly. "Oh, Simon!" Then the pale blur of face and shoulders no longer filled the window opening.

It required only the time taken for the horseman to dismount and move over to the doorstep for the heavy door itself to be flung open, and Marcia Ridley, barefooted and dressed in no more than her nightshift, hurled herself bodily upon him.

"Simon! Simon! Simon!" she cried. "You have come. I said that you would come. I said it!"

The man's arms closed around the warm shapeliness of her, and he smiled down at the dark head that was dunting itself against his chest. "Shush, shush, now. I said it too," he declared. "Och, now—hush-shush. Marry—here's a to-do. Quiet, dog—quiet! Down, dog. Marcia lass, see you . . ."

His hand, that had been running over the girl's dark hair,

181

paused. He raised his head. A lamp, held high, was coming down the wide stairway. Esther Ridley, a robe wrapped round her night attire, carried it. She did not run, as Marcia had done, but she came swiftly for all that, her lips parted, her eyes wide, saying no word.

Gazing over her sister's head, Simon's hand lifted, outstretched, towards her. His eyes were fixed on her's, those same deeply brown, warm-glowing kind and calm eyes that had been the saving of him one time—and many times since in retrospect—steady, tranquil, even by flickering lamplight in the middle of the night.

"My dear," he said, deep-voiced. "Here I am—as I said."

"Yes," she answered, simply.

That was all.

And at that brief exchange, Marcia looked up, staring at the man, then turning to look at her sister with the lamp, and back to Simon again. Then suddenly, abruptly, she thrust herself back from him, violent, almost falling in her urgency. "Oh!" she exclaimed. "Oh, God—I hate you! I hate you both!" And clapping her hands over her ears, as though to shut out the sound of her own voice—or, possibly, of his, and the tone that he had used—she went running, past her sister and up the stairs, leaving them standing. They heard her deep choking sobbing as she ran.

They watched her go. "I am sorry," Simon said, at length. "Very sorry." He shook his head. "I . . . I have brought you your father, Esther. Out of Scotland. He is sore wounded—as I was. He is here."

The girl's hand went up to her throat, and she bit her lip. Then, as with an effort, she nodded. "Thank you," she said. "Thank you, Simon."

Side by side they moved out through the open doorway.

XIX

THE task of getting Abel Ridley's heavy person, on its litter, down from the horses, into the house and upstairs to his own room, there to be unwound from his swaddling plaids, undressed, and his wounds unbandaged and looked to and treated, took up all their attention and effort thereafter for some considerable time. Only the kitchen-women and the one old manservant who slept in the house, and whose personal loyalty was beyond question, were brought in to assist, for Simon's safety's sake. Presently Marcia, clothed, dry-eyed, set-faced and silent, joined them, to do her share—and never to meet Simon's eyes.

Not that the man's eyes were so very active, for long. While the girls were busy dressing their father's wounds, Simon was set down at the great kitchen table before a plentitude of cold meats and wine, with instructions to leave little, if anything, to be cleared away afterwards. But with the best will in the world he could not fulfil those directions. Later, the young women found him sprawled across the table, head on arm, a chicken-leg still clutched in one hand, the viands but little demolished.

Reluctantly they roused him, to get him upstairs again in turn to the same good room that had been his sanctuary and his prison for so long. And however anxious they were for information as to what had happened, the Ridley daughters forbore, with major restraint, to question him there and then. Simon's muttered incoherencies about Hornshole and Hawick, a Roman road and the long miles of Tynedale, conveyed little to his hearers save the intimation of disaster. But their father's state and need was only too apparent, and details would have to await the morning. Simon, tugging off only his heavy riding-boots and doublet, slumped down on to his bed with regular breathing. His eyelids closed.

The girls stood looking down at the man for some time thereafter, unspeaking. Then Marcia turned away, slowly this time, and walked across to the door and out, without a word. For that lively creature, her footsteps dragged. Esther looked after her, trouble-eyed. Then gently she covered the sleeping figure with blankets—and the hand that drew them up to the haggard unshaven cheek lingered there for a moment or two.

Quietly she returned to her father's bedside.

Explanations and details had to wait for longer than any morning light. It was mid-afternoon before Simon awakened. But he was past any surprise at this; his capacity for sleep seemed these days to be practically unlimited—and it was notably by day rather than by night that he indulged it. Sitting up and stretching, he knew himself to be stiff but much rested, ravenously hungry—and sorely in need of cleansing and freshening up. He went padding out in search of the wherewithal to satisfy these requirements.

It was as well, perhaps, that he did not don his boots before so doing, otherwise his footsteps must have been heard in the hall below, and events might have taken a very different turn. As it was, hearing speech, including a man's voice, coming from the foot of the stairway, Simon halted at the top of it. Edging forward, he peered down.

It was the apothecary, Father Crispin, talking with the Ridley girls. Obviously he was just taking his leave. Simon had no wish to delay that leave-taking. He turned and tiptoed back whence he had come.

When the monk had departed on his palfrey, Simon went down to the kitchen, seeking food, water and a razor. Both sisters were there, and though each looked more dark-eyed and somewhat paler than usual, they made a lovely pair. At sight of him, Marcia flushed hotly and found something that needed attention over at the wide stone fireplace. Esther came forward, hands out, to greet him.

"Simon—you are well? Restored? You feel stronger, now?" she said. "You slept sound, of a truth . . ."

"Why did you not wake me?" he demanded. "Here was no

184

way for me to spend this day."

"If you have been to Scotland and back, since last we saw you, then you deserve longer sleep than that! Oh, Simon—how you must have driven yourself! Endangered yourself . . ."

He dismissed such talk with a wave of his hand. "I did only what fell to be done." But the thought reminded him. "That monk, Crispin, who has just gone—he does not know that I am here?"

"No. We did not tell him."

"But he came to see your father? He must . . . ? What did you say?"

"We sent for him. He can do more for Father than any other. We told him only that a young man had brought Father home. We said a—a stranger. Not a Hexham man. We knew that none must hear that it was you, Simon."

"Good!" he said relievedly. "That was well done. But . . . you must forgive me. How is he—your father? How fares he, now? Has he yet recovered his wits?"

"He has spoken to us, yes. A word or two. I think that he knows that he is home." She shook her head. "Oh, he is sore hurt. In a sorry state. Weak. But Father Crispin says that he will live, God willing. Thanks to you, Simon. You . . . you brought him from Scotland? All the way? You, alone?"

He nodded.

"But . . . the others? Nick? And Hal? And Jabez? From Anick Grange, here? And the rest, from Hexham—Master Harndean and his men? What of them? Father Crispin says that they have not yet returned. How came you, with Father, Simon? And, and why?"

"I came because there were none others to bring him. And because I had said that I would return," he said slowly. "I came because . . ." He paused, and shrugged, and let it stand.

"None others . . . ?" Esther repeated, and her words were husky, as though from a constricted throat.

He nodded "None."

"You mean . . . ? *None!*"

"Yes. All were slain. There was a battle. At the haugh of

185

Hornshole. On the Teviot. Near to Hawick. I watched it. Afterwards, of all the Hexham company I found but three men breathing, living. Sore wounded. One of these was your father. He had tried to escape, by the river. Of the other two, one died while I was there. Nor would the other live, I think." Simon's voice was harsh. "There was no more that I could do. And they had done grievous things in Scotland. I saw . . ." He shook his head again. "I took your father to my home, to Stirkshaws. My sister bound up his wounds, did what she was able. Then I brought him here. That is all."

Marcia had turned round now, to face him. They were both staring at him, horror in their eyes.

"All those men! Hal? Nick? All dead! Gone!" the younger girl gasped. "Oh, horrible!" And she covered her face with her hands.

"God rest their souls!"

"Yes." He looked at Esther. "It is war," he said. "It is . . ." He bit his lip. He found himself to be almost on the point of apologising to these young women, deploring what had been done to their menfolk—and knew the folly of that. The picture of what the same men had done to the hapless villages of Teviotdale was also in his mind—and would ever be. It was all wrong, all hopelessly wrong.

Esther seemed to divine his thoughts. "And yet, despite all, you brought our father home? All that way. Into danger. At the risk of your own life . . ."

"I could do no less." Deliberately Simon altered his tone of voice, his whole manner. "I am hungry," he said abruptly. "And I must clean myself. Wash. Shave my beard." It was the best way that he could help them—to give them excuse for busyness, something to do.

The sisters took appreciative advantage of the opportunity presented, occupying themselves with the blessedly humdrum tasks that could serve as a temporary screen between them and the contemplation of horror and violence. But later, when they were sitting watching the man at his meal, an uneasy silence settled upon them.

Marcia it was who broke it, her agitation not to be concealed or gainsaid. "What will you do, now?" she asked. "What next? You are in danger here . . ."

He nodded. "I must go again, with the darkness."

"Tonight? Back . . . back to Scotland? Away . . . for good and all! No more to return!"

"What else?" he said. He kept his eyes on the table. "Who knows—one day I may be able to come back again?" But it was flatly said.

"Must it be *this* night?" Esther asked, quietly. "So soon? You cannot be sufficiently recovered, strong enough, Simon?"

"I am well enough," he assured. "I rested well. The longer that I wait, the more hazard there is, for me—and for you also. If it was discovered that I was here, it would be the end of me. And dire trouble for you both." He looked up, now. "What befell when I had gone, before? When it was discovered that I had made off, fled? Was there . . . did you suffer for it, grievously?"

"No. Nothing to be named suffering—as you and others have suffered."

"But the Prior? He would be wrathful? You had given your word that I should be kept close, not allowed from this house. That man would not spare you . . . ?"

"He did not return to Hexham till yesterday. He had gone some way with my Lord Dacre, you will remember. We had not told anyone that you were gone, until Father Crispin came. He discovered it when he asked to see you. That was on the second day," Esther told him. "We believed that, by then, you would be safely away. Over the Border . . ."

"And the Prior? When he heard?"

"He was angry, yes. He summoned us to the Priory last evening. He named us many ill things. He talked of punishments and penances that he would impose on us, later. But he had much else on his mind, I think . . ."

"The gold!" Marcia interjected. "That was what weighed heaviest with my Lord Prior!"

"Yes. Mayhap. But with so many of his men away with the

187

Lord Dacre—more than six score—he is much exercised with the affairs of his manors . . ." Esther drew a quick breath as, obviously, the thought that none of those six score men would ever return to Hexham smote her anew.

Swiftly Simon spoke. "The gold, yes. Some of it, at the least, should have reached him by this. His messengers had been at Stirkshaws but a few days before I won home. A strange thing, was it not? Why they were so long in coming for the gold, I know not. There had been some mistake. My sister said that a messenger, a wandering friar, had indeed come to her, many months ago—but he asked for no money. He gave her only a message that I was alive and being cared for. And yet I said in my letter . . . I wrote about the gold. I cannot understand it. But I had no time to speak much of this matter with Ailie— to speak much of any matter." He shrugged. "But, be that as it may, these latter friars—two of them, there were—got half of the ransom, one thousand gold lions, away with them. That much Prior Anselm will now have. That much of my debt is paid . . ."

"Mary Mother! You talk of debt—*you*, who have given us back our father!" Marcia cried wildly. She turned on Esther, her full lower lip trembling. "He talks of debts—after what *I* did! He but the more shames me! I tell you, it is all my doing, my fault . . ."

Surprised, Simon considered her. "I do not understand," he said. "How can any of it be your doing?"

"Hush, Marcie," Esther exclaimed, hurriedly. "Such talk is folly. It will avail nothing. Nothing now, at all." She looked at her sister significantly, shaking her head. "Why should we waste time in talk of foolish gold? I would, Simon, that your sister had never sent one penny of it!"

"No," the man declared, definitely. "It was right and just that that gold should come here. But not all to your grasping Prior, see you. Half of those thousand gold lions are your father's. Those terms I bargained with him in the first place, for my life, on Flodden Field . . ."

"Stop! Stop!" Marcia all but shouted. "Will you drag us in

the mire—sellers of lives for gold? In sweet Mary's name—will you talk no more of accursed money!"

Simon nodded. "Very well. But a bargain is a bargain. And I would not have you think that I left this house, those five nights agone, that I might avoid the payment of my debt, my ransom. You understand that, do you not? I broke faith, broke *your* word to the Prior, because I could do no less and keep my self-respect. My people, Teviotdale, had to be warned if it was in my power to do it. I had to try . . ."

"You had to, yes," Esther agreed. "We know that. We understood what had made you go. We did not blame you, Simon. As I said, we told none of your going, until Father Crispin found it out."

"And were you in time?" Marcia demanded. "Did your warning save your people? Save Teviotdale?"

He sighed. "Yes—and no. Nothing could have saved all Teviotdale. But I was in time for the balefires to be lit and to signal their alarm. Some warning was given—but not enough. Some were able to save themselves—but not all. God knows, not all! The towns were given opportunity to put themselves in some state of defence. Hawick had time to muster . . ."

"Hawick, yes. And it was Hawick, you said, where this, this slaughter took place? Where the Hexham men died? Where Father fell?"

Simon looked down. "Yes," he admitted, slowly. "I fear that is true. Near to Hawick it was. They were advancing on Hawick—to burn it, like the rest. And Hawick was warned, ready. Another gave the final warning, that they were at this Hornshole. But, yes—you could say that it was because of my work, my beacons' alarm, that they were ready, that your people died." Evenly he said it. "I would not wish to deny the responsibility that is mine."

For a few moments there was silence in that room.

"You . . . you pay your debts, Simon Armstrong!" Esther said, at length, her voice less even than his. "All of them!"

He paused before he answered her. "There is one I owe *you*, unpaid as yet," he said.

He heard her gulp, and then the scrape of the form on which Marcia sat sounded loud as she pushed it back suddenly, rising to her feet.

"I shall go up—to look to Father," the younger girl said, shortly. "It may be that he needs help, attention." And turning, she hurried from the kitchen.

The man looked after her, and shook his head. "I have hurt that one," he said. "And that is a thing that I would not have wished to do."

"No," Esther told him. "I think that you are wrong. The hurt is not of your making. Let her be, Simon. She . . . she loves you well."

"Think you so?" He tapped his fingers on the table, frowning. Abruptly he said it, without looking at her, "And do you?"

When she did not answer, he turned to her, almost fiercely. "Well?" he demanded.

Meeting his eyes, haggard but burning, she inclined her head. "You know that I do," she said gently. "We both do."

It was the man's turn to thrust back his seat. He got up, to start to stride to and fro across the stone-flagged floor. "Both!" he cried. "There you have it! What use is that to a man—love after that fashion?"

She did not speak.

"Do you not see? Do you not understand?" he insisted. "And I am torn, as on a rack. I am your enemy. A foe. A hated Scot. I have nothing to offer you. And I have done you enough hurt."

"No," she said.

"Yes. And I would not hurt you more, by all the Saints of God! But it is hard . . ." Still at his pacing, he swung on her. "Help me, Esther Ridley. You came to me, once, when I was in sore need, when I was lost otherwise. More than the once. You came, and lifted me up, when I needed help most . . ."

"As I would come always, Simon, anywhere—if you needed me!"

"You mean that? Would you? Would you, lass? Then help me now. For I am tired, tired. In my mind, more than my body.

190

I cannot say what I would. And I must be out of this good house and away this night and over the Border and into Scotland before tomorrow. Away for long, it may be. Give me something to take back to Scotland with me, woman, that I may go in some sort of peace."

"It is yours for the asking," she told him simply.

"Say you so? Then, then, tell me that, one day, when these troubles are overpast, God willing, I may come back to Anick Grange and hope that you will by then hate Scotland less, hate it little enough maybe to, to go there, to take it for your own, to consider the exchange of it even for this England! That you will . . ."

Tense, earnest, as he was in that moment, the man stopped short, head up.

Esther, lips parted, was leaning forward. Her eyes widened.

"Listen!" Simon jerked. "Heard you aught? Were those horses? Hard-ridden? I thought . . ."

There was a cry from above, and the sound of hurrying feet. "Quick!" Marcia called down to them. "Simon—hasten! Here come men. From the Priory. Officers. Men-at-arms!"

"Oh—quickly! Quickly!" Esther cried, standing up. "Go back. Upstairs."

Their guest required no urging. With only a glance cast around the kitchen, and a word thrown to the girl, he went long-strided to the door and up the stairway three steps at a time. Marcia was hurrying down, skirts kilted up. As they passed, she gripped his arm for a moment.

"Into your room. Shut the door. Hurry, Simon," she panted. "I like it not. Lie quiet. Hidden. No—better. Into Father's room. Go there. If they come seeking, hide under his bed. They will never look there."

Simon ran on. He did not turn in at Abel Ridley's bedchamber, but went past to his own room at the end of the corridor. He would hide under no beds, for any man! Moreover, Priory men might be come merely to see the wounded steward himself. That might be all their mission. In which case he was better to be out of Ridley's room.

191

In his own chamber Simon went first to the settle whereon lay his sword, cuirass and morion. Swiftly he belted on the weapon, leaving the rest. Then he began to pull on his long riding-boots. He felt the better man immediately, despite the clatter and stamping of horses' hooves as men dismounted below his window.

Before the second boot was on, he heard the open front door being banged with an open hand, and then heavy footsteps clumping within. Men's voices were upraised.

Simon stood uncertain only for a moment. He crossed to the window and looked out, standing well back for fear of being observed. Four horses stood there on the cobbles, and one man-at-arms, dressed in the Hexham Priory livery, lounged beside them, waiting. All the Prior's fighting-men had not gone with Dacre, then, after all! The mellow evening light, flooding into the courtyard from the west, lit up the gold-painted saltire on the man's breastplate and helmet.

Simon listened, but could hear only the murmur of voices, no words. Holding his sheathed sword so that it might not clank or rattle, he moved over quietly to the door and out of his room, along the passage to the stair-head, tiptoeing, heedful that his spurs did not tinkle nor the floorboards creak. At the stout wooden banisters he halted, to crouch and peer down and listen.

And he frowned grimly at what he heard.

XX

". . . and I charge you to give me a fair answer for the Lord Prior, Mistress," a man's voice was saying, authoritatively. "We must have word with this fellow who brought him home. Who is he? Where is he?"

"I . . . I cannot say, sir," Esther's voice answered, less than confidently. "He was a stranger, as I said—not a Hexham man. He had brought our father far. We did not question him . . . in all the upset and distress. Where he was from, or whither going."

"Where is he now?"

"That I . . . I cannot tell you, sir."

"Mistress—say you that here was a stranger who brought Master Ridley all the way home from Scotland, wounded, coming to you in the middle of the night, and you did not give him the hospitality of your house? Did you not seek his name, where he was from?"

Esther's hesitation, however brief, was sufficient for Marcia to intervene. "He left us forthwith," she lied flatly. "He had far to go. To . . . to Morpeth, I think."

"Morpeth?" the man took her up quickly. "Was he of my Lord Dacre's own company then? He is lord of Morpeth, through his lady."

"No, I think not. Leastways, I do not know, sir." Hurriedly the girl answered. "He said but little, he was aweary and would be on his way. And we had much else to think on . . ."

"Father Crispin told my Lord Prior that you knew not whence this fellow was come? Now you say from Morpeth . . . ?"

Esther interrupted him. "Of what matter is it?" she asked. "Why, sir, should you seek this man? Surely all that is of concern is that our father should have reached home alive, safe, though sore stricken?"

"That is matter for rejoicing, surely, Mistress—and the

193

Lord Prior thanks God for it," the other declared unctuously. "But there is much that he would find out from this man, this stranger—much that it is necessary to know. And much that none other can tell us, it seems. For only this day we have had the evil word that all the rest of Master Harndean's company are lost. All dead. Slain, every one, in vile cowardly fashion while they slept, by the dastardly Scots. All the Hexham men gone. Save only Master Ridley, it seems. And this man who brought him home—whom you say is no Hexham man at all. You will perceive now, Mistress, why it is important for the Lord Prior to have word with him."

"I . . . we . . . it is terrible." Esther's voice was so low that Simon could only just catch her words. "I am sorry. How fearful a thing."

"Yes," said Marcia, as though her throat was compressed.

"It is a grievous loss. Over six score of good men lost. And their gear and beasts. It is a mortal blow to the Priory. There has been devil's work somewhere. Prior Anselm must know what befell. He is sore distracted. Sir Christopher Dacre, the Warden's brother, has seen the field—somewhere near to Hawick—but could inform nothing of how it fell out. Your father could tell us—but the monk Crispin says that he is not like to come to his senses yet awhile. So I have orders to find this other man, and bring him to the Prior."

"But, I tell you, that is not possible! He is not to be found. Not here . . ."

"No?" The man's tone hardened perceptibly. "I wonder? I questioned the old woman at the mill cottage, yonder. She said that she heard a horseman ride hither in the night—but none ride away again, thereafter!"

Simon bit his lip. The man was playing with the girls as a cat plays with a mouse.

"An old woman may fail to hear many things in the night, sir. And a man may ride out by other gait than he rode in." That was bravely said, but there was no hiding the evasion behind it. And their questioner's patience was exhausted, apparently.

194

"Do you swear, girl, then, that the man left this house last night? Swear it, by all that you hold holy?"

Simon rose to his feet, loosening his sword in its scabbard. He could not permit this to go on. There were things more precious to him than mere physical safety. He drew a deep breath. He would proclaim himself, and resolve this matter in a man's fashion.

But he was forestalled. Both girls cried out, Marcia railing shrilly at the Prior's emissary. Esther declaring that he was no priest or confessor to require holy oaths of them.

The other cut them short with what was obviously a blow of a clenched fist on the table. "Ha' done—the pair of you!" he cried. "You lie! You both lie. You are hiding the truth— hiding the man himself, I trow! Think you that the captain of the Prior of Hexham's guard is to be made game of by a couple of wenches? By Saint Wilfred, you'll learn otherwise! Enough o' this . . ."

"Master Crossley—I demand that you take us to the Prior!" Esther exclaimed. She spoke loudly, clearly, as well as force-fully—however strained her voice. "We shall speak only to Prior Anselm himself. Take us there, now—to the Priory, sir. You shall not speak to us thus, in our own father's house. Let us go—at once!"

Brave heart, Simon acclaimed silently. To get these soldiers out of the house, so that he might escape—that was her endeavour now. There was a woman that a man might die for, happily . . .

The officer Crossley saw the ruse as clearly as did the listening fugitive, however. Moreover, apparently he saw something else just then. For suddenly he laughed loudly, coarsely. "Ho, Mistress—is that it? So you will speak only with my Lord Prior, heh? And what will you tell him? That his captain interrupted you at your shaving—heh? That your beard is troubling you?" His laughter was joined now by that of two other men, hitherto silent. "This razor lying here is for one o' you, we must believe—since your father's beard is notable!"

Simon cursed beneath his breath. In his swift glance around

195

the room, before he left the kitchen, he had missed the razor. Esther had left it lying on the table, beside his viands, for his use when he had finished eating. There could be no denying that evidence that another man was in the house.

A silence descended then, for two or three seconds, the girls' inventive capacities halted before this eloquent witness. "It . . . it is nothing," Esther faltered, at length. "An old razor—that is all. Used for many purposes . . ."

"A truce to this!" the captain shouted. "You ha' lied enough. There is a man hidden in this house—that is clear. And any man that you must needs hide can only be an enemy. This man came out o' Scotland, with your father. An enemy, a Scot, the Prior's prisoner, broke from this house some days since. And there was treachery at Hawick! By the Saints o' God, Mistress—you ha' something to answer for! We search this house!"

"No! No! I forbid it! You will not . . ."

"Stand aside, woman. This is the Prior's house, and I speak in the Prior's name! Out o' my way . . ."

There was a cry, a scuffle, the sound of a blow, and a choked-off scream.

"Curse you, you hell-cat!" the man Crossley roared.

Simon waited for no more. Condemning himself for having waited for so long, he wrenched the sword from its sheath, and launched himself down those stairs.

The Scot's aim, in that downward rush, was elementary. It was merely to get himself past the people in the kitchen, out through the door of the house, brush aside the single guard set on the horses, mount one of them, and away. Nothing could have been more simple. And simplicity, with surprise, is the essence of success in such matters.

Down those steps he leapt, then, his feet barely seeming to touch the treads. But his progress, though spectacular, was not soundless. By the time that he reached the stairfoot, a man was within the kitchen doorway, tugging at the sword at his hip. Impetus meant everything to Simon Armstrong just then. He wasted no precious moments on sword-play. As he raced on down the stone-floored passage, he tucked his head down into his left shoulder, and so hurled himself bodily, like a battering-ram, at the man-at-arms emerging from the room. Though that surprised individual sought to draw back, at the sight, invol-untarily—as who would blame him?—he could not wholly withdraw himself in time. Simon's hunched shoulder caught him on the chest, and though protected by a steel breastplate, he staggered back. And almost in the same moment the fugi-tive's clenched fist, gripping the hilt of his sword, drove up under the other's chin. The unfortunate's head jerked back, and sagging at the knees, he toppled over, cannoning into the man who was seeking to push behind him through the door-way. Simon had the briefest glimpse of astonished faces, open-mouthed, evidently shouting, within the kitchen, and then he was past, lurching, stumbling, almost but not quite losing his balance. Recovering himself, his momentum but little im-paired, he went plunging out through the main doorway, into the courtyard.

So far so good. But the dash down the passage had been accomplished even less silently than had been the descent of the stairs. Outside then, the guard on the horses could not have failed to hear, and to realise at least something of what was going on. In consequence, though surprise there may have been, it was only partial. The man was there awaiting Simon's appearance, sword drawn—and he was standing between the door and the horses.

Simon, with no option, plunged straight into the attack, lunging fiercely, if possible to overwhelm the fellow before he was fully ready for swording—for there were no moments to spare. Almost he achieved his end, too, and had his footwork not failed to adjust itself immediately to the uneven cobble-stones of the yard, and thereby slipped a little, the steel that ripped the guard's doublet sleeve from elbow to shoulder undoubtedly would have pierced and put out of action the fellow's sword-arm. As it was, something was gained, for in instinctive self-preservation the other jerked his arm out of the way, thus deflecting and invalidating the parrying slash that he

197

had been going to deliver—and which in that headlong career his assailant could have done little to avoid. In the event, Simon sought both to halt his rush and to throw himself sideways, out of range of the man's weapon, all in the same motion. He managed it—but tripped, staggered and went down on one knee, sword clashing on the stones.

His opponent, a burly greying man, may not have been an artist with the blade, but he was no laggard nor coward. Raising his heavy brand high, he turned and flung himself upon his attacker. Simon, caught at a disadvantage, had only one course open to him to escape disaster; from his crouching position he thrust himself backwards explosively, using both hand and knee for purchase—and won clear of the other's hacking downward blow only by bare inches.

But that difficult leap, though a life-saver, finally brought to naught any hopes of Simon being able to jump on to a horse and away without a full-scale fight—for it took him away from the beasts, and left the guard between them and himself. And now two other men, preceded by their shouting, came running out of the house doorway, their swords drawn—though one of them, the more colourfully dressed, was being very obviously hampered and delayed by a young woman who clung to his arm and had to be dragged along with him.

Simon took in his new position with a single urgent sweeping glance. He might or might not be a better swordsman than these Priory bullies, but he could not hope successfully to fight all three, possibly four, of them simultaneously out here in the open, where he could be surrounded and struck down from behind. Since running would serve him nothing, with these others in possession of the horses, he had to cover his back— get something, some conditions to fight for him.

The courtyard was bounded on three sides by buildings— the house, a row of domestic outbuildings, and a range of stabling. Towards this latter, across the cobbles, the fugitive flung himself. At his back the others pounded.

There were three doors in this range of building—but only one stood open, and that was at the farthest inner end. With

198

only a yard or two between him and the pursuing steel, Simon had no time to reach that. He hurled himself over at the first closed door, kicking out his foot to open it as he reached it—since, he decided swiftly, in the constricted space within, in a stable, a lone sworder would probably have some advantage. But the door did not give to his push; it was latched presumably—and he had no time to seek out and open a latch. Whirling round, he pressed his back against the door planks—and lunged, at once.

He was only just in time. The officer, the man Crossley, had managed to shake off whichever girl had been clinging to him, and had outdistanced his minions. He had been right on Simon's heels, and his sword was thrusting even as the other turned. Simon's blade caught the oncoming steel in a parry that was not an instant too soon. The two blades screaked against each other as they were forced up and up, till the hilts locked. For a curious timeless moment the two men were frozen into immobility, straining against each other, wrist to wrist, chest to chest, eye to eye. Neither spoke.

But with the two other men coming running up, this was no occasion for immobility on Simon's part. Setting the sole of his foot against the planks of the door behind him, using it as a springboard, he thrust forward suddenly with a violent convulsive force and sought to channel most of the thrust into his sword-arm. The other went tottering back under the impact. And the Scot's point, sweeping down as soon as he disengaged, in a vehement half-circle, scored a thin scarlet line along Crossley's jawbone from ear to chin. An inch closer, and the Prior's captain would have been out of the fight.

There was no occasion for such reflections on Simon's part, however. He had to get back against the door, and his blade weaving, before either of the two men-at-arms could engage him. He only just achieved it. The former guard on the horses came in at his right hand, flailing his whinger like a windmill. Such tactics were not hard for a skilled swordsman to counter—if he was not too greatly preoccupied elsewhere. The second assailant was a jabber, crouching, shortening his sword, and using it as might a gladiator in the arena. Making a swift decision, Simon leapt sideways away from him, towards the windmiller, ducking almost double as he did so, to avoid the figure-of-eight flail of his steel, to shorten sword in turn and thrust savagely upwards, for the pit of the guard's upraised arm. The point touched home—but again an inch or so short, as the other sought to avoid it. Steel struck against steel, on the edge of the man's painted cuirass, and then glanced off, not into the vulnerable armpit but along the line of the shoulder, cutting doublet and flesh beneath—but not deeply. Gasping, the fellow staggered back, the sword falling from his hand with a clatter. Simon might have finished him then—but dared not neglect the jabber for another instant. Jerking round, immediately he had to contort himself, to arch his body inwards, away from a vicious stabbing thrust from below, snake-like in character. He felt the stuff of his doublet rip, at the stomach—but knew no deeper hurt. And his own weapon, whipping round and down in a flashing arc, spoke back. There was too much metal about the upper part of the crouching man, however, for a mere downward slash to be effective; his blade rang on morion and on breastplate, and then slid off into thin air, having drawn sparks but no blood. The jabber, alarmed, strove to withdraw himself, hastily, while still in that forward bending position, achieved a froglike backward hop, difficult and ungainly, tripped himself with his own spurs, and fell heavily.

Simon had no chance to deliver any *coup de grâce*, had he decided to do so. The officer Crossley, though dripping blood from his face and less steady on his feet than he had been, came on again. Moreover, the other man, the grey-haired horse-guard, was stooping down, groping for his sword with his left hand, despite his wounded shoulder. These Northumbrians were no cravens. And away beyond these, Simon glimpsed the fourth man, the one that he had first laid low at the kitchen door, emerging now from the house, dazedly shaking his head but on his feet once more.

It was perhaps strange that, noting all this in his urgent glance around, the hard-tried Scot failed to see, or at least consciously to note, that the remaining actors on that confused scene, the two Ridley girls, were still very much in evidence. No doubt his subconscious mind dismissed them, for the moment, as quite irrelevant to this grim man's business. If so, his subconscious mind was mistaken. For Esther, darting forward, flung herself down to grasp at the wounded man's fallen sword even as he stooped fumbling for it, wrenched it from his unsure fingers, and thereupon hurled it away from her, as far as her strength permitted. The thing fell slithering and ringing over the cobbles. Cursing, and aiming an angry but random cuff at the young woman, its owner went lurching after it.

Crossley was lunging now, and Simon, panting heavily, was on the defensive again. He parried, feinted and riposted—but the other drew back in time. He was an able duellist, obviously, and no heavy-handed swiper like the others. But he had one liability that his opponent was spared; even as he danced aside preparatory to another onset, Marcia Ridley rushed at his back, to grab at his sword-arm, and there hang on. She was fairly promptly and furiously shaken loose and thrown off. But Simon was thereby granted precious seconds of respite.

He used them to glance urgently round at the door behind him, seeking that latch that would open it. He saw it—a wooden pawl lifted by a simple pin. Unfortunately the same glance that showed him the latch, however, revealed, in the corner of his eye, that the jabbing fellow had picked himself up and was coming in again, on his toes, knees bent, sword hanging low, and mouthing imprecations. Simon had to turn to face him. But as he flickered his blade in the man's direction, to keep him at a distance, his left hand was feeling behind him on the face of the door, feeling, groping for that latch.

Esther, perceiving what he was doing, shouted something then, something about the door apparently, which the man failed to catch. Unfortunately the crouching fellow was shouting also. Possibly others were, likewise. Crossley was back in action again, too, having got rid of Marcia for the moment—though undoubtedly the fear of her further interference must have been distinctly distracting. The man from the house was

201

now coming to join the fray, if less than eagerly, his sword out. No doubt the wounded one would be back with his recovered weapon, any moment . . .

Desperately, as his steel wove its guardian glittering pattern before him, Simon's left hand was fumbling, searching for that latch behind him. This could not go on for much longer. He was gulping for breath, having to shake the running sweat from his eyes already. He required to be a fitter and fresher man than he was, to keep this up.

And then, abruptly, without warning, the door opened behind him—not as a result of any fingerwork of his. There was almost disaster, as he reeled back, all but falling. But Esther was there. She thrust her body against his, staying him up when he was off balance, and at the same time seeking to drag him within. Quickly Simon recovered himself, and leapt backwards, out of reach of those hungry questing swords, hope springing anew. As hurriedly, the girl sought to slam shut the door that she had opened. But that was not to be. Crossley, darting forward, got a knee and a foot within before she could close the gap. And another man hurled himself at the timbering, smashing the door wide once more.

But stimulated, revived in some degree by this new situation, Simon Armstrong's mind was working swiftly again. Obviously there must be another door, by which Esther had entered. Stables often had two doors, of course. Nobody must be allowed to get in at that other door, then, to take him in the rear. That was the danger. But it could represent an outlet for him, too . . .

"Esther!" he yelled. "The other door. Can you keep it shut? Barred? Must hold it . . ." He drove in at Crossley as he spoke—and had the satisfaction of registering a glancing wound on that man's thigh as he jostled with one of his fellows through the doorway. Simon raised his voice again, a hint of triumph in it.

"Marcia!" he shouted. "Marcia—do you hear me? The horses. Scatter them! All but one. Scatter their horses! Keep one—for me. The horses, Marcia . . ."

The fight changed its whole character and complexion now. Simon found himself in a narrow straw-littered passage-way at the side of a row of horse-stalls—in three of which his own beasts from Stirkshaws were tied. The partitions between each stall projected sufficiently to ensure that the lengthwise passage was no more than five or six feet wide. In consequence, though all four Priory men were now crowded into the stable after him, only two of them could engage him at one time—and even these two necessarily were somewhat hampered and constricted in their side-by-side sword-play. With his flanks and rear protected, Simon was able to keep their swords at arm's length. Retreating slowly, step by step, he backed down the passage-way.

This was good, a comparative relaxation and respite. But the inevitable happened. The two rearmost attackers—one of them Crossley, dabbing at his leg—perceiving that they could not get at their quarry thus, turned and hurried out whence they had come—obviously seeking the other door, by which Esther had entered, to come at Simon from the rear. The girl had disappeared—presumably she had understood his shouted instructions, and had gone to shut this other door. But could she hold it, against the assaults of two men outside . . . ?

Fending off his present assailants without any great difficulty, Simon presently heard a considerable banging and rattling from away behind him. Then Esther was back beside him, in one of the stalls.

"It is all right, Simon—they cannot get in," she gasped, breathlessly. "There is a bar. A swing bar. On the inside. They cannot come in there . . ."

"Good! Good!" the man nodded, never removing his glance from the two clumsy sworders in front. "Good . . . for you, lass. I . . . can hold these here . . . easily."

"Yes. But, Simon . . . better. There is another door. Inside. Just behind you. An inside door. Two stables there are. We can shut it. You understand?"

"Eh . . . ?" His mind raced to consider what this might mean,

203

might offer. "Another door? An *inside* door . . . ?"

"Yes. And we can bar it. From the other side. *That* side. Oh, Simon—don't you see . . . ?"

He saw. "How far back?"

"Only . . . a few paces now."

"Good. Be ready, then." Simon inched back and back, his blade cutting a rhythmic figure-of-eight design before him all the while. His two opponents must have heard the girl's panted information, but either its significance had not sunk into their preoccupied minds or else they left the thinking-out processes to their captain. At all events, they merely continued with their steady pressure.

Then, just as Simon found himself within the jambs of a doorway in the through passage, the other two soldiers came stamping back, frustrated in their attempt to break in at the barred second entrance to the stable. Or to the two stables, as it now appeared, linked together by this interior doorway in which Simon now stood. Crossley's leg did not seem to be troubling him greatly, for now he came pushing forward, shouting to his subordinates, and pulling at the shoulder of the wounded older man who was fighting with his left hand. He drew him back, and inserted himself in his place.

Simon decided to delay no longer. This inner doorway was fairly narrow. Two men could not fight in it at the same time. "Ready?" he jerked, tossing the word back. "Yes." Esther's voice sounded muffled. She must be standing behind the door itself.

"Right!" Simon stamped a foot, and lunged swiftly forward And again. And again. Three times there was the sudden aggressive flurry of furious steel. His adversaries pressed back, momentarily, to avoid his darting hissing point—and as they did so, Simon leapt rearwards himself. And into the cleared space Esther Ridley hurled herself and the door, slamming it to in the faces of the four men-at-arms.

Simon wasted not an instant. "Quick!" he cried. "Leave this to me. Outside and round, with you. Shut the other door behind them! The one we came through. Quick! Try to hold it." He was thrusting the locking bar home into its socket in the walling as he spoke, his shoulder against the door. Without a word the girl turned and ran, leaving him.

This inner door was not very heavy, he found, and the bar that held it far from stout. But it would hold for a time, it seemed. Already its timbers were shaking and quivering under a hail of blows from the other side. Simon, shoulder against it, waited, panting for breath. Let them hammer away at it. So long as they did not turn and run out through the open door behind them. They might not consider doing that at once, having already just tried the second outside stable door and found it holding against them. They must be led to assume that their quarry intended to hole up in here, meantime, like a badger, protected by the two barred doors.

There was more light behind him now—which indicated that Esther had flung open the other barred entrance and gone outside. He pressed heavily against the planking that was heaving and shaking still. He must keep them at that, for a little longer at least. Lifting his voice, Simon yelled abuse and jeers through at his antagonists, taunting them, urging them to come in and get him. Anything to keep them concentrating on that interior door.

Then, thankfully, he heard, above the thumping and banging and cursing, the more distant crash of the main stable door. Esther had done it, closed it. With not an instant to lose, now, and an unspoken prayer that the bar and socket here would hold for at least a little longer, Simon turned and went racing for the open air.

Out in the courtyard again, blinking in the last rays of the sinking sun, the man nevertheless took in the new situation at a glance. Esther was hanging on, as for dear life, to the wrought-iron loop that constituted the handle of that door— that same iron handle below the latch that he himself had tugged at vainly in an attempt to gain entrance. And close by, Marcia stood, a pitchfork in her hands, on guard, resolution in every line of her. Behind her stood not one horse but two. Of the other beasts there was no sign.

Gulping for breath, Simon came running up to them. The door that Esther was holding was not shaking at all, so far—evidently the men inside had not yet thought of coming out, but were still concentrating on smashing open the interior door. A swift glance showing him this, Simon reached over and took the pitchfork from Marcia. Turning, he strode to the door, and lifting the fork, inserted the long handle through the iron loop below the latch, so that one end overlapped each jamb of the doorway. Since the door opened inwards, this would act as a bar, and serve to hold it shut, for a little time, at least.

"Is there another?" he shouted to Marcia. "Another fork. For the other door."

"Not here. There are some round at the hay-barn . . ."

"The besom!" Esther cried. "Over there." Even as she spoke, she was hurrying over the cobbles, to take up and bring him the birch-twig broom, long-handled as were the pitch-forks, used for brushing muddy footwear, that stood a-lean beside the house door.

The man took it, ran back to the second stable door, out of which he had so recently come, and pulled it shut. It was identical with the other, with the same iron loop. He treated it in the same way with the broom handle. As he did so, he could hear the sound of splintering wood from within. The inner door must be yielding.

He had gained a few moments' breathing-space. It was not likely to be more than that. His four attackers were penned in the two stables, from which they could emerge only through the two barred doorways; there was no window in this range of outbuildings, glass being much too precious a commodity to waste on horses. But the long handles of the fork and the broom were slender things, and not fashioned for use as bars—though admittedly it would be difficult for the imprisoned men to exert full pressure on them from within . . .

Marcia had brought the horses along to him. "Quick!" she cried. "Do not tarry, Simon. Away with you!"

He required no urging. Sheathing his sword, he grasped the

206

saddle, to pull himself up. "Away with the other beast," he panted. "I need only the one."

"No," Marcia answered him. "That is for Esther." She turned to her sister. "Up with you. Oh, hurry! Hurry!"

Simon, one foot in a stirrup, one still on the ground, swung round, to stare from one girl to the other. And, for almost the first time, he saw the elder sister's glance to be unsteady, unsure, as she bit her lip.

"Go on!" Marcia exclaimed, urgently. "Why do you wait? Do not delay, for sweet Mary's sake!"

"But . . ." Simon began. And got no further.

"I cannot leave you," Esther said then, her voice as uncertain as her eyes.

"You must. You *shall*! He needs you."

"Yes." That single word was strangely, levelly, enunciated, accepted. "Yes. But Father . . . ?"

"I shall look to Father. Think you that I cannot do that? He does not need us both."

"No." The swift acceptance again, reinforced by a brief nod. "But . . . I cannot leave *you*—to all this." And Esther's hand waved, to indicate all the situation in which they found themselves.

"Why not? I will hold them as long as I may . . ."

"Not that. The Prior. And this Crossley . . ."

"*That* for the Prior and his bully!" Marcia snapped her fingers. "I am in trouble with the Prior already, am I not? What more can he do to me? A few more penances! A few more Aves!" She tossed back her head. "He is welcome to them. And he needs Father, remember. More than ever, now—now that so many of his men are dead. All his other stewards gone. The Prior must needs save Father, now—at any cost. And Father will save me! Never fear. You know that is true."

"It may be so," her sister agreed. "But, my dear—I . . ."

"Oh, fools! Fools—both of you!" the younger girl cried. "Will you go, while you may? Listen! Listen to them! They will be out . . ."

Certainly the door, the door that was held only by the frail

207

bar of the broomstick, was rattling and shaking now, quivering under a hail of blows and tuggings from within. Marcia ran over to it, to grasp that bar, and hold it tight in position.

Simon looked at Esther, and though he found no words to utter, his eyes were eloquent.

That young woman shook her dark head. "The cost, Marcie," she said. "The price! The price is too great . . ."

"Oh—do you not see?" her sister pleaded. "The price has been paid already! I paid my price, *before*! It is a *favour* now that I am seeking of you—of him. Cannot you see it? For my peace of mind. For my conscience' sake. Can you not understand? Will you not give me this—and go? If you love me . . ."

For a long moment Esther eyed the other girl, while the door behind her shook and banged, and the shouts from inside rose to a crescendo.

"See! This will not hold much longer," Marcia declared, her voice breaking. "For *his* sake, Esther—for Simon's sake, if not for mine—go now! At the least, set him on his way. He needs that. Lead him by the swift secret ways. Across Acomb Fell and the Colwell Moss. These others will catch him, otherwise, knowing this country better than he. Oh, waste no more time, Sister, for our good Lord's sake!"

Esther threw up her head. "Yes," she said, in a different voice. "I will do that." She ran forward, and cast her arms round her sister, and for a second or two the girls embraced each other there, leaning against that heaving door. Even as they stood, the bottom foot or so of one of the planks flew out, smashed by the kicks of a heavy boot.

That was enough for Esther. Turning, she came hurrying back to Simon, skirts held high. The man's arms went out to her, and grasping her round the waist he swung her up high, in a single sweeping movement, on to the back of the horse that he himself had been going to mount. Pulling herself up, kicking aside the hampering folds of her gown, somehow she managed to work herself astride the heavy soldier's saddle. Then, ignoring the stirrups, weariness forgotten, Simon vaulted up on to the other beast.

"You are a woman in a thousand, Marcia Ridley!" he cried. "May Mary Mother keep and protect you. And to aid her in that same, hear this!" He raised his voice notably. "You, in there!" he shouted. "You spawn of Satan, you churchman's jackals! Hear you this. If the least hurt or harm comes to this young woman—to either of these young women—now or later, on account of this day's work, as God is my witness, I will come back here from Scotland, sooner or later, and slit me the throat of each one of you! I will hunt you down, each and all, wherever you may hide yourselves, day and night—yes, and your Prior too, curse him! Tell him that, from Simon Armstrong. He has had a deal of my gold—he shall taste my steel too, tell him, priest or none, should a hair of these women's heads be touched. You have it? I pay my debts. I have brought him home his steward. I shall not fail in my debt to these women—so help me God!"

There was a sudden silence from the stable. The two young women looked at the man askance almost, for a moment, blinking at the intensity of ferocity in his voice. Here was a Simon Armstrong that neither of them had met hitherto. Into the hush it was Marcia who spoke.

"I . . . I seek to pay my debts too, Simon," she said, falteringly. "Go, now . . . and try if you can to think kindly of Marcia Ridley."

"I could do no other, lass—from now till eternity!" he assured her, deep-voiced. "Fare you well—so very well!" He raised his hand high, in salute—and brought it down hard in an open-palmed slap on the broad rump of his mount. "Come!" he cried.

Esther dug her small heels into her heavy horse's flanks, promptly, unhesitant now, and clattered out over the court-yard cobbles of her home only a length behind the man. She did not look back.

Just to be heard in the tattoo of their beasts' hooves, the beating and banging on the door resumed.

XXI

WHETHER any of the Priory men actually came after them or not, the man and the woman did not know. They saw no sign of pursuit, at any rate, while still they were in the open tilled lands and pastures around the Grange, and thereafter the spinneys and woodlands of Beaufront swallowed them up. They rode hard through the gently fading light of the May evening—and Simon was gratified to perceive that he had no need to slacken his pace or choose easy going on Esther's account. Though far from dressed for the part, she was obviously an excellent horsewoman. She directed their route even if she did not physically lead the way—and quite evidently she had a close knowledge of the countryside and its possibilities for horsemen.

They did not follow even approximately the route that Simon would have done, had used hitherto, avoiding the Tyne altogether, and striking north by east over gently rising terrain dotted with scattered woods, for the high ground of Acomb Fell, shunning the vicinity of all farmeries and cottages. And presently, climbing the open braes of the Fell, they looked back over the wide vale, with Hexham town rising on its hill in the midst, and saw no sign of chase or horsemen. That was not to say definitely that no one followed them, down there amongst the shadowy copses and thickets—but at least no pursuit was close behind. They did not slacken speed, however, in consequence.

Indeed, only the roughness of the country across which Esther guided the fugitive reduced their pace over the next hour or so. They went by a succession of whinny commons and reedy mosses and hillocks that embosomed ponds and lochans small and large, mile after mile into the north, keeping always well to the east of the low ground of Tyne, till eventually the shadowy narrower valley of another river opened before them, and they had reached the Rede. Beyond it, black, monstrous now, against the pale lemon sky in which the first stars were twinkling faintly, rose all the vast and daunting barrier of the Cheviots.

They reined up, under a jutting tall rock that stood at the very lip of the valley, beside the broken grass-grown mounds of a Roman fort—for the last miles they had been following the green deserted highway of Dere Street; Simon, for one, would not cease to bless those busy Romans hereafter. Esther raised a hand to point.

"Yonder lies the Rede," she said. "The Romans built a causeway, under its waters, to cross it down there, near to Woodburn. The causeway still is there. Yonder light is Woodburn, and Otterburn is but five miles higher." She raised her head a little. "And yonder are your great wild hills, Simon. Yonder lies Scotland."

"Yes," he said.

"You will be safe now, I think."

"Yes."

"It is . . . I have done . . . what I said that I would do."

"Yes."

There was a pause. The man sat his sweating horse, silent, seemingly withdrawn. But something appeared to compel the woman to go on talking.

"You can ride on . . . for hours yet. All night, if you will. There will be half a moon. And no clouds. It will never be wholly dark."

"No."

"You could go on up Redesdale, and over the Redeswire and Carter Bar. But I think that you would be safer in the wild hills. My Lord Dacre's men could still be returning home, down Rede."

He nodded.

"It would look strange for you to be riding in the wrong direction. And at night."

"Yes."

"And you must not fall into . . . into English hands again,

211

Simon."

This time the man turned to her, as though he would remark on that. But instead he only bit his lip and shook his head.

"It cannot be more than fifteen miles to the Border now, I think. As flies the crow?"

"No."

He heard her swallow. "Scotland . . . Scotland is not so very far away . . . from Hexham . . . after all!"

She had her answer this time, and his voice rasped harshly. "It will be as far away as darkness is from light!" he said.

A tiny sound escaped her, a sad small sound. And, after a moment, "I was afraid of that."

And now they were both silent. A curlew was calling, calling, across the dark valley somewhere, with all the hopeless longing of creation in its plaint.

Simon roused himself, as though with an effort. "And you?" he demanded.

She made no answer.

"This is where you meant to come? When Marcia said . . . when you said that you would set me on my way?"

She inclined her head, unspeaking. It was the man's turn to do the talking.

"It was good of you to come so far," he said, levelly. "It is a long way."

"No. This Roman road will take me back."

"Back to Hexham?"

"Where else? Back to Hexham," she repeated.

"I am sorry," he said.

"You need not be. I shall be quite safe. I know the road."

"It is myself that I am sorry for," he told her.

"Oh."

He nodded. "Leaving you here, Esther Ridley, is going to be more than I can bear, I think."

"Oh." That was a very small exclamation indeed. "And, and how far, sir, how much farther would you have me go with you?"

"By all the saints of God—to the end of my road itself, girl!

212

To the very last end of it," he cried. "I think, see you, that I might rather be in your Prior's cell, and you near, than in Stirkshaws Tower, with all broad Scotland before me . . . and you otherwhere." His voice cracked strangely. "You see what you have done to me, woman!"

And now she had no lack of words. They came fast, breathlessly. "I see, yes—I see. And I give thanks for what I see! Oh, Simon, Simon—I had hoped. Hoped, and prayed even. And feared. Feared most. Feared so many things." Her hand now was on his own arm. "Feared that it could never be so. An Englishwoman—daughter of the man who had bargained your life for a price. Or even, if that was possible, that it might be Marcie, perhaps—Marcie, who is so much more fair and gay and winsome. Feared . . ."

"Marcia I like well, my dear. But you—you are my own true love. Have been ever since you lifted me up out of the very borders of darkness. You, and you only. You it was who had the keys at your belt, you see! Not Marcia." He was standing in his stirrups now, leaning over to her. "You brought me up that long long road, girl. You have been with me every mile, every hour, waking and sleeping since. How far will you ride my road with me, then, Esther Ridley?"

"Farther than this Redesdale, my love," she said. "Farther than the Border. Farther than Scotland and your Stirkshaws. To the world's end, indeed, Simon Armstrong—and beyond that too!" Her voice, husky no longer, rang clear as a bell.

He reached out his arms to her. "What need of two horses on that road, then, my love?" he cried. "Come you."

She came.